2-2-07

Books by G.A. McKevett

Just Desserts

Bitter Sweets

Killer Calories

Cooked Goose

Sugar and Spite

Sour Grapes

Peaches and Screams

Death By Chocolate

Cereal Killer

Murder à la Mode

Corpse Suzette

Published by Kensington Publishing Corporation

G.A. McKevett

Corpse Suzette

A SAVANNAH REID MYSTERY

KENSINGTON BOOKS
www.kensingtonbooks.com

KENSINGTON BOOKS are published by

Kensington Publishing Corp.
850 Third Avenue
New York, NY 10022

All Kensington titles, imprints, and distributed lines are available at special quantity discounts for bulk purchases for sales promotion, premiums, fund-raising, educational or institutional use.

Special book excerpts or customized printings can also be created to fit specific needs. For details, write or phone the office of the Kensington Special Sales Manager: Kensington Publishing Corp., 850 Third Avenue, New York, NY, 10022. Attn. Special Sales Department. Phone: 1-800-221-2647.

Kensington and the K logo Reg. U.S. Pat. & TM Off.

Library of Congress Card Catalogue Number: 2005928276
ISBN: 0-7582-0462-0

First Printing: May 2006
10 9 8 7 6 5 4 3 2 1

Printed in the United States of America

Lovingly dedicated to Michael Paul.
Your smiles and laughter light our world.
What a miracle you are!

Acknowledgments

I would like to thank Joyce and Lloyd Eaton for the title, *Corpse Suzette*. Their wit, love, and loyalty never fail to amaze and amuse, year after year. What special, precious people you are!

Also, I want to thank all the fans who write to me, sharing their thoughts and offering endless encouragement. I enjoy your letters more than you know. I can be reached at:

sonjamassie.com
or
gamckevett.com

Chapter

1

"Wanna go watch Loco Roco?"
"Sure."
"Same place?"
"I'll be there in ten."

"There" was the Patty Cake Donut Shop, which frequently served as a meeting spot for Savannah Reid and her old buddy, Dirk. Police work could be lonely when nobody in the department was willing to be your partner. And Detective Sergeant Dirk Coulter was frequently a lonely man.

But generally not for long.

Now a private detective, Savannah had once been his partner in another lifetime . . . before she and the San Carmelita PD had parted ways under less than amiable circumstances. And once in a while, when she "got a yen," as her Southern granny would say, for an old-fashioned stakeout, she accepted one of his invitations.

He invited her constantly. He enjoyed her company and the homemade snacks she frequently brought along to fuel the long, tedious hours. She accepted once in a while . . . when there were no good forensic shows on TV and no unread romance novels on her nightstand.

But she always accepted when the subject was Loco Roco.

She was every bit as determined as Dirk to catch that lowlife doing something illegal, immoral, or fattening and put him back in the joint where he belonged. Roco had made a lifelong career of robbing convenience stores and on his last job had pistol-whipped a clerk into a coma. With Savannah's help, Dirk had arrested him, only to have the most serious charge thrown out on a technicality: prosecutorial error.

They'd never gotten over the disappointment that Roco was back on the street after only eighteen months. They knew it was just a matter of time until he lapsed into his old pattern, and they intended to be there when he fell off the wagon and violated his parole.

They had been watching Loco Roco for weeks. So far, he hadn't even jaywalked or spit on the sidewalk. To their consternation, he was Mr. Law-Abiding Citizen, while his latest victim was still in physical therapy, relearning how to walk. But Savannah and Dirk weren't the sort to give up easily.

And that was why Savannah arrived at their rendezvous spot in eight minutes rather than the estimated ten.

When she pulled into Patty Cake's parking lot, she found Dirk sitting in his old battered Buick Skylark in the rear near the alley. She knew the drill. He was waiting to see if she had brought any cookies, pie, brownies, or cake before he went into Patty's. Cheapskate that he was, he was hoping he'd only have to buy coffee. His mood—which usually wavered between morose and sullen—would plummet when she emerged from her classic Mustang, bagless.

Tough.

Her company didn't come cheap. The scintillating conversation, the benefit of her vast law-enforcement experience, the occasional slap upside his head to keep him awake . . . it all had a price. And the cost was two maple bars . . . or a giant chocolate-frosted Boston cream if she was in the throes of PMS.

He rolled down his window as she approached the Buick, a scowl on his face.

"No fried apricot pies?"

"You ate them all when you were over Saturday night," she said as she opened the passenger's door and brushed some Taco Bell wrappers off the seat and onto the floor.

"That was two nights ago. You've had plenty of time to make some more."

She slid in next to him and fixed him with a baleful eye. In her thickest Georgia drawl, she said, "Ye-eah, buddy . . . and I've had time to go clean that filthy house trailer of yours, wash your pile of dirty laundry, and perform an unnatural sex act on you that I'm sure you'd just love. But we both know none of that's *ever* gonna happen, so go get me some donuts, boy. Two maple bars *and* a Boston cream. And make it snappy!"

Dirk's jaw dropped. "*And?*"

"And."

"Now you're just bein' spiteful."

She grinned and winked at him. "You think?"

Half an hour later they were parked across the street from Burger Bonanza, watching the rear door of the fast food joint, waiting for a skinny, grungy thirty-year-old named Roco Tessitori to exit.

"How sure was his parole officer that he's going to get fired tonight?" Savannah asked as she licked the chocolate frosting off her fingertips.

"Sure, sure. The manager here called the P.O. this morning and said he was gonna let Loco go as soon as his shift's over. Said he's been late every day, doing next to nothing on the job, and he threatened one of the girls who works here. The manager figures his public service obligation's been fulfilled. He's done hiring ex-cons."

"And you figure our buddy's going to take his firing hard and go off the deep end?"

Dirk smiled, a nasty little grin that Savannah knew all too well. "Oh yeah. Loco's pretty predictable. When things don't go his way, he reverts to his old way of life. And besides, I'm feeling particularly lucky. I got two out of five on a Lotto scratch-off card this afternoon."

Savannah shot him a sideways glance to see if he was serious. He was.

She decided not to mention that getting two out of five on a scratch-off was an everyday occurrence for most Lotto enthusiasts. No point in dampening Dirk's cheerful mood which for him was as rare as getting all five on a scratch-off card . . . while sitting naked on the back of a bull elephant . . . under a blue moon.

She took the last bite of her Boston cream and washed it down with her last sip of coffee. Okay. The food was gone; it was time for this stakeout to end.

"So," she said, "you figure he'll knock off another convenience store before the night's out?"

He took the empty donut bag, crunched it into a ball, and tossed it onto the back floorboard. "Tonight. Tomorrow night. Next Tuesday. It'll happen, and it'll be worth the wait. After all, I'm a very patient man."

Savannah sniffed. "Yeah, right. This from a guy who has a conniption if he has to wait three seconds for a light to turn green, who pitches a fit if a waitress takes longer than five seconds to re-fill his coffee cup, who—"

"All right, all right. I . . . hey . . . heads up."

He pointed to the back door of the burger joint, where their quarry had just emerged, wearing a bright red uniform with the white "BB" Burger Bonanza logo on the back. Roco stomped across the parking lot to an old, decrepit Chevy. Opening the trunk, he peeled off the shirt and pitched it onto the ground.

"The boy looks downright disgruntled to me," Savannah said with a snicker.

"Oh, he's had better days," Dirk agreed.

They watched as the guy dropped the red pants, kicked off his shoes, and yanked the trousers off his ankles.

"Well, would you get a load of that," Savannah said. "Right down to his bloomers, here in front of God and everybody."

"I oughta bust him for exposin' himself right now," Dirk replied.

Savannah took a pair of binoculars from the glove box and focused them on Roco's rear end. "Or for wearing those briefs. They say 'kiss me under the mistletoe' and Christmas was two weeks ago. That's gotta be some sort of fashion felony."

Roco had thrown the pants onto the ground beside the shirt, then retrieved a pair of jeans from the trunk. In less than a minute, he was wearing the jeans and a black sweatshirt, and his sneakers were back on his feet.

As Roco got into his car, Dirk restarted the Buick and Savannah fastened her safety belt, happy for a bit of action. If there was anything she hated it was a boring stakeout once the goodies were gone.

A few seconds later, Roco peeled out of the parking lot, going out of his way to drive over the discarded uniform. They followed him onto the freeway, where he chose the northbound entrance ramp.

"He lives south of here," Savannah said.

Dirk smiled. "I know. Like I said, I'm feeling lucky tonight."

"I don't know what to make of this," Dirk said as Roco disappeared inside Kidz Emporium. Having followed him to a strip mall on the outskirts of town and the large toy store, they had parked a discreet distance away and watched as he entered the establishment.

Savannah shrugged. "Do you figure he'd go shopping for a nephew's or niece's birthday or whatever, right after getting fired from a job he badly needed?"

"Can't imagine it. Maybe he needs a video game to while away the idle hours now that he's unemployed."

Savannah got out her cell phone and called information, then dialed the store's number. "Security, please. Yes, hello. I'm with the San Carmelita Police Department"—she gave Dirk a sideways smirk—"and I was wondering if you could discreetly surveil a gentleman who's just entered your store and let us know what he purchases, if anything. Yes, Caucasian, thirty, black hair, dark eyes, six feet, one hundred and forty pounds, jeans and black sweatshirt. Sure. I'll hold. Thanks a bunch, darlin'."

A few minutes later, Savannah thanked the security guard again, tossed the phone back onto the dash and chuckled. Elbowing Dirk in the ribs, she said, "You're right, big boy. Today's your lucky day. You're not gonna believe what that moron just bought."

Fifteen minutes later, they were still sitting in the car, but this time they were parked at the outer edge of a convenience store's lot. Roco was standing beside his car, fumbling with the small orange bag he had carried out of the Emporium.

"He's going to do it," Savannah said. "He's crazier than I thought. He's actually going to try to knock over a Quick Stop with a toy gun."

"I guess he's got some urgent bills to pay and can't take time to score a real piece on the street." Dirk shook his head and laughed. "Fine with me. Now I can let him go through with it and hang himself good before I have to intervene. Hell, he can't even give a clerk a decent pistol-whipping with a toy gun."

Roco tucked the plastic pistol into the front of his jeans, pulled his shirttail over it, and strode toward the store's entrance. Savannah and Dirk checked their own weapons in their shoulder holsters and got out of the car the moment he disappeared inside.

In seconds they were at the front door. They looked through the glass, ready to duck if he was facing their way. Having arrested him before, they were sure he'd recognize them on sight, and this was one crime they didn't want to interrupt . . . at least, not at first.

Timing was everything.

They slipped inside unnoticed and made their way along the wall that was lined with soda-filled refrigeration units. Savannah glanced down each aisle they passed, but other than Roco and the elderly lady behind the counter the store appeared empty.

Roco was hanging out by the candy display, making a show of choosing some gum. With a couple of packs in hand, he made his way to the front.

Weapons drawn, but pointed at the ceiling, Savannah and Dirk followed him.

He approached the clerk and slapped the gum onto the countertop. "Gimme these," he barked.

The clerk was a petite, silver-haired woman with bright blue eyes that narrowed at hearing his rough tone. "And will that be all?" she asked with forced courtesy as she rang up the sale.

"No, that ain't all." He reached into his waistband and pulled out the toy weapon. Pointing it at the woman's head, he said, "Gimme the money in that register, too, while you're at it. And hurry up about it, too, or I'll blow your fuckin' face off."

For a moment, Savannah had a horrible thought: What if the old lady died of sheer fright? What if she had a heart attack and dropped dead then and there?

Maybe they should have intercepted him before he'd gotten this far!

But over Roco's shoulder she could see the woman's face and the hot fire of anger that leapt into the elderly lady's eyes. Savannah decided not to worry about this one. She had seen that look in her own Granny Reid's eyes, and she knew this woman wasn't one to be scared to death . . . literally or even figuratively.

She felt Dirk tense beside her. He was ready to make his move.

She lowered her gun and trained it on Roco's back.

She wouldn't take the shot. Not with the clerk also in her line of fire. But Roco wouldn't know that.

In her peripheral vision she saw Dirk do the same. In another second, he would announce and then they would—

Boom!

The explosion shook the store, and Savannah felt its reverberations throughout her entire body. Her ears rang as her brain tried to process. Instinctively, she dropped to one knee and ducked her head, her Beretta still pointed at Roco.

A gunshot.

She knew the sound all too well.

She did a split-second mental check to see if she had fired. No. She hadn't put her finger on the trigger yet.

A quick, sideways glance at Dirk told her that he hadn't fired either. He looked as confused as she was.

Roco had fired a shot?

With a plastic gun?

Roco. She looked back at him and saw an ugly, dark red stain appearing on the back of his thigh. He was starting to shake, violently. Then he dropped to the floor like a sack of flour.

Now Savannah had a clear view of the old lady behind the counter . . . all of her . . . including the Colt .45 in her hand that still had smoke curling from its barrel.

"That'll teach you!" the clerk said as she slowly lowered the weapon and laid it on the counter. "Try to rob *me* will you! And with a toy gun?! You oughta be ashamed of yourself. I'll bet you thought I was just some poor, helpless old woman. Well, I served in the Women's Army Corps, buster! You just held up the wrong woman!"

Dirk wasted no time rushing the counter and securing the .45 before Annie Oakley, Sr. could do any further damage with it.

Savannah holstered her own weapon and turned her attention to Roco, who was lying on the floor, bleeding profusely from his leg wound.

So far, he hadn't said anything. He wasn't even moaning or groaning in pain. He looked like he was in complete shock as he stared up at Savannah with blank eyes.

"How bad is he?" Dirk asked her.

She looked down at the wound and saw that blood wasn't just flowing from it; it was spurting. Annie O. had hit an artery. "Pretty bad." Savannah turned to the clerk. "Do you have any sanitary napkins in here?"

"What?" The old lady looked confused. "I . . . uh . . . there are some tampons on that shelf there. I—"

"No, I need sanitary napkins . . . pads . . . if you've got them. To stop the bleeding."

"I don't carry anything like that."

"Paper towels?"

"I got regular old napkins over there by the coffee machine," the clerk said, "but I'm not getting them for you if it's to help him."

Dirk ran to the coffee station, grabbed a handful of napkins, and thrust them into Savannah's hands. She used them to apply pressure to the wound but the blood quickly saturated them, welling between her fingers. She silently cursed herself for not having a pair of gloves. "Roco, my man, you better not have AIDS," she muttered. "Call 911," she told the clerk. "Tell them to get an ambulance here, code three."

The lady shook her silver head. "I'm not calling anybody. I hope he bleeds to death right there on that floor. Then he won't be holding up some other poor soul who *hasn't* served time in the military."

Dirk made the emergency call himself.

He also brought an entire box of the napkins over to Savannah, knelt next to her, and tried to help her staunch the flow.

She glanced down at Roco's ashen face, his dark eyes wide with pain and fear. She had to admit; she felt just a little bit sorry for the guy . . . until she thought of his previous victims . . . the guy he had pistol-whipped, who still couldn't walk.

Then she decided that maybe Lady Justice wasn't such a bad old broad after all.

"Guess this *was* my lucky day," Dirk said as he tossed away a handful of soaked napkins and grabbed some fresh ones. He looked down at Roco. "*You*, on the other hand . . . you're going to the hospital and then right back to prison."

Savannah could hear sirens approaching. She could also hear the clerk talking on her cell phone. She was saying to somebody, "Yeah, I got him good. Right in the leg. He's the third one I've shot in only five years! Sure, let's get together tonight at O'Henry's and celebrate."

Savannah nudged Roco to keep him conscious. "Stay awake for me, there, buddy. Help's about here." She shook her head. "Boy, you're just havin' a bad night, aren't you? You get fired from a job, you pick the only convenience store in three states with a gun-totin' granny WAC behind the counter, you violate your parole and get a hole blown in your leg . . . all in one hour. How piss-poor unlucky are *you*?!"

"I sure appreciate you letting my cousin stay with you," Tammy said as she brought Savannah a second hot-from-the-oven cinnamon bun on a china dessert plate. "I just don't have room for her there in that tiny little apartment of mine, and you have a nice extra bedroom upstairs. It's just so much handier, and you're so nice to do this for us and . . ."

She babbled on as she placed the roll on the end table next to Savannah's easy chair, then fluffed up a pillow and shoved it under Savannah's feet, which were resting on an ottoman. Still in her bathrobe, pajamas, and fluffy slippers, Savannah looked the picture of Saturday morning leisure. Except that it was Tuesday.

Tammy tried to grab the mug out of Savannah's hand. "Here, let me refresh that cup of coffee for you and—"

"Hey, hey . . . hold on." Savannah clutched the mug to her chest. "Not that I don't enjoy having my hiney kissed like this first thing in the morning, but the homemade rolls are enough. You don't have to wait on me hand and foot, too."

"I don't mind. Really, I don't. Here, is that enough cream in your coffee? Enough frosting on that bun?"

Savannah paused mid-slurp to watch her assistant over the rim of her Mickey Mouse mug.

Something was up.

Tammy Hart had been Savannah's so-called sidekick for years, a delightful addition to her Moonlight Magnolia Detective Agency, not to mention a close personal friend. Tammy was always energetic, eager to please, and beaming with exuberance— often more exuberance than the less feisty Savannah could stand.

But the tall, slender, athletic, and health-conscious blonde despised junk food of any kind. She considered the "three deadly whites," Sugar, Flour, and Salt, to be the greatest evils upon the face of the earth—far ahead of Lust, Gluttony, Sloth, Greed, or Envy.

So why would she appear on Savannah's doorstep first thing in the morning with a piping hot pan of cinnamon rolls? And why was she scurrying around like a chamber maid in a queen's court? A grumpy queen, who was likely to scream, "Off with her head!"

"Tell me more about this cousin of yours," Savannah said, keeping her voice even, her face expressionless.

Tammy shot her a quick look as she poured a dollop more cream into her cup. "Uh . . . Abigail? Mmmm . . . yes. Abby's well, she's . . . . What did you want to know about her?"

"What she's like. If you two were close growing up. And why you feel so guilty about dumping her off on me."

Bingo. Tammy's golden tan turned two shades paler. She spilled some of the cream onto the floor beside Savannah's chair.

Instantly Savannah's two black cats, a couple of mini-panthers named Cleopatra and Diamante, scrambled off the windowsill and began to lap it up.

"Guilty?" Tammy choked on her own spit—always a bad sign. "I just hope the two of you will get along. That's all."

"Why wouldn't we? You said she's a big girl, like me. She probably likes to eat and cook. We'll swap recipes."

"Well, actually, Abigail's bigger than you. Quite a bit bigger, in fact."

Savannah shrugged. "Good. Then she'll probably have better recipes."

Tammy set the creamer on the end table and sat down on the sofa. "Abby's really big. Really heavy. The family is all worried about her health. That's why I entered her in the contest."

"The makeover thing that new spa is offering?"

"Yeah. The place is called 'Emerge,' and the woman who runs it is this famous Beverly Hills surgeon, Dr. Suzette Du Bois." The guilt briefly left Tammy's face and her eyes sparkled with enthusiasm. "She's been running a spa for movie stars in the Hollywood Hills—"

"The Mystic Twilight Club . . . yeah, I've heard of the place.

But you have to have a bazillion bucks to even get through the gates."

"That's there, but this new place, Emerge, is for the average person."

"The average person with money to burn, you mean."

"Well, yes, I'm sure it's expensive, too. I mean, plastic surgery and personal trainers and fashion consultants, they don't come cheap, but what they can do there is amazing! The idea is, you go in as a disgusting old caterpillar and *emerge* as a beautiful butterfly!"

"And you're going to send your cousin, Abigail, through this . . . process?"

"Yes! I won it for her! Dr. Du Bois had a contest; people wrote in to enter the people they love and to recommend them for a metamorphosis. I had to write this long letter all about Abigail and how she deserved to enter the program and find the true, beautiful self she has hidden under all that . . . you know . . . inside."

Savannah took a sip of coffee, then said quietly, "Don't you consider Abigail beautiful, as she is?"

"Well, yes, but . . . she could be so much more . . . or less . . . or . . . You know."

Savannah stifled the urge to take offense. As a woman who carried some extra pounds above what the weight charts considered "ideal," she was a bit sensitive to disparaging remarks aimed at less-than-svelte folks. But she knew that Tammy, for all of her own weight-consciousness, wasn't really prejudiced against any group of people.

Tammy meant well. She had a good heart. And that was the only reason Savannah hadn't shoved the carrot and celery sticks that she was always offering up her left nostril.

You don't do serious damage to nitwits who mean well. It was a motto Savannah lived by, most of the time.

"How does Abigail feel about you entering her into this contest?" Savannah asked.

Tammy shrugged. "I haven't told her yet. I thought I'd wait until she gets here this afternoon. Then I'll surprise her with it. Don't you think she'll be thrilled? I mean, this is the chance of a lifetime! Who wouldn't be?"

Who wouldn't be thrilled to know that their cousin entered them into a contest for a total physical makeover—an ordeal involving torturous exercise, a starvation diet, and having your body carved, vacuumed, and stitched—the chance for a big, fat "caterpillar" to emerge as a socially acceptable "butterfly"? Yeah, who wouldn't be just jazzed about that? Savannah mulled that one over.

"When is Abigail getting here?" she asked with lackluster enthusiasm.

"I'm picking her up at LAX this afternoon. She's flying in from New York. I figured I'd bring her straight here from the airport. She thinks she's just here for a California vacation: some sun, some beach, Disneyland. Wait until she finds out! She's going to be so happy!" Tammy bounced off to the kitchen and quickly returned with yet another roll.

Savannah took it and held it close to her nose, breathing in the warm, cinnamon-scented sweetness. Yes, she intended to savor this frosting-coated bit of bribery. Because, in spite of Miss Tammy-Pollyanna's optimism, Savannah had a feeling that before Cousin Abigail's California visit was over, she was going to earn every stinking, guilt-laden calorie.

Chapter

2

"I thought you'd made a New Year's resolution not to let any relatives come visit you," Ryan Stone said as he dished up bowls full of Savannah's banana pudding and handed them to her for the mega-dollop of whipped cream.

Savannah shrugged. "Yes, but you know as well as I do that New Year's resolutions don't even last as long as the Christmas fudge. Besides, I meant any of *my own* crazy Georgian relatives. I forgot to include Tammy's family."

Ryan leaned over her to pull another bowl out of the cupboard, and Savannah had to remember to breathe. Even after years of friendship, Savannah hadn't gotten over her crush on Ryan. He was straight off the pages of one of her romance novels: tall, dark, and heart-stop handsome. A simple smile from him could set her knickers aquiver, but having him close enough for her to smell his two-hundred-dollar-a-half-ounce cologne was enough to cause all of her vital systems to shut down.

But long ago, Savannah had given up any dreams of sharing anything more than banana pudding-scooping with him. And the reason had just walked into her kitchen: Ryan's life partner, John Gibson.

"May I be of any assistance?" John asked in his velvety British accent. His thick silver hair glowed against his pale blue cashmere sweater, which was the same shade as his eyes. John wasn't exactly hard to look at either. And he was the epitome of grace and generosity.

"Why don't you go ask Tammy and Abigail if they want coffee or tea," she suggested. "I made both . . . Earl Grey for you, John, of course."

He leaned over and gave her a kiss, tickling her cheek with his lush mustache. Lowering his voice he said, "Must I? I was hoping to escape for just a moment or so. Ryan, would you be so kind?"

Ryan gave him a withering look. "Right, send *me* back in there. No thanks. Savannah asked *you* to do it."

They looked at each other, then at Savannah, and they both gave her sheepish grins.

"What is this?" she said. "Neither one of you wants to go back into my living room and visit with my guests?"

Ryan chuckled. "We love Tammy."

John nodded. "It's true. We've always had a special fondness for Tammy, darling girl that she is."

"And Abigail is her cousin," Savannah said, "and this little party is to welcome Abby to California, so go get welcoming. Why do you think I invited you guys over here tonight?"

"Uh . . . to dilute the bitter cup of social tea brewing in your household," John replied evenly. "At least, that would be my guess."

"Mine, too," Ryan added. "I know if I had to contend with . . . that person . . . for any length of time, I'd be inviting *you* over to smooth out the bumpy patches."

"That bad, eh?"

John sighed. "I merely mentioned something about a fascinating program I'd watched on the Discovery Channel about the hippopotami of the Congo, and she took offense. Asked me if that were some sort of wisecrack aimed at her."

Savannah placed the bowls on a serving tray along with some spoons and napkins. "She does seem to be a bit touchy about the topic of weight. But we need to be patient. It isn't easy being overly-curvaceous in a supermodel-skinny world."

"But I love curves," Ryan said, giving Savannah an approving once-over.

John nodded vigorously. "As do I! We both appreciate the sensuous beauty of a voluptuous woman."

"Oh, shut up," she snapped. "You're both shameful teases."

She took the last bowl from Ryan and emptied the remainder of the whipped cream on top of it. Then she shoved the tray in John's direction. "Here, take that in there, give them a bowl, and find out what they want to drink. And whatever you do, don't give Abigail the one with the extra whipped cream . . . unless she asks for it. She's bound to get riled if you do."

John and Ryan didn't stay long. Not nearly as long as Savannah would have liked. She had hoped they would at least hang around long enough for Tammy to work up the courage to tell Abigail about her "gift."

But they were long gone, and it was just the three women and the two cats when Tammy dropped her bombshell.

Savannah was sitting in her comfy chair, letting Cleopatra lick whipped cream off her fingertip when it happened.

"I have a really special reason why I invited you to come visit me," Tammy began. She was sitting on Savannah's footstool and facing Abigail, who was on the sofa, her feet propped on the coffee table.

Normally, Savannah didn't allow people to put their shoes on the table. It had been Granny Reid's and that made it sacred. But there was something about Abigail that didn't invite criticism, advice, or even a simple request. Savannah wouldn't have admitted that she was actually afraid of Abigail Simpson, but she was.

In the first place, Abigail wasn't what she had been expecting. Savannah knew that Tammy came from a well-to-do East coast family, and knowing that Abigail lived in New York she had anticipated a stylish dresser. But Abby was less than Fifth Avenue chic. If she had, indeed, been walking down Fifth Avenue, she probably would have been mistaken for a bag lady.

Tammy had called her "grooming impaired" and that was kind.

Her waist-length hair hung in a limp braid down her back and looked as though it hadn't been washed in a month of Sundays. She wore no makeup of any sort on her sallow face, and while Savannah didn't particularly wear a lot herself, she couldn't help thinking that even a bit of color on Abigail's cheeks and a dab of lipstick would have made her look better. Maybe even . . . alive.

Her blouse and skirt hung in shapeless drapes around her, the top a bright paisley print and the skirt an equally brilliant plaid. Her shoes were scuffed black boots with laces that were knotted in several places.

The only sign of vanity or personal fashion statement was her jewelry. She wore enormous gold hoops in her ears and at least eight or ten bangles on each wrist.

Yes, "grooming impaired" was kind.

Earlier that afternoon, upon opening her front door and seeing Abigail standing there in all of her frumpish glory, Savannah had decided that this "Emerge" idea of Tammy's was a pretty good one, all in all.

But after a few hours in Abigail's company, Savannah was afraid for Tammy's life. Abby seemed to take offense at absolutely everything that might even be remotely weight-related. If she glowered when told she would have a really "big" time in California, how would she take the news that her cousin thought she needed "making over?"

"You invited me here for a *special* reason?" Abigail's eyes narrowed. "What special reason? You said it was because Mom told you I needed a vacation after working so hard this last semester."

"Well, it is, partly." Tammy scooped the cat off Savannah's lap and held her tightly. She looked like a scared kid clutching a teddy bear. Savannah winced when Cleo growled and switched her tail back and forth. If Tammy kept squeezing her like that, she was going to be on the receiving end of fang and claw.

Cleo knew when she was being used.

"It's really a . . . a wonderful surprise," Tammy stammered. "You're just going to love it!"

"I doubt it," Abigail replied with a sniff. "If I were going to love it, you wouldn't be beating around the bush like this. Spit it out."

"I won something for you."

"What is it?"

"It's a stay at a spa. A new luxury spa here in San Carmelita that—"

"I don't do spas."

"But . . . but . . ." Tammy shot a panic-filled look at Savannah.

"It's a very high-end spa," Savannah offered, deciding to dive headfirst into the deep end with her friend. *Hey, what are friends for?* she thought as she heard herself add, ". . . with all sorts of extras besides just the massages and—"

"I don't do massages." Abigail crossed her arms over her chest and stuck out her chin. "That's just what I need . . . some skinny woman massaging my naked body, thinking of the wisecracks she's going to make to her friends the minute my back is turned."

Savannah thought of the kind, gentle, nonjudgmental therapists who had soothed her aching muscles when she had been fortunate enough to afford a massage. "I don't think they're all that way," she said. "They see and touch bodies all day long and the vast majority of us don't look like runway models."

"And the majority doesn't look like me either," Abigail snapped. "That's what you're thinking. You might as well go ahead and say it."

Savannah's temper flared. "That isn't what I was thinking at all. And I don't like people telling me what I'm thinking, especially when they're just flat dab wrong about it. You've been doing that ever since you got here, and frankly, I don't appreciate it."

"Uh, well, um . . ." Tammy interjected. "This spa isn't really known for its massages anyway. It has a lot more to offer. It's run by this doctor, Suzette Du Bois, and she's famous. A lot of movie stars go to her for . . . um . . . rejuvenation and stuff."

Abigail's nostrils flared. "What kind of rejuvenating *stuff*?"

"Well," Tammy continued as Cleo growled, "she's a surgeon, and she does all sorts of amazing things like . . . uh . . . liposuction and tummy tucks and butt lifts and skin resurfacing and . . . you know . . . stuff that anybody would just *love* to have if they could only afford it, but I could never afford it, and I suppose you couldn't either, so I put your name in the drawing and told them what a fantastic person you are, and how deserving you are, and they said, 'Okay, she wins!'" Tammy took a deep gulp of air and added, "Now isn't that just about the best news you ever heard?"

What they heard was nothing.

Nothing at all.

Silence reigned for what seemed like ten and half years.

Then Cleo yowled, bit Tammy on the thumb, jumped out of her lap and ran away.

Abigail sat there, smoldering for another eternity before she said in a quiet, deadly tone, "Let me get this straight. You 'won' me a chance to have some butcher carve up my body and—"

"And liposuction!" Tammy offered feebly. "Don't forget the liposuction! That's not cutting anything, it's . . ." Her voice faded away as she watched her cousin's face grow purple.

"Carved up and vacuumed away. My body hacked up and parts of it thrown away as biohazard material just because you and society think there's too much of me! And that's why you invited me to come visit you here in sunny California? Is that what you're saying to me, dear cousin of mine?"

Tammy sat there on the footstool, holding her bleeding thumb, opening and closing her mouth like a goldfish who had just jumped out of his bowl, and staring at Abigail. "I . . . I . . . well . . . I . . ."

Savannah couldn't take anymore. "I'm sure it seemed like a good idea at the time," she said in her most conciliatory tone, "but knowing now how you feel about it, Tammy can just contact the people there at Emerge tomorrow morning and gracefully decline on your behalf. And you, Miss Abigail"—she fixed her with the no-nonsense, big-sister glare that she had perfected over the years when dealing with eight younger siblings—"can assume that your cousin had nothing but your best interests at heart. You can say a simple, 'No, thank you,' and spend the rest of your vacation lying on the beach, soaking up some of our golden California sunshine and thanking Tammy that you're not back there in New York City, enjoying that foot and a half of snow the weather man says they just got."

Abigail glared back and said, "Oh, yes, that's just what I want to do . . . go lie on a beach with all the skinny California girls in their bikinis, who look like heroin addicts or escapees from a concentration camp, who starve themselves to conform to society's standard of . . ."

Savannah sighed and shook her head. Some days it just didn't pay to gnaw through the restraints.

The next morning, Savannah, Tammy, and Dirk were sitting at the picnic table in Savannah's backyard, eating a lunch of fried bologna sandwiches and potato salad that Savannah had fixed for them. At least, Savannah and Dirk were eating it. As usual, Tammy had brought a healthier selection of her own, a Tupperware container full of salad.

"I swear, I never saw a body do a turnaround like that so fast in all my life," Savannah said, spreading mustard thickly on a slice of bread. "Last night Abigail was madder than a wet hen, squawking about how degrading the very idea of a makeover was. And today, she comes downstairs to the breakfast table, sunshine and light, and says she's rarin' to go!"

Tammy beamed. "I know! I can't believe it myself, but she couldn't wait for me to take her over to Emerge and get her started. You should have seen the fuss the staff was making over her, TV cameras and news crews everywhere. Abby was eating up all the attention."

Dirk took a swig of lemonade and cleared his throat. "Sounds suspicious to me. She's up to something."

"Yeah, that's what I think, too," Savannah added. "I saw a gleam in her eye that my nephew gets right before he pulls the tail off a lizard."

"Don't say that." Tammy winced.

"Sorry, but I think that kid's a budding serial killer. Vidalia had better get her bluff in on him before he gets much older or—"

"No," Tammy said, "I mean don't say that about Abigail. Have a little faith, will you two?"

"In what?" Dirk wanted to know.

"Humanity."

He grunted. "That'll be the day. I'm a cop, remember? I see every day what 'humanity' is up to. And it ain't pretty."

Tammy Sunshine shook her head in disgust. "Not *everybody* is up to something. Some people are good and kind and—"

"Only the ones who are afraid of getting caught and punished." He gave her a nasty little smirk. "That's where I come in. I keep the regular folks honest."

Savannah chuckled. "Oh, yes, Dirk. That's it. Everybody in society is law-abiding because Dirk Coulter is on duty. We live in fear. We tremble in—"

"Yeah, yeah, enough already." He held out his glass. "Gimme some more of that lemonade and mark my words: She's up to something. It's just a matter of time until we find out what."

In less than forty-eight hours, around nine in the evening, Savannah got the phone call. She was sitting in her favorite chair, her feet on the ottoman, a cup of double-fudge hot chocolate on her side table, a romance novel open on her lap, and a cat on either side of her feet—kitty foot warmers, she liked to call them.

Dirk's surly voice barked at her through the phone. "Where is that houseguest of yours?" he asked without preamble.

"She went to bed an hour ago. Why?"

"How did she seem?"

"Seem?"

"Yeah, you know, her mood. Was she grouchy, grumpy?"

"Not particularly. Not Sneezy or Bashful, either. She spent the day there at Emerge, getting her blood work done and other things to get ready for her surgeries. They've scheduled her liposuction for the day after tomorrow. She seemed a little tired . . . wanted to go to bed early. What's this about?"

"I just caught a case."

"What is it?"

"Missing person."

"What's this got to do with me?" she said, glancing down at her half-read romance novel. In the last chapter, the virgin heroine had finally trusted the swashbuckling hero enough to take a moonlight sail on his ship. He had "trusted" her right back . . . very nicely, and in graphic, steamy detail. So well, in fact, that Savannah suspected the newly deflowered lady would allow him to trust her in the next chapter, too.

Something to look forward to.

Dirk's timing had always left a lot to be desired.

"It's Suzette Du Bois who's gone missing," he said. "The plastic surgeon who's supposed to operate on your girl there. The one who owns the joint where she's—"

"You're kidding! When?"

"Last night was the last time anybody saw her. She didn't show up at the clinic this morning. Didn't Abigail mention it to you? Apparently, everybody there was talking about it."

Savannah glanced at the staircase and wondered about her houseguest upstairs. Now that she thought about it, maybe Abigail had seemed a little weird tonight. But then, with Abigail, who could really tell?

"Where are you?" she asked.

"On my way to Du Bois's house, down by the marina. Her business partner has a key to the place. He's going to meet me there and let me in."

"Want some help?"

"I don't need help."

Savannah rolled her eyes. "Of course not. What was I thinking?"

"But I'd like to have your company. Got any more of those chocolate chip cookies . . . the ones with the nuts in them?"

Chapter

3

Like many Southern California coastal towns, San Carmelita was longer than it was wide, with the ocean forming its western border and the eastern edge a row of sage-covered foothills.

Spring rainstorms would temporarily green the hills until they looked like the mountains of Killarney, but the rest of the year they were a relatively boring tawny beige. Their only adornment: sprinklings of prickly pear cactus and the occasional gnarled oak tree.

When those spring rains were generous, it was easy to forget that Southern California was basically a desert, each community a man-made oasis. But when spring came and went with only minimal rainfall, it became all too apparent to the residents that they were desert dwellers and that every drop of water counted.

As Savannah left her home in the middle of town, halfway between the beach and the foothills, and drove toward the waterfront area and the marina, she noticed that her neighbors' yards, like hers, were extra crispy this year. Watering lawns—like washing cars, rinsing down sidewalks, showering alone, and flushing a "number one"—was temporarily outlawed.

But if March brought its usual tropical storms, Savannah and her fellow Californians would be building sandbag dams around their houses to prevent the rivers of water that coursed down the streets from rushing through their front doors. The mansions, perched on the hillsides for the optimal ocean view, would be sliding down onto their neighbor's mansions, mountains of mud and rock would be cascading onto the Pacific Coast Highway, traffic would be backed up from Santa Monica to Santa Barbara, and Southern California would be back to "normal."

Sometimes Savannah missed the relatively uneventful weather of the small, rural Georgia town where she had been born and raised. She missed it most during earthquakes. But about the time she waxed too nostalgic, she would round a corner and see the sparkling Pacific spread out before her, lined with golden beaches and majestic rows of graceful palms, and she forgot all about peach orchards and pecan groves.

Tonight the ocean was particularly beautiful, sparkling in the silver light of a full moon. On the distant Santa Tesla Island she could see the occasional wink of the lighthouse's beam as it made its rounds.

Yes, this Georgia peach was usually quite contented and happy to be transplanted.

As always when she entered the waterfront areas of town, she noticed that they had more than their share of stately palm trees. Apparently palms grew best in soil enriched with *beaucoup de* bucks.

Luxury cars did, too. Everywhere she looked she saw some version of Mercedes, Jaguar, or BMW, along with the perfectly restored classic Chevrolets, Fords, and Rolls Royces.

Savannah felt right at home in her own '65 Mustang, except for the black smoke coming out of her exhaust pipe—another issue she would have to address if she ever got another client. At the moment they weren't exactly knocking down her door.

She found the address quickly, an elegant Spanish-style home that backed up onto one of the many channels that interlaced this area. Around the rear corner of the house she could see what appeared to be at least forty feet of dock and an ocean-worthy sailboat.

Not bad, she thought, looking over the multilevel dwelling with its glistening white stucco walls and red-tiled roof. *That's what my little house is going to be when it grows up someday.*

But, ever-practical, she reminded herself that she didn't want a spread like this. The taxes alone would be more than her mortgage, utilities, and Victoria's Secret bill combined. There'd be no money left over for bubble bath or Godiva chocolates. And a lady had to keep her financial priorities in order.

She considered pulling into the driveway next to Dirk's Buick, but decided instead to park on the street and drip oil on public property.

A late-model Mercedes sat next to the Buick, and she saw no radio cars, ambulances, or medical examiner's wagon. No yellow tape across the door. Apparently Dirk hadn't found anything too alarming. Yet.

Most likely, there was a perfectly good reason that the doctor was missing. Most people disappeared, temporarily or permanently, of their own accord. Although, not usually wealthy, successful, well-rooted types like Dr. Du Bois. From the look of her real estate, Suzette Du Bois had spent a lot of time and money establishing herself in this community. She wasn't likely to just walk away from it all.

As Savannah left her car and walked up to the front door of the house, she couldn't help noticing the landscaping. Although the yards in this part of town were miniscule—with every inch of waterfront property a precious commodity—Suzette Du Bois or her groundskeepers had made the most of the tiny lot. Strategically placed lights illuminated the terraced flower beds, which brimmed with Martha Washington geraniums, glistening white alyssum, and deep blue lobelia. Ivy climbed the stucco walls and intertwined with equally hearty bougainvillea, adding an old-world charm to the house that was obviously new.

When she approached the front door she saw that it was ajar, and she could hear male voices coming from inside the house. One of them was Dirk's.

Through the sparkling beveled glass sidelight next to the door, she could see him standing in the well-lit foyer with a tall, dark-haired fellow who appeared to be in his late forties or early fifties.

Pushing the door open, she stuck her head inside. "May I come in?" she asked.

Dirk gave her a curt nod, then turned his attention back to the man. "And that was the last you or anyone you know saw her?"

"Yes. She was leaving the office."

"You saw her drive away?"

He nodded. "In her BMW, which is in the garage. I checked. So, at least, she made it home," he said with what sounded to Savannah like a less-than-genuine Italian accent. A number of things looked less than natural about the guy, from his heavily-gelled hair, which was a suspiciously intense shade of blue-black, to the eyebrows perched halfway up his forehead and the perpetually surprised look on his face. Apparently, he had had a few too many face-lifts in the losing battle against looking his age.

He also looked worried. Worried and tired . . . as if he hadn't slept for days.

Savannah wondered why he would be so tired. Suzette had only gone missing today.

She walked over to them and stood next to Dirk. When he said nothing, but continued to scribble on his notepad, she held out her hand to the man. "I'm Savannah Reid, a friend of Sergeant Coulter here."

Dirk glanced up and grunted. "Oh, sorry. Yes, she was my partner on the force for years. Now she's a private investigator. I ask her to hang out with me once in a while. You mind?"

The man didn't seem to mind at all. In fact, he visually perked-up at the mention of her being a P.I. "I'm Sergio D'Alessandro," he said as he took her hand and gave it a hearty shake. At the same time, his eyes traveled up and down her body, giving her what she called, the "elevator look," stopping at several floors along the way to window-shop.

Apparently, he liked what he saw, because he flashed her a dazzling smile. A bit too dazzling. Savannah suspected he was one of those males who hadn't met a female he didn't like since hitting puberty.

She pulled her hand out of his and resisted the urge to wipe her palm on her pants.

"Nice to meet you," she said through only slightly gritted teeth. "And you are . . . ?"

He visibly swelled with indignation. "*I* own the Mystic Twilight Club, an exclusive spa that caters to only those of the most refined taste and—"

"I know the place," she said. "I meant, who are you in relationship to the missing pers—"

"I'm Dr. Du Bois's business partner. Have been for years. And she was also my ex-wife."

Savannah lifted one eyebrow ever so slightly. "Was? I should think she still *is* and always will be your ex-wife."

He shrugged. "You know what I meant. I mean she's missing now and . . ."

And you're already referring to her in the past tense, she thought, but she kept any further comment to herself. There was little to be gained by letting a potential suspect know how suspicious they appeared.

And if, indeed, Suzette Du Bois was a missing person or a victim of foul play, ex-husbands and current boyfriends were always at the top of the suspect list.

She could feel Dirk tense slightly beside her, and she knew he had picked up on it, too.

He cleared his throat and took on an even more officious tone. "Is Dr. Du Bois in the habit of missing work?"

"Never. Never, never. She was a workaholic and she knew more than anybody how important it was for her to show up today to start this new Emerge campaign."

Again with the past tense.

Savannah decided something then and there. For all of his high-falutin' name, Brioni suit, and Tutima watch, Sergio D'Alessandro wasn't that sharp. Obviously, he knew or strongly suspected his former wife was dead, and he was too dumb to realize he was exposing that fact.

And while most people might fear that possibility if an otherwise responsible, predictable person went missing for twenty-four hours, experience had taught her that most innocent folks continued to speak of their loved ones in the present tense, even after they were confirmed dead. It was only natural.

"All right," Dirk said, flipping his notebook closed. "I'm gonna have a look around. You can get back to whatever you were doing before you drove over here."

Sergio shifted from one Bruno Magli to the other. "Don't you want me to stay . . . in case you need something or . . ."

"Nope. You let me into the house. That's all I need or want from you right now," Dirk replied with his usual lack of charm. "Don't call me. I'll call you. And stay in town. Don't go takin' no unscheduled vacations to Tijuana or Vancouver, if you know what I mean."

He turned and walked away, leaving D'Alessandro standing there with an aggravated look on his face.

When Dirk was out of earshot, Savannah sidled up to him. "There's something you should know," she said. "Sergeant Coulter's bite is a lot worse than his bark."

"Huh? Don't you mean . . . ?"

"Nope. I meant what I said. You should probably leave now."

The next thing she saw was the back of Sergio D'Alessandro's fancy suit, walking briskly out the door. She couldn't help but think that the atmosphere improved with his absence. There was something about the man she didn't like . . . beyond his basic smarminess. And her instincts seldom led her astray in that regard.

Yes, if anything had actually happened to Dr. Suzette Du Bois, she would give ol' Sergio a second look. Maybe a third and a fourth.

She found Dirk in the kitchen, listening to the messages on an answering machine on the counter.

"Anything good?" she asked.

"Just the usual crap," he replied. "A couple of calls from somebody named Myrna, wanting to know why she wasn't at work this morning."

"I think Myrna is the secretary or receptionist at Emerge. She's called at my house and talked to Abigail a couple of times to schedule things with her."

Savannah glanced around the room, noting that, although it was a gorgeous, modern kitchen with lots of architectural accents like beveled glass inserts in the cupboards, an ornate wrought iron pot rack, a brick oven, and marble countertops, it was a mess.

Dirty dishes sat in the sink in a bath of scummy, greasy water. Pans half-filled with dried food littered the stove top. With one finger Savannah opened the dishwasher and it, too, was full of crusty dishes.

"It's a little hard to tell if she ate here last night or this morning," she said. "Most of these dishes look pretty old."

"Eh, she's a pig. She may have a fancy joint here, but my trailer is cleaner than this mess."

While Savannah wouldn't label the woman quite so quickly or harshly, she had to agree that, even though Dirk lived in an old, rusty mobile home in a trailer park on the bad side of town and decorated it with plastic milk crates and rickety TV trays, his place was basically sanitary at all times. And she, herself, had been raised by Granny Reid to believe that a "filthy kitchen" was one where the dishcloth hadn't been thoroughly rinsed and neatly hung on the rack to dry.

"There's no excuse for bein' nasty," Gran always said in her soft, Georgian drawl. "Maybe a body can't help being poor, but everybody can afford a bar of soap. There's just no reason for dirtiness, not a-tall."

"I'm going to go look for her purse," Savannah said.

He nodded. "I'll check out the bedrooms."

Savannah found the pocketbook quickly. It was on an accent table in the living room, next to the door that led into the foyer. And beside the Louis Vuitton bag was a set of keys and a cell phone.

The living room resembled the kitchen in that it was beautifully decorated with high-end mission style furniture but was cluttered with magazines, newspapers, clothing, and a plethora of used wine glasses. Savannah noticed that nearly all of the glasses were smudged with the same shade of bright red lipstick. Apparently, Suzette Du Bois drank alone . . . and a lot.

But there was more than just the usual disorder caused by messy housekeeping . . . or a lack thereof. Books had been pulled off shelves and the drawers of an entertainment center were open, their contents on the floor. A desk against the far wall had been rifled through, as well.

Suzette Du Bois's home had been searched.

And Savannah had seen enough houses that had been burgled

by professionals to know that whoever had searched this house was an amateur. Somebody had been looking for something, but wasn't very good at finding it. She wondered whether they had.

On the floor near the sofa sat a miniature bed, and at first glance, Savannah thought it was for a doll. With a red velvet tufted headboard and a coverlet of the same fabric, it looked like something out of a tiny boudoir. But when she walked over to it, bent down, and examined it more closely, she saw the name "Sammy" embroidered on the bedspread.

Something told her that Sammy was a pet of some sort. And the fact that there was no hair on the velvet ruled out a cat. *Probably a poodle*, she thought. *Or some other type of pooch that doesn't shed.*

"There's some kind of mutt living here," Dirk called from the bedroom. "The damned thing's got a whole wardrobe of ridiculous junk to wear in here."

"And a bed for it in here," she yelled back.

"Somebody tossed this room," Dirk hollered. "All the drawers are open."

"In here, too."

On the coffee table, amid the heap of magazines and next to a nail file and bottle of polish lay a small leather dog collar. It was bright pink, studded with purple rhinestones. *How gaudy*, she thought, fingering the tiny collar. Cleopatra and Diamante wore only black with *clear* rhinestones. In Savannah's household, no self-respecting pet would be caught dead in *purple* rhinestones. Especially if his name was Sammy!

Dirk walked into the living room just as Savannah was picking up a daily planner from a side table next to an easy chair. She thumbed to the current date and found two entries. "AS workup" under 9:15 A.M., and "Lunch—Toscano's" under 1:30 P.M.

"The barking rat's not here," he said, "or it would already be nipping at our heels. I checked all the other rooms. No sign of her or Fido."

"AS work-up," Savannah muttered. "I'll bet that is for Abigail Simpson, Tammy's cousin. Wonder if Suzette made her luncheon date."

"What makes you think she had a date for lunch?"

"Toscano's is one of the most romantic restaurants in the county. No woman would go there alone."

"Maybe she was meeting another chick."

"Maybe, but I doubt it. 'Chick' lunches, as you call them, usually go down at Kimberly's Garden or Casa del Sol."

"So, we gotta check Toscano's first thing when they open tomorrow," he said.

"Nothing in the bedroom?"

"Nope, nothing but more mess, like in here and the kitchen."

"Was her bed slept in?"

He shrugged and looked puzzled. "How can you tell?"

Savannah thought of the tiny cubicle in Dirk's trailer that served as a bedroom and its perpetually mussed sheets and blankets. "Never mind," she said. "She probably doesn't make hers daily either."

"I never did understand the logic behind that," he replied. "I mean, you're just going to get right back in it again, so what's the point?"

"The same could be said for doing dishes and changing your underwear. It's what separates us civilized folks from the heathens."

"Or us practical people from the fusspots."

"Whatever."

"You always say that when you're losing an argument."

"Or when I'm tired of a stupid one." She glanced around the room once more. "What do you think?" she asked him.

"I still think you quit every time I'm getting the best of you."

"I meant about Suzette Du Bois."

"I think she's dead."

Savannah nodded thoughtfully. "Me, too. She leaves her car, her purse and keys, her cell phone. Is her makeup in the bathroom?"

"Yeap. You taught me to always check that first when it's a broad who's gone. A woman goes off without her face, that's a bad sign."

"The worst. But what about Sammy?"

"Sammy?"

"The dog."

"How do you know its name?"

Savannah pointed to the bed.

"Oh," he said. "Well, there's a nice little sweater with four arm—or leg—holes in it, layin' on the bedroom floor, and it's a chilly night out."

"And his rhinestone collar is there on the coffee table." She took a deep breath, then let it out slowly. "I agree. I've got a sinking feeling that Dr. Suzette Du Bois is a goner. And things don't bode so well for Sammy Du Bois either."

Chapter

4

Savannah stood in front of her stove, spatula in hand, watching the breakfast eggs fry in the skillet, the grits bubble on the back burner, and Abigail stew at the kitchen table.

"I can't believe they'd cancel the press conference this morning," she was complaining to Tammy, who sat across from her, her elbows propped on the table, her head in her hands. "Why? Why would they do that!"

"Because Dr. Du Bois has gone missing," Tammy said for the fifth time in the past fifteen minutes. "Dr. Du Bois owns Emerge. She *is* Emerge. They can't have a press conference to announce the opening of Emerge without her there! I'm sorry you're so disappointed, Abby, but . . ."

Savannah left her position at the stove and walked over to the table with a basket of hot biscuits and a jar of Granny Reid's peach preserves. She set them in front of Abigail, hoping that the sight of fat-filled, carbohydrate-rich foods would improve her mood. Hey, it always worked for *her*.

"Yes, Abigail," she said as she shoved the butter plate in Abby's direction, "why *are* you so disappointed? Frankly, I'm a little surprised. In the beginning you were so opposed to the

whole idea and now you're plumb beside yourself that everything's been put on hold. What's that about?"

Abigail fixed her with a baleful eye, then reached for the biscuit basket. "I didn't like the idea at first, but I had decided to go
ahead with it. At least until . . ."

Savannah searched her face, but Abigail would have made an
excellent poker player. Other than general anger and habitual an-
noyance, nothing more registered on her features.

"Until what?" Savannah prompted. "You were going to go
ahead with it until what?"

Abigail shrugged. "I don't know. I just figured when the time
was right, I'd . . ."

"What?" Tammy said, dropping her hands from her face. She
looked as suspicious as Savannah felt. "What were you up to,
Abby? I want to know, too. I think I have a right to know, since
I'm the one who—"

"Who got me into this mess in the first place?" Abigail dropped
two of the biscuits onto her plate and started to slather on the
butter. "I know. I owe you one, too, cousin."

Savannah didn't like Abigail's tone. It wasn't the sort of "I owe
you a nice lunch some time" tone she would have preferred. It
was more like an "I'm gonna get you, sucker, in a dark alley some
night" tone.

And the "too" stuck in her craw even more.

She walked back to the stove, and, while she tended the eggs,
she glanced at the woman sitting at her kitchen table and wondered what was behind that angry face. A world of hurt. She was
sure of that.

And Savannah understood that pain all too well. Living as an
unsvelte woman in a svelte-worshipping society . . . hurt was in-
evitable. Deep, soul-scarring hurt.

On most days, Savannah could fend off the barbs and arrows
with her own inherent self-confidence. Who cared if your butt

was big if you had great boobs and helped take a bad guy off the streets so that he couldn't hurt anybody else for a while? She'd be damned if she'd hate herself and her own flesh just because somebody else thought there was a bit too much of it.

But Savannah knew that not everyone was as satisfied with their life as she was, and not everyone had benefited from having a grandmother who had raised them with such daily helpings of wisdom as: "Don't fret about such nonsense as a number on a scale, Savannah Girl. People measure everything by numbers in this world—mostly so's they can feel they've got a leg up on everybody else—and most of what they're measurin' ain't worth squat in the overall scheme o' things."

Savannah strongly suspected that Abigail Simpson hadn't been raised to believe that she was far more than just a number on a scale. Sadly, there weren't enough Granny Reids in the world to go around.

But was all that hurt and anger a danger to society? More specifically, was it a threat to the missing owner of Emerge—an establishment that symbolized the intolerance that caused Abigail and others so much pain?

Savannah slipped into detective mode and made a quick mental note of Abigail's whereabouts since she had arrived. She realized there were numerous holes in Abby's schedule that were large enough to allow for mischief.

But if Abigail had actually done something to cause Dr. Du Bois to disappear, that would involve far more than mere mischief. And looking at the woman who was sitting at her table, eating her biscuits and peach preserves, Savannah found it hard to believe that Tammy's cousin was capable of kidnapping. Or worse.

She decided to talk it over in detail with Dirk later, when they met at Emerge as planned.

After a few more unpleasant exchanges with Abigail, Tammy

left the table and walked behind Savannah to the refrigerator. Pouring herself a glass of apple juice, she shot Savannah a haunted look. Savannah shrugged. There was only so much she could do. Abigail might be staying in her house, but she was Tammy's guest.

Lucky Tammy.

"Why don't you take Abigail over to the pier today?" she suggested. "Check out the carousel and get your palms read. Have one of those giant ice cream waffle cones."

"Is that what you think I do all day? Eat?" Abigail snapped while chewing on a biscuit. "Is that why you're suggesting stuff like that and feeding me every minute?"

Savannah slipped the eggs onto a plate and shoved them in front of Abigail, along with a bowlful of grits and a platter of bacon and sausages. "I don't know how much you eat, Abigail," she said, "and I don't give a hoot what you eat. I have a lot more interesting things to think about on any given day than your dietary habits. I just know what *this* kid"—she nodded toward Tammy—"has for breakfast, and I wanted to spare you eating a bowl of sawdust covered with soy milk. Don't get your dander up, sugar. I'd do it for anybody."

Abigail's mouth dropped open for a moment, then she snapped it closed and smiled.

She actually smiled, Savannah thought in wonderment. *I got a grin out of her!*

"Well," Abigail said, "as long as you'd do it for anybody."

"Yeap. Anybody. You ain't nearly as special as you think you are, Miss Abigail," she said with a sweet, soft tone that sounded in her own ears a lot like Granny Reid. "Leastwise, not special in *that* way."

Tammy gave a little gasp, and for a moment, a heavy, awkward silence hung in the air between them.

Then Abigail threw back her head and laughed. It was a

hearty, throat-roaring laugh that echoed throughout the house, startling both Savannah and Tammy and the cats, who left their feeding bowls and raced for the living room.

When Abigail finally caught her breath, she studied Savannah for a few long moments and then said, "You're a pisser, Savannah. I think I like you."

Savannah dumped another biscuit onto her plate. "Yeah, yeah . . . well, you don't know me yet. Wait'll I make you my usual, run-of-the-mill Southern fried chicken dinner with all the fixins. That'll probably be more of an insult than your system can handle."

Abigail's eyes softened, and for a moment, Savannah noticed that she really could look pretty. Quite pretty, in fact. "You go ahead and make that dinner for me, and I won't take offense," Abigail said. "Throw in some old-fashioned cream gravy, and I'll even be nice and say 'Thank you.'"

"Well now, we don't have to go that far. You go straining yourself like that, you might bust somethin'."

Savannah had driven past the building site for the new Emerge facilities many times, as it was situated on a major road that skirted the foothills at the edge of town. Like too many areas in San Carmelita—in Savannah's opinion—that section of the city had been "improved" by chopping down the orange and avocado groves and planting commercial buildings and condominiums in their stead.

Savannah missed the strawberry fields and lemon trees. While a giant office supply store and a sprawling home improvement center might be handy when you needed an ink cartridge for your printer or wallpaper and paint, they didn't smell half as sweet when warmed by the morning sun.

But she had to admit that the new Emerge building was a beauty. Set back from the road, a wide driveway took the visitors to an elegant, contemporary facade. An asymmetrical arrangement of rose-colored granite walls and brass-trimmed windows and doors set with copper-tinted glass, the establishment exuded both modern sophistication and warmth.

The word "Emerge" and a simple butterfly were displayed in brass over the wide, double front doors. Savannah drove into a parking area to the right and behind the building, where she found Dirk, sitting in his Buick and waiting for her.

She glanced at her watch. It was two minutes past nine.

She was late. Two whole minutes. Mr. Fidget Britches would be having a hissy.

He glowered as he saw her approach the car and tapped a finger on the dial of his wristwatch.

"Yeah, yeah, yeah," she said, casually opening the passenger door and climbing inside. "Get over yourself. Like your schedule's any more important than anybody else's."

She reached into her oversized purse, pulled out a wad of aluminum foil, and tossed it into his lap.

"What's this?" he asked, brightening instantly.

"Biscuits. Still warm from the oven."

"Wow, Van, thanks!" He dug in immediately, ripping away the foil. "Did you butter them?"

"Of course."

"Peach jam?"

"Yes, shut up and eat."

He bit into one and groaned in gluttonous, orgiastic pleasure. "Oh, man, that is heaven," he said. "Pure heaven. I forgive you for being late."

She sniffed. "That's big of you."

He glanced over toward her bag. "Where's the coffee?"

"What?"

"You brought me biscuits and *no coffee*?"

"I figured you'd have your own."

His smile evaporated. His shoulders slumped. "Well, I guess I can just gag them down without—"

She snatched the foil out of his lap. "Forget about it! I do something nice for you and you bellyache about it?"

"Gimme those biscuits, woman, before I fly into a blind rage!"

She laughed and handed them back. "Did you get over to Toscano's yet?"

"Yeah. Nobody was there but the cleaning crew, but they let me in. I looked at their reservation book. There was a one-thirty entry for a 'Lawrence.' The other names were marked through, but Lawrence wasn't. I figure that's because they didn't show."

"Likely. But does Du Bois know a Lawrence?"

He shrugged. "Don't know. But I'll keep my eyes open for a Larry. How was our girl Abigail this morning?"

"Testy after she got the phone call from Myrna, Emerge's receptionist, this morning. She told Abigail that not only was the press conference cancelled, but the whole kit and caboodle has been put on hold for the time being."

"That Abigail's up to something, I'm telling you. There's just something sneaky about her."

"Yeah, I think so, too. But 'sneaky' is a long way from kidnapping or murder."

"Did you say anything to Tammy?"

"Over breakfast we discussed the fact that Suzette Du Bois is missing, but of course I didn't mention that we were wondering about Abigail. You don't seriously think she's done anything . . . you know . . . like that, do you?"

Dirk brushed the biscuit crumbs off the front of his shirt and back onto the foil. "Naw. I can't see her doing anything drastic. But she's up to no good of some kind. You wait and see."

As they left the car and walked to the front door of the building, Savannah thought of Tammy, so kind and well-intentioned. The young woman didn't have an evil or even cranky bone in her body. It was hard to imagine that she and crabby Abigail were even related. Savannah couldn't bear the thought that Abigail intended to cause any serious trouble that would bring grief to Tammy, who had only intended to benefit her cousin.

"Whatever's gone wrong here," Savannah said, "I'm sure it has nothing to do with Abigail."

"We'll see," Dirk replied.

He opened the front door and held it as Savannah passed through. Savannah liked that about Dirk. He opened doors for women, even in this day and age, and he preferred his ladies well-cushioned—*his* term, not hers—in all the right places. You could forgive a guy for a lot—cheapness, impatience, and occasional indelicacies—in exchange for opened doors and comments like, "Eh, she's too skinny for my taste. Looks like she needs a few cheeseburgers and milkshakes."

But the moment Savannah stepped inside, she forgot all about Dirk's virtues—both of them—as she felt herself caught up in an unexpected, magical environs. Sunshine flooded the lobby, streaming golden from enormous skylights overhead. The walls were the same rose-colored granite as the building's exterior on either side, but straight ahead was a long wall of floor-to-ceiling glass. On the other side of the glass was an atrium, a sunlit fantasy garden of tropical greenery with a misty waterfall, moss-covered rocks . . . and butterflies. Hundreds of breathtakingly beautiful butterflies flitted from plant to plant, from rock to rock, their iridescent wings glimmering with jewel-rich shades of gold, sapphire, emerald, and amethyst.

She walked over to the glass and resisted the urge to press her palms and nose against it like a mesmerized child. "Wow," she said under her breath. "Look at that! Did you ever see anything so beautiful?"

"Why, thank you," replied a male voice behind her. And it wasn't Dirk's.

She turned and saw that Dirk had left her and walked over to a desk on the right side of the room. And behind her stood the most truly beautiful man she had ever seen. Probably in his late twenties or early thirties, he had an ethereal quality about him— cream-colored skin that was as flawless as a cover model's, platinum blond hair, and eyes that were the palest sky blue.

He was dressed in a long-sleeved, ivory silk shirt and linen slacks of the same color. His build was slight but muscular, and although he was a couple of inches shorter than Savannah, his long legs and proportions made him appear taller.

He stepped closer to Savannah and gazed into the atrium, his eyes following the flight of one of the butterflies as it fluttered near the glass where they stood. "It's nice to see people enjoying it," he said with quiet pride, "taking time to really appreciate it. People don't take enough time for beauty these days."

"That's true," she said thoughtfully. He sounded older than his years, and there was a quiet air of wisdom and grace about him that seemed ageless.

She extended her hand to him. "I'm Savannah," she said, "and you are . . . ?"

He took her hand in his and gave it a firm but gentle shake. "I'm Jeremy Lawrence," he replied. "the stylist here at Emerge."

"Stylist?" She glanced at his hair. It was a nice, standard, GQ cut. Nothing too fancy. "You're the hairdresser?"

He smiled . . . a patient smile, like that of a teacher with a student. "No," he said, "we have another person who does the hairdressing. I'm more of a style consultant. I coach our clients in developing their own unique styles . . . in all aspects of their lives. Hair and makeup are certainly part of that, but we also offer guidance while they find the best ways to express their inner selves through clothing, jewelry, home furnishings, social etiquette, entertaining, even leisure activities such as music and the arts."

"And you do all that?"

"I help. I guide whenever possible," he said with quiet humility.

Savannah glanced over at Dirk, who was having a conversation with a woman at the desk, a highly made-up, overprocessed, sixtyish blonde who looked as though she would have benefited from this young man's input.

"May I help you with anything?" Jeremy asked. "Are you a member of the press, or . . . ?"

Savannah opened her mouth to say, "No, I'm with that guy over there," but at the last moment, she swallowed the words and decided, on instinct, to lie. "Yes," she said. "I'm with *San Carmelita Today* . . . the magazine in the Sunday paper. I'm sure you've seen it."

"Of course. I read it every weekend."

He was lying, too; she could tell. But at least he was blackening his soul in an attempt to be polite. She wasn't sure why she had given him the cover story. Maybe she was getting too old to trust young men who were prettier than she was.

"Is he with you?" he asked, nodding toward Dirk.

"No," she said, "I overheard him tell the lady there at the desk that he's a detective with the San Carmelita Police Department."

A look of pain crossed Jeremy's face. "Is he here about Suzette? Did you hear him say if he's here because she's . . ."

She waited for him to fill in the blank. When he didn't, she added, "Missing? Yes, I think I heard him say something about that."

"I hope nothing's happened to her," he said, then he seemed to realize he was talking to a "member of the press" and a guarded look crossed his face. "I suppose you came for the press conference today. I'm afraid you've made a trip for nothing. I thought Devon had called everyone to reschedule."

"Devon?"

"Devon Wright, our publicist. I'm surprised you haven't met Devon. She's the one who usually deals with the press."

His pale blue eyes studied hers with an intensity that made her uncomfortable. Her own eyes were a deep, cobalt blue, and long ago she had learned to focus their laserlike intensity on suspects and make them squirm in their interrogation seats. She wasn't accustomed to being on the receiving end of such scrutiny.

"Devon Wright. Ms. *Wright*. Oh, of course I've spoken to her before on the phone. I didn't know her first name."

"And she didn't call you about the press conference being postponed?"

"Oh, she probably did. My assistant at the paper is a dingbat intern. Always forgets to give me my messages. Has the news conference been rescheduled?"

"Here's Devon now." He nodded toward a petite young woman who was striding down the hall to the left, coming toward the lobby. "You can ask her directly. I have to be going now. It was nice speaking with you."

"And with you."

She noticed that he gave Dirk one more sad, anxious look before he retreated down the hallway to the left, passing Devon Wright. He paused to say a couple of words to her before disappearing into one of the doors that lined the corridor.

As the publicist approached her, Savannah decided rather quickly that she didn't particularly like Devon Wright. Hyper people got on her nerves . . . even more so if they were hyper salespeople.

And Devon was wearing the tissue-thin grin of a salesperson as she scurried up to her, her high-heeled boots clicking on the granite floor. Her brightly embroidered, skintight jeans, fringed leather jacket, and super-short, red-tipped, black hair were, no doubt, intended to announce to the world that she was quite "hip" . . . a "with-it" sort of professional.

But to Savannah, she just looked *un*professional.

And Savannah was also willing to admit that maybe she, herself, wasn't all that "hip" or "with-it" anymore.

Getting older did that to you.

"Hello, hello!" Devon greeted her, hand outstretched, fake grin broadening. "I understand you've come for the press conference. I'm sorry you weren't contacted, but we've had to postpone it for today."

"I'm sorry to hear that. I was looking forward to learning more about what you're doing here at Emerge. This is just beee-autiful!"

Devon's eyes glistened with a nearly maniacal gleam. Savannah had seen the same fire of enthusiasm in the eyes of vacuum cleaner salesmen on her front doorstep . . . seconds before she threw them off the porch.

"Oh, isn't it though!" Devon gushed. "This place and the work we'll be doing here is *so* important! Literally changing lives! Women—well, men, too—will walk through those doors sad and ugly worms, and emerge as the glorious butterflies they were meant to be!"

"Worms . . . turning into butterflies . . . hmmm. . . ." Savannah considered for a moment how Abigail would react to that particular terminology. She hadn't even warmed up to the idea of being called a fuzzy caterpillar. She'd probably pitch a fit, and Savannah couldn't blame her.

"They emerge . . . as they were *meant* to be," Savannah mused, "versus, how they were actually born into this world."

"Exactly! Isn't that a mind-shattering concept! Everyone, even the simplest people in society, being able to come to a place like this and transform themselves, fulfill themselves, live life as the person they always wanted to be!"

Savannah returned the too-bright smile and adopted the carnival barker tone of voice. "And they only have to take out a second mortgage on the house, sell the kids, and hawk the family pooch to pay for it all! Ya-a-y-y!"

Devon's grin vanished, replaced by an aggravated, suspicious scowl. "Emerge offers payment plans for the underprivileged . . . upon credit approval, of course."

"Oh, of course."

After several moments of awkward silence, Savannah decided to make a bad situation worse. "I hear that Suzette Du Bois has gone missing," she said.

Yes, every vestige of Devon Wright's faux smile evaporated. "Where did you hear that?" she snapped.

"I overheard that police detective over there asking your receptionist about her." She shrugged. "Hey, I *am* a reporter, after all. I keep my ears open. Of course, I could be persuaded to keep what I heard off the record for the time being. . . ."

Devon opened and closed her mouth several times as she seemed to search for the right words.

"That would be . . . um . . . nice. I mean, there isn't really anything to report now anyway."

"And in return for my . . . waiting . . . you might give me the first phone call when you do have something substantial to report?"

Devon looked doubtful, but she said, "Okay. Give me your business card, and I'll see what I can do."

Business card?

Savannah paused, thinking fast. The cards in her purse represented her as a private investigator, not a newspaper reporter.

"I don't have any with me right now, but I'll leave my number with your receptionist at the desk."

"You don't have a business card, Ms. . . . ?"

Savannah's mental gears whirred. "McGill. Savannah McGill."

Devon's eyes narrowed. "And do you have your press pass with you, Ms. McGill?"

"Darn. No. It's in my other purse . . . with my cards . . . you know, changed pocketbooks last night to go out to dinner at this fancy-schmancy place, forgot to put everything back into my everyday purse. Do you ever do that? I just hate it when I do that."

"Maybe you should leave for now, Ms. McGill. Emerge isn't really open to the public today. You can come back when we have our press conference."

"When they find Suzette Du Bois, you mean. When they figure out what's happened to her."

The publicist's eyes narrowed even more, and Savannah saw a light shining there that made the hackles on her back rise. Devon Wright might be dressed as a bebopping, hip-hopping fluff-head, but underneath the frivolous facade was a dangerous woman.

"You should go now. Really," she said. "I'll walk you to the door."

Savannah glanced over at Dirk, who was still hanging out by the desk, questioning the aging, floozy receptionist. "Thanks, but I can find my way to the door," she said, "since it's only twenty feet away. I'm quite resourceful that way. Toodle-ooo. See you later."

Devon didn't reply. Or walk her to the door. But she did stand there and stare after her, boring eyeholes into her back. Savannah half-expected her sweater to burst into flames somewhere between her shoulder blades.

Savannah willed Dirk not to call out to her, to inquire about her untimely exit. And he didn't. They had worked together long enough to know that they should save potentially embarrassing questions for behind closed doors.

Once outside, she returned to her car and waited for him to join her.

It didn't take him long. Five minutes later, he rounded the side of the building and walked across the lot to her Mustang. She rolled down the window. "Let's go somewhere else to talk."

He nodded. "The pier?"

"Sounds good. Follow me over."

"Nope. *You* follow *me*."

"Eh, bite me."

She knew he would break at least five major traffic rules to beat her to the pier. Dirk was just . . . such a guy. He couldn't help himself.

Savannah had worked on him for years, trying to smooth out the rough spots. And she had succeeded in a few instances. He no longer propped his feet on her coffee table without first removing his sneakers, and he remembered to lower the toilet seat at her house at least fifty percent of the time. That was about as civilized as Dirk Coulter was ever likely to get.

But Savannah loved him anyway. When she wasn't plotting creative ways to murder him and dispose of the body, she appreciated the fact that his bravado, bordering on aggression, masked a heart that was remarkably soft toward the half a dozen people Dirk loved in the world.

He was as loyal as they came.

She and Dirk had known each other since way back when. "Back when," for her, meant "fifteen years and thirty pounds ago." For him, it meant a bit more hair and less around his middle.

But one of Dirk's sweetest qualities, the one that endeared him most to Savannah, was the fact that he hadn't really noticed those years or pounds. She was pretty sure that, at least in his eyes, she was still that feisty, sexy young cop who had been assigned to work with him . . . and had agreed to, although everyone else in the department had refused.

Dirk had always been difficult, rebellious, a pain in the neck . . .

the proverbial loose cannon that everyone wanted to throw overboard. Other men on the force couldn't stand him. The females had the hots for him, responding to that tough-guy-with-street-smarts appeal, not to mention more than his share of brawn. But none had lasted longer than a couple of days in the field with him . . . until Savannah.

She didn't care if he broke a few rules. She bent plenty herself . . . especially those she considered stupid. And so what if he leaned a little hard on a particularly unsavory suspect to get to the truth? He had good instincts and didn't "lean" unless he was sure the guy was a bad one.

Together they had taken a lot of dangerous criminals off the streets and just as importantly, they had brought justice and closure to a lot of victims. Savannah had decided long ago that was a good way to spend a life. And she had also decided she could put up with most of Dirk's less pleasant habits to achieve that.

She reminded herself of that when she pulled into the pier parking lot and saw him sitting there in his Buick, a nasty little smirk on his face.

He had beaten her there.

Big whoopty-do.

The fact that she had lost the unofficial race meant that she would have to join him, rather than vice versa. Sitting in his grubby Buick was the price to pay for law-abiding driving.

But he had chosen the parking space nearest the beach and the view today was great, so she didn't mind too much.

The midmorning sun had broken through the haze and Southern California's idea of a winter day was simply magnificent.

She got into his car, rolled down her window, turned her face toward the sun and closed her eyes, letting it warm her soul. Palm trees rustled overhead in the onshore breeze. A few seagulls cawed, some children laughed further down the beach, someone's boom box was playing "California Girls." All was well with the world and—

"Did you get a load of that dumb broad back there? Boy, was she a piece of work or what?"

Savannah tried not to let his words or the grating tone of his voice pollute the purity of her perfect California-Zen moment. "I beg your pardon?" she asked with all the tranquility she could muster.

"That stupid broad back at Emerge. Talk about a brainless twit! Why she—"

"Do you know," she said, eyes still closed, her voice a monotone, "that you are the only man left in the world who still calls women 'broads'?"

"So, what's your point?" he snapped.

"Point? My point?" Eyes still closed. Still tranquil. Still in the serene consciousness of the moment. "No point. I have no point. It was just a simple observation."

"No, you were bitching at me. Criticizing my language, like you always do. I know when I'm being criticized. If I wanted some br . . . *woman* to bitch at me, I'd get married."

"If you could find some broad who'd have you," she muttered under her breath, losing the Zen.

"What?"

"Nothing." She opened her eyes and shook herself back to reality, grim as it might be. "What were you saying? You don't like somebody. What else is new?"

"I don't like that gal who's the receptionist or secretary or whatever back there at that Emerge place."

"Any particular reason?"

"She's a bimbo. And worse yet, an *old* bimbo."

"Young bimbos are somehow better than old ones? Why? Because they're easier on the eyes? You don't mind a woman being an ignoramus as long as she's firm and perky?"

"What?" He stared at her for a long moment, obviously confused. "No, it's not that. Firm and perky? That's stupid. It's just that if a gal's older, she's had more time to figure out how to smarten up. She doesn't have any excuse for being a bimbo past... oh, thirty-five or so. After that, she oughta be wiser."

Savannah studied her old friend's face and saw only sincerity. She gave him a sweet, warm smile. "I love you," she said.

He looked pleased but confused. "Okay. First you criticize me, then you say something like that. You're nuts."

"But not a bimbo?"

He smiled back. "Not even in the ballpark with bimbo."

"Tell me more about the receptionist."

"She's gotta be pushing sixty, but she was flirting with me, actually coming on to me." He shut his eyes and shook his head as though trying to shake out the very thought. "Yuck. She could almost be my mom. And that wouldn't even matter, except that she's had a ton of bad plastic surgery. Her eyebrows are up to her hairline, her nose is as pointed as a just-sharpened pencil, and her lips are all plumped up like she's been bee-stung. It's gross, I tell you. If she'd had one more face-lift, I swear she'd have a beard."

Savannah groaned. "That's an old one."

"But applicable in her case. She asked for my number. Can you believe it? She was commenting on the fact that I'm not wearing a wedding ring and wanted my home phone number."

"Did you give it to her?"

"Hell no. I gave her Ryan and John's."

"You're a bad boy."

He snickered. "I know."

"Did you get a read on her about Suzette?"

"Just that she doesn't like her. Has worked for her and ol' Sergio forever, but doesn't have an ounce of respect for either one of them."

Savannah shrugged. "Well, I can understand that where Sergio's concerned. He seemed more than a bit smarmy to me."

"And Suzette lived like a pig."

"She was a bit sanitation-challenged, yes. . . ."

"And who was that pretty boy you were talking to over there by the butterfly cage?"

"The gentleman by the atrium was Jeremy Lawrence, Emerge's style consultant."

His eyebrows raised a notch. "Lawrence?"

"Yeap. How much do you want to bet he was Suzette's luncheon date that didn't show at Toscano's?"

"Gotta be. I'll be talking to him next. And the gal with the weird hair and the sprayed-on jeans?"

"Devon Wright. She handles public relations for Emerge. We don't like her much either."

"Oh, why not?"

"Because *she* doesn't like *me*. Didn't believe me when I told her I'm a reporter with *San Carmelita Today* magazine."

"That newspaper thing that comes out on Sunday?"

"That's the one. And just because I didn't have a press pass or a business card, she didn't buy my story."

"You're slippin', gal. Once upon a time, you'd have had a business card for at least six businesses at a given time in your wallet."

"I know. Tammy hasn't printed any for me lately. It's her fault. Anyway, I—"

Her cell phone began playing an obnoxious tune from her purse. She made a face as she reached inside and pulled it out. "Damn it, Dirk," she said, "I told you to stop messing with my phone. '*La Cucaracha*' just ain't my song."

"You started it, setting mine to play 'Wind Beneath My Wings.' Embarrassed me to death in the middle of a meeting with the chief."

"Shhh," she said as she pressed the Talk button. "Hello?" She gave Dirk a quick, knowing glance. "Uh, yes, Sergio. It was nice meeting you earlier, too. How can I help you?"

"What does *he* want?" Dirk whispered. She reached out and put her free hand over his mouth.

"Yes, I'm alone. We can talk freely. What is it?"

She listened for a long time, then said, "Of course I'm very discreet about my investigations. No, Detective Coulter wouldn't need to know anything at all. Yes, I'd be interested. Good. I'd be delighted. See you at noon."

She clicked the phone off and sat there grinning at Dirk for as long as she could hold the secret. Then she spilled it. "Sergio D'Alessandro wants me to investigate Suzette's disappearance privately for him."

"And not tell me anything about it."

"That's right."

They both grinned . . . big, evil, face-splitting grins.

Then Savannah sang, "In the mornin', in the evenin' . . ."

And he replied with, ". . . ain't we got fun!"

Chapter
5

Savannah made a practice of arriving at appointments early. Funny how much you could learn sometimes just by being someplace a few minutes before someone expected you.

And by arriving at the San Carmelita Marina fifteen minutes early, she learned something about Sergio D'Alessandro and Devon Wright. As Granny Reid would put it, they were "carrying on."

From her vantage point on a second-story balcony of Café Carolina, she could see the front of the harbor condominiums where Sergio lived—according to Tammy, who had done a quick computer check for her. The restaurant where he had suggested they meet was only a stone's throw away. So she had a clear view when he left his condo, walked Devon to a black Corvette convertible in the parking lot, and passionately kissed her good-bye. The farewell had included a quick, not particularly discreet butt feel, which sealed Savannah's opinion that they were, indeed, "carrying on."

She mentally added that to the list of things she was not supposed to tell Dirk, but undoubtedly would.

As Devon drove off and Sergio strolled her way, she decided to take her glass of iced tea and move to a table inside. No point in letting him know that she knew about Devon. What he didn't know wouldn't hurt him . . . or, more importantly, cause her any grief.

He came swaggering into the room a couple of minutes later, looking like he had just stepped off a yacht, wearing crisp white slacks, a navy blue blazer, and a red mock turtleneck. The smile he flashed her way told her that he was most impressed with himself and expected her to be, too.

She smiled back and lifted her glass in salute. If he had only known what she was thinking: that she should get one of those outfits and ship it back to her brother, Macon, in Georgia. He needed a git-up like that to wear when he was changing transmissions on trucks there in his garage.

"Ms. Reid . . . the private investigator," he said as he pulled out the chair across from her, unbuttoned his jacket, and sat down. "Or is it Ms. McGill, reporter at large?"

Savannah chuckled. "Well, I guess I'm just plain ol' Savannah right now, until you tell me what you want from me."

He motioned to the waitress and ordered a vodka martini on the rocks. Then he looked around the restaurant and waved a hand, indicating the giant palms, the tropical ceiling fans that swirled overhead, the heavy wicker furniture, and the expansive view of the marina. "You like?"

She nodded. "I like. Nice choice."

His eyes skimmed over her outfit, taking in the simple Aran sweater and beige twill slacks. Her only adornment was a pair of plain gold hoop earrings that Granny Reid had given her for her twenty-first birthday.

She could tell he wasn't impressed, and that was just fine with her. Occasionally, her private detective's income allowed her to splurge on something nice from the Victoria's Secret catalogue, but she wasn't about to tell ol' Sergio that she was wearing a rather daring silk teddy under that tame exterior. Her bloomers weren't—and never would be—any concern of a guy who dyed his hair "Midnight Black" at the age of fifty-something.

"I checked up on you, *bella*," he said, his Italian accent thick as Georgia sorghum and about as sickeningly sick. "You're quite a detective. You've solved some rather important cases here in San Carmelita over the years . . . you and that friend of yours, Sergeant Coulter."

"One or two, here and there," she replied.

She said nothing as the waitress gave him his martini, but as soon as she walked away, Savannah fixed him with a mischievous grin and said, "I've done some checking on you, too, since you called this morning."

He froze, his martini halfway to his lips, and said, "Oh? And what did you find out?"

She glanced around, but no one was seated near them. She lowered her voice anyway. "Oh, a couple of things. First of all, you're from a little-known area of Italy. . . ."

He took a sip of martini and gulped it down. "Yes . . . ?"

"A little-known, western part of Italy, called Bakersfield, California. Name on birth certificate: Leonard Roy Hoffman. Graduated from Thurston High School, class of '71. Finished number 273 out of 275 students. You've had a number of aliases over the years: Mario Barbarino, Stephano Gucci, Salvador Donatello. Served time in Lompoc for embezzlement of company funds from a designer in the LA garment district." She paused for a breath. "How am I doing so far?"

He found his voice and croaked out a simple. "Fine. And . . . ?"

"You and Suzette Du Bois weren't actually married. You had a church wedding, close friends and all that, about five years ago, but nobody bothered to fill out the proper forms and get them to the county courthouse, so it wasn't really legal. Which was handy because you didn't actually have to go to the trouble of getting a divorce about a year later when she kicked you out . . . for fooling around with other women."

He nearly choked on his olive. "How did you know that!?"

She resisted the urge to laugh. Although she and Tammy had verified all the rest on the computer an hour before she had left the house to join him at the restaurant, she had just guessed at the reason for the split-up. Sergió-Leonard wasn't a difficult book to read.

"I'm good," she said. "Don't you think?"

"Maybe a little too good," he replied. "I wasn't hiring you to check up on *me*. I know more than I need to know about myself."

"And now, so do I. But you'll find me a very nonjudgmental person. I've known a lot of perfectly lovely people who've gone by a dozen other names, swindled, lied, and cheated, and served time in federal prisons. I'd never think any less of you for it."

He studied her a long time over the rim of his martini glass, a scowl on his otherwise line-free brow. Then he said, "I want you to look for Suzette. That's all I want you to do. And I'll pay you extra well if you find her."

"How well?"

He named a figure that set her head to spinning. Visions of Victoria's Secret shopping sprees floated in her head along with the prospect of repaving her driveway and giving Tammy a raise.

"Okay," she said. "You cover my expenses, and I think we can work with that number. You can drop by my office and my assistant, Tammy Hart will have you sign the appropriate papers. Then we can—"

"There's just one thing," he said.

A catch. There was always a catch.

"What's that?"

He glanced around the restaurant, leaned forward, and lowered his voice. With not even a trace of an Italian, French, or

Spanish accent, he said, "You have to find that thieving, double-crossing bitch before the cops do."

"Why?"

"Because she's got something of mine. And I want it back."

"So, you're the one who trashed her house, looking for your property?"

He glanced away and cleared his throat. "I might have."

"Okay, that's a 'yes.' What did she take from you? Money?"

He hesitated, then shrugged. "Oh well, you'll find out sooner or later, I'm sure. So I might as well tell you. Yes, money. A lot of it."

"How much is a lot?"

"Now *that* is something you don't need to know." He drained his martini and motioned to the waitress for another. "Just find her, Savannah. Find her, help me get back what's mine, and you and I will both be a lot richer."

Savannah liked to think that she didn't work for money. She worked for the soul-deep satisfaction of bringing bad boys—and occasionally girls—to justice. What was money when you could look in the mirror and see a person who served the community, who made the world a better place?

If there was anything better than that, it was looking in the mirror and seeing a woman who had righted a wrong . . . *and* was wearing Victoria's latest silk and chiffon peignoir set.

She lifted her tea tumbler and clicked his martini glass. "Sergio, darlin', you've got yourself a deal."

Savannah stood at her kitchen window and looked out at Abigail, who was reading in one of her chaise lounges in the back yard. Tammy stood next to her at the counter, slicing lemons and placing them in a pitcher of mango sun tea.

"How did your morning go?" Savannah asked, although she already had a clue, judging from the glum look on Tammy's normally sunny face.

"Lousy," she replied. "I offered to take her to the beach, to Lookout Point, to the old mission, even Disneyland or Six Flags, but no-o-o, she wouldn't budge out of that chair. Who comes to Southern California to sit and read?"

Savannah shrugged. "Hey, some people actually go to Las Vegas to see the shows and eat cheap shrimp cocktails. Go figure. I gather you're sorry you invited her here in the first place."

"Sure I am. Especially now that it seems she's not even going to get the makeover. If Emerge's plastic surgeon is missing . . . who knows what's going to happen." She plopped the lemons into the pitcher, grabbed a spoon, and stirred. "Do you think Suzette Du Bois is dead?"

"I did last night. This morning, too. Now I'm not so sure."

"Because Sergio D'Alessandro hired us to find her?"

"More because D'Alessandro has explained a motive for why she may have disappeared on her own."

"The money she's supposed to have taken?"

"Right. He had huge dollar signs in his eyes when we were talking. I didn't get the idea it was five or even six figures."

Tammy froze, knife in hand. "Really?"

"Really. The guy lives in one of those marina condos and owns a fifty-foot yacht that even 'well off' folks could only dream about. He showed it to me after we ate lunch. Offered to take me out for a spin around the harbor, but I told him 'no thanks.'"

"He's not your type?"

"No, a potential murderer is definitely not my type. Especially one who's fifty going on thirteen."

Tammy reached up into the cupboard and took down a glass. "I'm going to take this out to Abigail. How much do you want to bet that she'll find some reason to bite my head off again?"

"Has she always been this crabby?"

Tammy thought for a moment, then nodded. "Yeap. Ever since I can remember."

"Then *why* did you set this up?"

A sad look crossed her face. "I've always felt sorry for Abby."

"Because she was a heavy kid?"

"No. I mean, she was, but I didn't feel sorry for her because of that. I was superskinny, and I got teased, too. When you're a kid you're always either too much this or not enough that. I felt sorry for her because of her parents. My mom is her dad's sister. But they're very different. My parents are great, but Abby got the crummy ones. Her dad was never around, never paid her any attention, like my dad did me. And her mom wasn't there for her either." Tammy looked out at the woman on the chaise lounge and a kind of understanding dawned on her face. "In fact, all I remember my Aunt Betty ever doing was lying around, reading books and magazines. I guess the apple doesn't fall far from the tree and all that."

"Guess not. Anyway, I still think it was sweet of you to set this up for her, whether she understands and appreciates your motives or not."

"Thanks. Wish me luck."

"Good luck. Take the knife with you in case things get ugly."

Tammy snickered, grabbed the pitcher and glass, and headed outside.

Savannah looked down at the black cat, who was doing figure eights around and between her ankles. "It isn't dinnertime yet, so don't even start with me," she told her. "Cleo, go bite your sister or whatever. If you trip me again, I swear I'll—"

The front doorbell rang, and she hurried to answer it, nearly stepping on the cat's tail in the process.

It was Dirk. And he had his cop face firmly in place.

"I gotta talk to you and that Abigail What's-Her-Name, too," he announced without the preamble of a "hi" or "how do you do?"

"Nice to see you, too," she said, opening the door wider and ushering him inside. "What's up?"

"Not a lot on my end. That's why I want to know what you and that Sergio dude had to say at your lunch."

She followed him into the living room. He plopped himself on the sofa, and she sat in her easy chair. He looked tired. Dirk frequently worked around the clock on a murder investigation. And this was as close to a homicide as you got without a body, so she wasn't surprised that he was tired and cranky.

She also wasn't impressed with his cranky self. "Mr. D'Alessandro is now my client," she said, grinning at his scowl. "You know that what I discuss with my clients is confidential."

"Since when?"

"Since he promised me a big ol' bundle of bucks if I find her before you do."

"Oh yeah?"

"Yeap."

"Why would he do that?"

"Maybe because she absconded with a ton of his money. Or maybe not, I'm not at liberty to say."

He sniffed. "Good thing you're so discreet."

"Ain't I though?"

"Did he give you any good leads about where you might start looking for her?"

"Nope. But he gave me the keys to her house and permission to search it thoroughly, no warrant needed or any of that messy legal stuff."

"It's *her* house, not *his*. Where does he get off giving you permission to search her property?"

"Don't know, don't care too much. I'm not planning to hoist any flags up the pole announcing I'm there . . . when I do my searching, that is."

"In the dead of night."

"You betcha."

"You gonna start tonight?"

"Just waiting for the sun to set and the moon to rise. You want something to eat or drink?"

"No. I want a lead on where this gal is. The captain threw me a real homicide, a drive-by over in the east end. Some druggie's momma got herself shot, sitting and watching TV, eating a pizza and minding her own business."

"You figure they were gunning for him and got Mom instead."

"Ain't that just the way it always happens. Some innocent kid sitting on a porch, behaving themselves, some guy walking with his baby down to the corner store for a quart of milk. And then, *blammo.* Anyway, I don't have time to mess with this Du Bois thing, when we don't even know for sure if it's foul play or her taking an unscheduled trip to Vegas."

Savannah studied her old friend and noticed the dark circles under his eyes and how he seemed to have no energy at all. Maybe he was getting burned out. He couldn't pull all-nighters anymore without paying a price.

And if he refused free food and beverages, he might be worse off than she had thought.

"You okay?" she asked, her voice soft with affectionate concern.

"Who me? Yeah. Sure. Why?"

"You look tired."

He shrugged and grunted. "Hell, Van. I've been tired since 1990. What else is new?"

She tried to remember. "What happened in 1990?"

"I don't know. Just made that up. Lemme talk to that Abigail chick so that I can go get a nap before I go back to the drive-by scene."

"She's out in the backyard with Tammy. I'll get her."

He started to hoist himself off the sofa. "I'll go out there."

"No you don't. You stay here."

"I'm not *that* tired. You're sweet, but you worry too much."

She sniffed. "I wasn't offering for *your* sake. I want you to question her in here, where it's easier for me to eavesdrop. In fact, move in to the kitchen table. I'll pretend to make chocolate chip cookies while you squeeze her."

"Pretend? Just pretend?"

He looked interested. She started to relax; Dirk wasn't ready to go toes-up on her any time soon.

"Do I need a lawyer here? Is this a real interrogation or what?" Abigail wanted to know as she faced off with Dirk over Savannah's kitchen table.

"Naw," Dirk replied, "if it was a real interrogation I'd have you handcuffed to your chair and I'd be smacking you with a telephone book. This here is just a friendly chat."

For once, Tammy had decided that she would help Savannah bake, even if it meant touching the toxic white substances— sugar and refined flour. She stood next to Savannah, stirring the sugars and shortening together in a mixing bowl.

Savannah leaned over her shoulder and whispered, "How's it going there, Betty Crocker?"

"Sh-h-h. I want to hear this."

Savannah chuckled and went back to measuring the dry ingredients.

"So, what do you want to know?" Abigail asked, her arms crossed over her chest, an ugly frown on her face. "Whatever it is, I don't know anything about it."

"I want to know how your day went yesterday."

"Minute by minute?"

Dirk returned the sullen look. "For right now, I'll settle for hour by hour."

Abigail sighed and rolled her eyes. "Savannah got me up about seven-thirty and gave me breakfast. Then Tammy took me to Emerge."

"Did you go inside with her?" Dirk asked Tammy.

"Yes, for a few minutes," Tammy replied.

Dirk turned back to Abigail. "And what happened when you got to Emerge?"

"We went in and that trashy blonde receptionist, Miranda or Maria or whatever her name is . . ."

"Myrna," Tammy supplied. "And she was really sweet, even though she . . . well, you know."

"Looks like a tramp." Dirk nodded. "And Myrna did what?"

"She greeted me; congratulated me for winning the make-over." Abigail made a face that looked like she had just sucked on a wedge of lemon. "Then she led us down the hall to a waiting room."

"Yeah, it was really neat," Tammy said. "They had these really cushy couches with fancy pillows and a fireplace going—a fake one, but it looked homey and cozy—and they had fresh fruit in bowls for us to eat and a pitcher of water with ice and slices of fruit and—"

Savannah shot her a "button your lip" look, and Tammy went back to stirring. "Anyway, it was neat."

Dirk sighed. "Now that we've established how 'neat' the waiting room was, can you tell me what happened next?" he said to Abigail.

"We waited for at least a half an hour. I was getting pretty sick of it. You can only eat so much fruit and drink so much water. Then a gal named Devon came in and introduced herself. Said she was public relations, or something like that, and apologized for the delay. She said that Dr. Du Bois was late, but was expected to arrive soon. Then she gave us a tour of the place."

Tammy brightened and opened her mouth. Savannah gave her another look, and she snapped it closed.

"I'm sure the rest of the place was 'neat', too," Savannah whispered. "But Dirk's just not that big on décor."

"Gotcha," Tammy whispered back.

"How long did the tour take?" Dirk wanted to know.

Abigail shrugged and looked at Tammy. "I don't remember exactly. Maybe an hour?"

Tammy nodded. "That's about right."

"And then?" Dirk asked, scribbling on a small notepad he had taken from his inside jacket pocket.

"And then I left," Tammy interjected.

"Good." He gave her an irritated glance, then turned his attention back to Abigail. "But you stayed?"

"Yeah. A nurse took several vials of blood from me. They weighed and measured me. All of that sucked."

"I'm sure it did," he replied.

"But after that, it was sorta nice. They gave me a pretty good lunch and served it outside on a patio. And Jeremy ate with me."

Savannah watched as Abigail's face changed at the mention of the style consultant's name. She looked quite pretty when she smiled. Her eyes had a dreamy quality, and as Savannah recalled Jeremy Lawrence's handsome features and quiet charm, she couldn't really blame Abby.

"Jeremy?" Dirk asked. "You mean Jeremy Lawrence, the hairdresser?"

"Yes, but he's not a hairdresser," Abigail replied. "He's a stylist; a person who helps you find the best ways to express who you really are inside through the way you dress, act, decorate . . . all kinds of things like that."

"Yeah, whatever." Dirk kept scribbling.

Abigail bristled. "No, not *whatever*! Jeremy Lawrence is a really classy, special person. He treated me with dignity and respect. We talked for more than two hours about *me*, about what *I* like, about what *I* want from my life, about how *I* would like the world to perceive me. We talked about clothes, among a lot of other things, and the whole time he was making suggestions and giving me advice. But he never once said anything like, 'Wear this because it will make you look less fat' or 'Big women shouldn't dress like this because it makes them look even bigger.' He didn't even mention my size."

She paused to take a breath from her outburst, and a heavy silence hung in the room.

Savannah broke it by placing a pitcher of lemonade on the table. "I talked to him, too, and he seemed like a very intelligent, charming person."

"Eh, he looked gay to me," Dirk said with a sniff.

Savannah's nostrils flared, but she kept her tone even when she replied, "Now, Dirk . . . you think that *everyone* who's intelligent and charming is gay. So, we can't go by you."

"I don't think he's gay," Abigail added. "He told me that I'm a beautiful woman and that he was going to help me find new ways to reveal that to the world. And he had a certain gleam of interest in his eyes when he said it. I think he likes me."

"Yeah, okay," Dirk replied. "So we've established that Jeremy Lawrence is a peach. A straight peach. What else?"

"Then that Myrna gal showed up and said that since Dr. Du Bois still hadn't shown up, I could just hang out there at the spa for the afternoon. Get a massage, a facial, manicure and pedicure . . . stuff like that."

"And did you?"

"I skipped the massage and went for the rest."

"Then you came back here?"

Abigail glanced away, hesitated a moment, then said, "Well, not straight back here. I took a cab downtown and walked around a little. Looked in some of the antique shops and boutiques. Then I took a stroll on the boardwalk and had dinner at one of the restaurants there."

"Which one?"

"What do you mean 'which one'? I thought you wanted to know if I could give you any new leads on what happened to Dr. Du Bois, but you're actually checking *me* out here. You're trying to see if I have an alibi."

Savannah stuck a panful of cookies into the oven and set the timer. "Don't get riled, Abby," she said. "Dirk checks *everybody* out. He's sorta like you New Yorkers. He doesn't trust anybody."

Abby turned back to Dirk. "Okay. I ate at a Mexican restaurant there on the beach. Maria de . . . something or the other. I had a beef tamale and a chicken enchilada with extra cheese and two margaritas. Okay? So it wasn't exactly lowfat or low-carb, but—"

Dirk held up one hand. "I don't give a damn what you had to eat or drink. Cheez, chill out."

"Are we quite done?" Abigail rose from the table and pushed in her chair.

"Did you come back here after dinner and stay here until you went to bed?"

"Yes, I did. Ask Savannah if I didn't."

"I will." He flipped his notepad closed. "We're done here. And thank you for your cooperation."

Abigail turned on one heel and marched outside.

Dirk shook his head. "Tammy, I gotta tell you, kiddo, your cousin is one bristly bit—"

"Watch it. That's my family you're talking about," Tammy said.

"Yeah, and my houseguest," Savannah added.

He stood and tucked his notepad and pen back into his pocket. "Can I take a couple of those cookies to go?" he asked wearily. "If I don't get horizontal soon, I'm gonna pass out."

"Sure." Savannah stuck a few into a plastic bag and zipped it closed. She handed it to him as Tammy walked out the door, following her cousin. "You're right, you know," she said. "Abby is bristly."

"And she's a bitch, too."

Savannah smiled. "Yes, she is. But then, the value of good, honest bitchiness is highly underrated in our society."

He just grunted.

She slipped her arm through his and guided him toward the front door. "Go home and take a nap, sugar," she told him. "You know you're not worth shootin' if you don't get enough pillow time. Go home, put on your Mickey Mouse jammies, crawl into bed and—"

"You know I don't wear pajamas! Real men don't wear pajamas."

"Yeah, yeah . . . or wipe their feet at the door, or use a napkin, or drink wine, or . . ." She smiled. "You bad, Dirk. We *all* know it. You ba-a-a-ad."

Chapter

6

Savannah stood in the middle of Suzette Du Bois's tumbled living room and closed her eyes. Unlike Granny Reid, whom everybody knew had a psychic streak, or as Gran preferred to call it, "the good Lord's gift of knowledge," Savannah didn't claim to know anything above what her five senses told her.

Yet, more than once, she had stood in the center of a crime scene and felt something that her high school science teacher couldn't have explained. She had sensed the victim's fear, horror, and pain as palpably as any human touch on her skin.

But tonight, although she closed her eyes and willed her mind and her own emotions to be still and open to impression, she felt nothing out of the ordinary in the doctor's home.

All she felt was a creeping uneasiness at being in a place she wasn't really supposed to be, doing something relatively illegal.

Downright illegal, she reminded herself. *There's police tape over that front door and you crossed it, girlie. That's a definite no-no.*

Then she chuckled to herself. Funny how the voice of reason and caution in her head always had a soft tone with a strong Georgian accent . . . just like Granny Reid's.

Savannah had left Tammy and Abigail sitting on her sofa with

a big bowl of popcorn and a couple of movies. She had told
Tammy where she was going and Tammy had begged to join her
for a bit of "sleuthing," as Tammy-Wanna-Be-Nancy-Drew called
it. But neither of them thought it a good idea to share the details
of their investigation with Abigail, and they couldn't think of any
plausible excuse to leave her at home by herself.

So Tammy was at the house, pouting and watching chick flicks
with her grumpy cousin while Savannah had all the fun.

If you want to call this fun, she thought, as she looked around at
the mess that had once been Suzette Du Bois's home. *Still might
be her home for all I know*, she reminded herself. *And she might come
waltzing in here any minute and want to know who I am and what I'm
doing here.*

But Savannah didn't waste much time thinking about that.
She had lied her way out of far too many situations in the past to
suffer any serious pangs of conscience or angst at this late date.

She did have to admit, however, that she would like to have
Tammy with her tonight. The silence in the empty house was
deafening. And even if she didn't feel any spiritual residue of recent evils committed inside the walls, the place was still creepy
enough for her to wish she had some company.

Dirk was busy on his drive-by shooting case. And when she
had called and invited Ryan and John, they had gracefully de-
clined, having tickets to a dinner theater production that they
had been looking forward to for months.

So, she was on her own and not particularly enjoying her own
company.

As best she could, she shook off the feelings and concentrated
on the job at hand, which was hard enough even when you didn't
have the heebie-jeebies. Trying to find something, when you
didn't have the slightest idea what you were looking for, was always a challenge.

She had already gone over the living room, looking for anything she and Dirk might have missed before. Finding nothing, she decided to check the bedroom next.

Down the hallway and to the right, she found the master bedroom. She flipped on the wall dimmer switch, then quickly lowered the light. There was no point in announcing to the neighbors or passers-by that someone was home.

Especially if the "someone" wasn't the homeowner.

As Dirk had said, the bedroom was a disaster, like the rest of the house. Originally it had been decorated in a rustic but elegant old-Spanish style, with a mixture of dark, heavy furniture, cream-colored plaster walls, and light, gauzy fabrics. The four-poster bed was draped with a sheer white canopy and the floor-to-ceiling windows were framed with the same delicate material.

The paintings on the walls were of exquisite old-world gardens in the Mediterranean.

But that was where the loveliness and grace ended.

Like the rest of the house, the room was a muddle of clutter and confusion. As she walked around, she distinguished between what was simply bad-housekeeping—the dirty dishes stacked on the bed tables, the piles of books and magazines beside the bed, the crumpled clothes tossed in the corner near the bathroom door—versus the results of what she assumed was Sergio's searching: dresser and chest drawers open with clothing tossed onto the floor, the desk in the corner emptied, and the closet doors opened with clothing and shoes piled in a heap just outside.

"Thanks for making my job even harder," she whispered to the unseen Sergio. If he had just left everything as it was, she would have had a much better reading on what was going on with Dr. Suzette right before she evaporated.

She walked over to the nightstand that had a phone and alarm clock on it. Experience told her that if you wanted to know which side of the bed the head of the house usually slept on, look for the phone and alarm clock.

Opening the drawers of that stand, she was somewhat surprised at the contents. There was the usual array of reading glasses, antacids, and sleeping pills, an address book, pens, and a couple of notepads.

What she wasn't expecting was the array of pictures, magazines, calendars, and other memorabilia, all dedicated to one woman.

Marilyn Monroe.

While she might have understood such a collection in the bedroom of a sixty-plus-year-old man, it was unusual in a woman's nightstand. Especially a woman who was born after the actress's death.

Two pictures in particular interested Savannah. One was a close-up of Marilyn, dressed in typical silver screen glam, a white fur stole around her bare shoulders and flashy earrings with emerald-cut sapphires surrounded by diamonds.

The other picture appeared at first glance to be a duplicate. But after taking a second look, Savannah realized that it wasn't Marilyn at all, but a very good look-alike. This woman lacked the charismatic sparkle and sensual quality that Marilyn had exuded in her prime, but the features were markedly similar and the clothing and jewelry an exact replica.

Although Savannah hadn't been shown a picture of Suzette Du Bois, she didn't need anyone to tell her that this was the doctor, striving to look like her idol.

It struck Savannah as somehow pathetic.

Suzette was obviously a pretty woman in her own right. Why would she want to look like someone other than herself? And why Marilyn Monroe in particular? Marilyn had been a beautiful woman, but . . .

Savannah had heard of people who sought out plastic surgeons who would cut and stitch them into a facsimile of some famous person, and she had always thought such folks must be sad, lost souls with little going on in their own lives. Who would have thought a talented doctor, famous for her own abilities and accomplishments, would have been tempted to do such a thing?

Savannah put the pictures back into the drawer, closed it, and continued to look around. The small wastebasket beneath the nightstand held only a small amount of trash. She pulled it out and looked inside.

Some used tissues, a wadded piece of paper, and what appeared to be an empty prescription medicine bottle were all she found.

She uncrumpled the bit of paper and saw a string of ten numbers, separated by several dashes. It looked like a credit card number or maybe a bank account number. Beneath the number was a single word: *rosarita*.

A bank account number and password?

The thought also occurred to her that if Sergio had searched the house for his lost money, maybe he should have been looking for something less obvious than the actual cash. She reminded herself that, these days, one saw less and less of the real green stuff. People were paid in direct deposits and often one's money was nothing more than a string of numbers on a sheet of paper or a computer screen. Gone were the good old days of tossing a pound of cash onto the bed and rolling naked in it.

Not that I ever had enough to actually do that with, she reminded herself. It was one of those dreams of hers that would probably never be fulfilled, along with getting naked—or even semi-naked—and rolling on absolutely anything with Mel Gibson.

Wishing upon a star, contrary to Jiminy Cricket, didn't always work.

She took a small tape recorder from her jacket pocket, turned on the record button, and read off the numbers aloud, along with the password.

Then she reached for the small, brown medicine bottle.

Instead of some drug store chain's logo, as she was expecting, the label had the name and address of a local vet. In fact, it was the veterinarian where she occasionally took Diamante and Cleopatra for their checkups. Dr. Desiree Harney. The prescription was for Sammy Du Bois: phenobarbital, half a pill, to be taken every twelve hours.

She noted the date on the bottle and the quantity of pills and counted the days. If Sammy had been given his meds faithfully, this prescription would have run out three days ago.

Again, she flipped on the recorder. "Check with Dr. Desiree about Sammy Du Bois's phenobarbital," she said, "if a refill was picked up, and by whom."

She was just leaving the bedroom, flipping off the light when she heard a sound, a rattling from the front of the house.

She froze, her heart pounding in her throat.

Instinctively, she reached inside her jacket for the Beretta in her shoulder holster. The feel of the rough textured grip against her palm was reassuring, but not enough to take away the jelly feeling in her knees as the adrenaline hit her system full force.

She eased down the dark hallway toward the foyer, being careful to step lightly and not make a sound on the marble floor.

She could hear muttering, male voices, speaking low to each other, but she couldn't make out any words. And she recognized the rattle. Someone was picking the lock on the front door.

Just as she neared the end of the hallway and the moonlit foyer, she heard the door creak open.

She pulled her weapon and pointed it toward the ceiling.

Finger off the trigger, she reminded herself.

Of course her subconscious knew the drill. It had been second nature to her for years now. But where firearms were concerned, you always reminded yourself. You took only conscious actions.

The door was open, she could tell by the change of light in the entrance. She could see their shadows stretching long across the floor only a few feet away.

She remained around the corner, wondering what to do next. She couldn't exactly jump out, see who it was, and demand they explain their presence. Not when she had no business being there herself.

"Do you think she's here?" one of the voices said.

"She has to be. Her car's half a block away," replied the other.

They were talking about her! She had parked the Mustang down on the corner rather than directly in front of the house. It had to be someone who knew both her and her vehicle. The thought was more than a little unsettling.

"We'd better watch ourselves," said one of them. "She might shoot us."

The other one snickered and with a distinctly British accent replied, "We'd better use caution, indeed. She's an excellent shot, that one. Why only the other day, she and I were at the shooting range and—"

Savannah reached over and flipped a wall switch, illuminating the hallway where she stood. She stepped out of the shadows and said, "You two like to have scared the piddle right outta me. I thought you had a dinner theater to go to."

Ryan closed the door behind them, and John hurried over to embrace her. "Savannah, love, we were just talking about you," he said.

"I heard." She reholstered her gun and gave him a hearty hug.

John turned to Ryan. "See . . . she had her weapon drawn and everything. I'm telling you, we had a close brush with the Grim Reaper just now."

She playfully shoved him aside and gave Ryan a peck on the cheek. "You should have called me on my cell and let me know you were coming. I would have met you at the door, and you wouldn't have had to pick the lock."

"We thought about it," Ryan said. "But it's good practice for us, picking a lock now and then, and besides, an ill-timed cell phone ring can spell trouble. I'll never forget, I was sneaking up behind a suspect one time, my phone started playing Beethoven's Fifth and . . ."

He grinned down at her with that breathtaking smile of his, looking fantastic in his evening wear, a smartly cut black suit and white shirt with French cuffs. She grinned up at him. "Oh, don't worry, darlin'," she said. "When I'm expecting a call from either of you, I always set my phone on vibrate."

They laughed, and John said, "Savannah, my love, if we ever decide to take a wife, it will be you. No other woman on earth would do."

"You're darned right," she said. "That's just understood."

Ryan glanced around. "So, where are you in this break and enter escapade of yours?"

"B and E? I prefer to think of it as a clandestine search for truth. And I'm finished, thank you very much."

John beamed. "Ah, then our timing was perfect. Let us take you to a late dinner."

She glanced down at her simple slacks, casual sweater, and loafers. "I'm not dressed for it."

Ryan quickly slipped off his jacket and tie and rolled his sleeves halfway up his forearms. "You are now," he said.

John did the same and offered her his arm as though she were royalty and he her courtier.

"Well, if you put it that way," she said. "How's a girl to resist?"

A couple of hours later, Savannah arrived home, sated with fine French cuisine, a glass of even finer French wine, and the company of witty, intelligent, not to mention sexy, men.

She parked the Mustang in the driveway, too tired to mess with putting it in the garage. "The occasional night out won't hurt you," she told the car as she walked away from it and up the walkway to her front porch.

It was late, and Savannah had assumed that her houseguest would be in bed. Tammy would have gone home by now and Abigail, still on New York time, would have retired.

But as Savannah was about to put her key in the front door, she noticed a flickering of light in the window. The television was on in the living room. And she could hear music, a strange, exotic, Middle Eastern sort of melody coming from inside.

She paused. Then, rather than going directly into the house, she stepped softly over to the window and peeked inside.

What she saw astonished her.

Abigail was watching something on the television. Savannah couldn't see what from where she was standing. But Abby wasn't just watching. She was standing in the middle of the living room floor, dancing, swaying to the music, lifting and moving her arms in the most graceful, feminine motions.

Her long hair was loosed from its braid and flowed in gentle waves down her back nearly to her knees. As she moved, her body tilting to one side then the other, hips rolling, her hair nearly sweeping the floor when she dipped, she was the picture of womanly grace and sensuality.

Savannah watched, transfixed. There wasn't a trace of the sullen, homely, graceless woman who had sat, sulking, at her kitchen table that afternoon. This lady was beautiful, exuding an elegant sexuality all her own.

When Savannah recovered from her shock, she left the window, walked back to the door, and stood there, wondering what to do next. She sensed that this was a side of Abigail that the lonely woman never showed to the world. And sadly, as lovely as she looked, Savannah was sure Abby wouldn't want to be seen in what appeared to be a private moment of self-expression.

So, Savannah took as long as she could and made as much

noise as possible messing with the front lock and opening the door. Then she waited in the foyer, making a production of putting down her purse, removing her gun, and locking it in the coat closet safe before finally strolling into the living room.

When she did, she found Abby, hair pulled back and twisted behind her, a DVD in her hand and an awkward, irritated look on her face. The television had been turned off.

"Oh, hi, Abby," Savannah said brightly. "I'm surprised you're still up."

"I was just going to bed," she snapped, shoving the disk into the pocket of her skirt.

Without another word, she headed for the stairs.

"Good-night," Savannah called after her. But all she received in return was the sound of Abigail's booted feet, heavy on the stairs, and then the bedroom door shutting firmly behind her.

Savannah shook her head and marveled.

"Yes, Gran," she whispered to her far away, Georgian grand-mother. "You're so right. It just takes all kinds to make the world an interesting place to live."

Chapter

7

The next morning, Savannah was grateful that Abigail slept late because it gave her some private time with Tammy and Dirk. While Tammy sat at the desk in the corner of the living room, typing away at the computer, Savannah and Dirk stood behind her, leaning over her shoulder, staring at the screen.

"Emerge appears to be on good footing financially," Tammy said, studying the screen in front of her. "The Mystic Twilight Club, on the other hand, is in trouble. Looks like they were fine until about six months ago. Their credit rating started to decline last summer, and now they're running ninety days late on many of their payments to creditors."

Savannah stared at the screen, trying to see what Tammy was seeing, but the columns and figures there might have been a foreign language for all they meant to her.

"I'm glad I've got you, kid," she said, patting Tammy's shoulder. "You're worth every penny I pay you."

Tammy looked up at her, a bright grin on her pretty face. "You pay me? Since when?"

"Maybe since this weekend if Sergio gives me that retainer

check today. I'm going by Emerge in a little while to shake him
and see if it falls out of his pockets."

"Yeah, yeah . . ." Dirk shifted from one foot to the other. "And
how about this guy's finances? How's he sitting?"

"Pretty, just like Dr. Du Bois," Tammy replied. "That condo
on the water costs him a bundle. So do the cars, the private clubs
he belongs to, not to mention his jewelry bills. Apparently, he
keeps himself and some females in sparkling style."

"Any engagement rings?" Savannah asked, thinking of Devon
and that passionate butt-feel in the parking lot.

"No. Three-carat, princess-cut earrings and a pinky ring for
him, but no diamonds on ladies' fingers."

"And he's not up to his neck in debt?" Dirk wanted to know.

"Nope. Credit is perfect. He looks great, at least on paper."

"And Suzette's finances seem fine, too," Savannah told him.
"No obvious money problems to prompt any skullduggery."

Dirk grunted. "Most people don't need prompting. They can
be rotten for no reason at all."

Tammy looked up at him and rolled her eyes. "You are so negative, Dirko. Do you get enough fiber in your diet?"

He returned the look. "Do you have to get that head of yours
aired up regularly like a leaky tire or—"

"Okay, okay. Enough of that." Savannah gave them both a
swat. "We've got work to do. I'm headed over to the vet's office.
Then I'm off to Emerge. I'm meeting Sergio there at ten. Tam,
you see what you can do with that account number and password
I gave you. And keep working on Suzette, too. Her finances may
be in order, but something's got to be amiss somewhere. Whether
she disappeared on her own or had some serious help, there has
to be a reason."

"I've got to get back to my drive-by," Dirk said. "Until we find
some of the doctor's blood or body parts, I'm not going to spend
much time on this thing. Unlike you rich private detectives, I'm

not getting paid to chase down women who decide to run away with their good-looking, stud-muffin poodle groomer."

Tammy closed down the computer and stretched a kink out of her neck. "I'm going to have some breakfast, and then I'll work on that account number until Abby gets up. I promised I'd take her to the old mission today. It's sorta spooky and gloomy. Thought she might like it. Unless we hear from Emerge, that is. They've kind of left her hanging."

"I'll see what I can find out about that, too, while I'm there," Savannah said. "How long do you think she'll be with us . . . if the makeover is off, that is?"

Tammy squirmed in her seat. "Not too much longer, I hope. I'm sorry that she's such a pain. She's always been a bit on the negative side, but I swear she's a lot worse than I remember. I know it's been hard on you having her here."

Savannah thought of the woman dancing in her living room the night before. She recalled how nicely Abigail had smiled when she had teased her, how well she had taken good-natured ribbing. She thought about the lonely little girl, the "fat kid" in every class, the absentee parents.

Savannah's parents had been absent, too. But she had been fortunate enough to have Granny Reid. And she knew her life would have been sadly much different without Gran's loving care and input.

Without Gran, she might have been a lot like Abigail . . . without the dancing.

"Enjoy the old mission," Savannah told Tammy. "There's a great bookstore in the museum next door to the church. Abby might like that. I'll bring home something good for dinner."

Tammy smiled. "Thanks, Savannah."

"No problem. And don't worry about how long she stays. I'd like the chance to get to know her better."

* * *

Savannah resisted the urge to hold her breath the entire time she was in the vet's office. The odors of pet urine and medicines made her remember every time she had showed up here, a sick or hurt pet in tow, and the associated traumas. The last time she was there, Cleopatra had something stuck in her throat, a piece of plastic from the seal around a water bottle. One hundred and fifty dollars, and five painful scratches later, Cleo was plastic-free but Savannah's nerves had been shattered and her monthly budget left in tatters.

Yes, going to the vet's office was only slightly less stressful than a Pap smear.

So, she didn't waste time, but strode up to the receptionist's window.

The young woman behind the desk recognized her instantly. "Hi, Savannah. How's Cleopatra?"

"You remember our names. How sweet."

"I remember the patients who give me scars." She held up a forearm, exposing a inch-long white mark.

"Oh, sorry. Cleo's fine, thanks, but not any better about taking pills."

"Do you need a refill on her methimazole?"

"Thanks, but we're set with that." Savannah glanced around and, although she could hear conversations and occasional barking down the hall, there was no one else around. "Actually, I'm here in sort of a professional capacity."

"Professional?"

Savannah flipped open her investigator's ID. "I'm a private investigator. I just want to ask you a couple of quick questions . . . totally off the record, of course."

The receptionist looked skeptical. "What do you want to know?"

"Just one little tiny thing." She leaned into the window and lowered her voice. "Can you tell me, when was the last time Dr. Suzette Du Bois filled Sammy's prescription?"

The receptionist squirmed in her chair. "Well, we aren't really supposed to reveal confidential information like that."

Savannah flashed her brightest, warmest, down-homiest smile. "I know. And as one of your patients, I really appreciate your discretion. But I'm a little worried about Sammy. We're trying to find Suzette, and I know he needs that phenobarbitol twice a day. He's such a sweet little dog, and . . ."

"You won't tell anybody that I said anything?"

"Honey, wild horses couldn't drag it out of me. I just need to know for myself . . . and Sammy, of course."

After a quick glance down the hallway, the receptionist whispered, "Four days ago."

"She came in here four days ago and got a refill?"

"Well, not Dr. Du Bois. She never comes and gets it herself. She sends her secretary."

"Her secretary?"

She nodded. "Blonde gal, lots of makeup, late fifties maybe. I can't remember her name. . . . It might start with an M."

"Myrna?"

"That's it. Myrna. She came in and got the new bottle."

"Thanks a bunch. And I'll do you a big favor in return."

The receptionist brightened. "Really?"

"Yeah, I'll send you a box of Godiva chocolates, anonymously, of course, and the next time Cleo or Di needs a shot or to get something pulled out of their throats . . . I'll take them somewhere else."

"Really?"

"Cross my heart and swear to swallow my bubble gum."

"You got it!"

Myrna, the receptionist, was the first person Savannah saw when she stepped through the doors of Emerge. She greeted

Savannah with a warm but curious "hello" as Savannah walked up to her desk.

"Hi," Savannah replied, taking her first close look at the woman Dirk had described as "trampy looking." And while it was obvious by her too-high eyebrows, too-pronounced cheekbones, too-plump lips, and too-bleached hair that Myrna had fought the losing battle against aging a bit too vigorously, she seemed like a nice person. Her smile—though suspiciously white and perfect—was sweet enough.

"My name is Savannah," she said, "and I have an appointment with Mr. D'Alessandro at—"

"Savannah, like in Georgia?" Myrna asked.

"Yes. Exactly."

"How nice. What a lovely name that is. A lot better than Myrna. Were you born in Savannah?"

"No, but my mom had a thing about Georgian names," she replied. "My siblings are Atlanta, Marietta, Macon, Waycross, Vidalia, and so forth."

"Cute."

"Yes, a little *too* cute, but Mom's a little . . . well. . . . About that appointment with Mr. D'Alessandro . . . ?"

"Of course, I'll let him know you're here." She picked up the phone, punched a couple of numbers, and said, "A lady named Savannah is here to see you. Okay, sure, I'll tell her."

She hung up and looked a bit apologetic. "Sorry, but Mr. D'Alessandro will be a few minutes. He's on a phone call to London. May I get you a bottle of spring water while you wait?"

"No, I'm fine." Savannah leaned her elbows on the countertop and assumed what she hoped was a casual, conversational pose. "I'm happy for the opportunity to visit with you, if you aren't too busy."

Myrna laid down her pen and interlaced her fingers. "No, I'm not that busy at all. If you don't mind me saying so, I'm surprised you're here today. There isn't much going on, unfortunately. You *are* a reporter, right?"

Savannah nodded with only a twinge of a conscience pang. Thanks to Granny Reid's strict teaching against the evils of lying—more than one trip behind the barn to dance to the tune of a willow switch—Savannah had never gotten used to telling a bold-faced lie. And in her line of work, that was a bit of a handicap.

At least now, thanks to Tammy's creative ingenuity, she had several business cards in her purse to give to anyone who demanded one.

She figured that if you're going to sully your soul with lies, you might as well have good props to back you up.

"I'm here to talk to Mr. D'Alessandro—and anyone else who will talk to me—about the disappearance of Dr. Du Bois."

Instantly, a guarded look came into Myrna's hazel eyes. She glanced down at her desk, picked up her pen and began scribbling on a piece of paper that looked to Savannah like some sort of release form.

"I don't know anything about that," Myrna said. "We don't even really know for sure that something's happened to her. Dr. Du Bois could just be . . . taking a few days off or . . ."

"Was she in the habit of doing that?" Savannah asked.

"Well, no, but I guess a person could get really tired of . . . you know . . . things . . . and need a break."

"Was she tired of . . . things?"

Myrna's eyes wouldn't meet hers. "She might have been. She'd been working hard, and the last day we saw her here, she was—"

She stopped abruptly, leaving Savannah dangling on that unfinished sentence.

"She was . . . ?" Savannah prompted.

"Well, she was a bit upset, and sometimes people need some space for a little while when they're upset."

"What was she upset about?"

Myrna glanced warily down the hallway. "I'm not sure exactly. She had just had a bad day, some arguments and . . . I'd better not say any more. You should ask Mr. D'Alessandro about it."

"Oh, I will," Savannah said, "but you know how men are. They always give you the *Readers' Digest* condensed version, and they leave out the really good, juicy stuff."

Myrna snickered, then caught herself and went back to scribbling on her papers. "Yes, but I don't know if we really want Emerge's 'juicy stuff' showing up in your magazine."

"That's very discreet of you. I'm sure that Dr. Du Bois and Mr. D'Alessandro appreciate that sort of loyalty on your part."

For half a second, a look crossed Myrna's face—sour, angry, maybe a bit hurt—then disappeared. But it was so intense that Savannah knew right away: all wasn't well with Myrna and her employers.

There was definite animosity there. But with whom? One or both?

Savannah donned her most sympathetic face. "I can't imagine that Mr. D'Alessandro is all that easy to work for. I had a boss one time that I couldn't stand, and between you and me, Sergio reminds me a lot of him."

Again, the look.

Myrna didn't reply verbally, but the expression on her face said it all. Yes, Ms. Myrna definitely qualified as disgruntled.

Savannah decided to take a stab in the dark as to why Myrna might not have been all that fond of Suzette, either. "I've never met Dr. Du Bois," she said, "but I know how irritating it is when bosses ask you to run frivolous personal errands for them on your own time."

She had struck pay dirt. Myrna nodded vigorously and promptly discarded her right to remain silent. "No kidding!" she said. "Like you don't even have a life of your own. Trips to the dry cleaners, the drugstore, the grocery store for heaven's sake! Heaven forbid that somebody's run out of fresh basil!"

"And some bosses will even have you go to the vet for them!" Savannah added. Might as well stoke the fire a bit. "Picking up medicine for her *dog*, of all things. You must just hate that."

Just as quickly, Myrna's demeanor softened. "Oh, I don't mind that. Sammy's a little sweetheart. And I love animals. It's the trips to pick up her favorite bath gels that I resent. And having to go shopping to buy skimpy lingerie for his latest girlfriend. *That* I mind!"

"And who wouldn't! Can't Devon pick out her own garter belts, for heaven's sake?"

Myrna's eyes widened. "You know about Devon?"

"Oh, honey, I know just about everything worth knowin'. Being nosy is my job, and I gotta tell you, I'm very good at it."

Myrna laughed and Savannah felt a bond, a girl-connection, had been made.

She had a new friend at Emerge.

No time like the present to take this new friendship for a practice run. So, she leaned even closer and whispered, "Also, just between us, I can't stand that Devon. She should fall down a flight of stairs and into a pit of crocodiles, as far as I'm concerned. She irritates the daylights outta me."

"Oh, absolutely. I hate her! She thinks she's so hot and so smart."

"And that's particularly irritating to those of us who really are."

Myrna snickered, then shook her head. "I don't understand what Sergio sees in her, or any of the rest of the bimbos he dates . . . except that they're young and don't have any wrinkles or sags."

The depth of sadness in the woman's eyes touched Savannah's heart. She could tell by looking that Myrna had once been a beauty. And if she hadn't been cut, stitched, and tucked into an unnatural caricature of herself, she still might have been.

"I don't think men like Sergio date young women because their skins are smooth," Savannah said softly. "I think it's because they feel more comfortable with a woman who hasn't been around very long . . . long enough to figure out how little a man like that really has to offer her. Us older gals see a guy like him coming and we tuck tail and run."

Myrna studied Savannah's face for a moment, then said, "You aren't as old as I am. Judging by your lines, I'd say you're in your midforties."

"Very good. You could work at a carnival, guessing ages and all that."

"It's like a carnival here. Strange characters everywhere and—"

The phone on her desk buzzed. She answered it and then told Savannah, "Mr. D'Alessandro can see you now—now that he's finished with his call to London . . . which is code for 'talking dirty on the phone with the bimbo.'"

Savannah flashed her a warm, down-homey smile. "Thank you, Myrna. I'm glad we had this little girl talk. Let's chat again, soon, huh?"

Myrna returned the smile. Yes, Savannah decided, she definitely had an "in" at Emerge.

"You got it," Myrna replied. "Good luck with your magazine story. I can't wait to read it. But remember . . . don't quote me directly on any of that."

"Wouldn't dream of it."

Yeah, I can't wait to read that story too, Savannah thought as she headed down the hall toward D'Alessandro's office door. *And if the story has a bad ending, which I think it's going to . . . I want to read it in the form of an arrest warrant.*

Down the hallway and to the left was a door with a brass plaque that read, "Sergio D'Alessandro, President."

She had to admit, Sergio D'Alessandro sounded a bit spiffier than Leonard Roy Hoffman. It certainly looked better on a brass door plaque. But she'd never trusted people who changed their names as frequently as the papers on the bottom of a parakeet cage. One changed names and bird-cage papers for the same reason: because the shit was piling up.

She knocked once, then opened the door and stepped into one of the most opulent offices she had ever seen. From the China-red walls to the black lacquered furniture, the plush oriental rugs and oversized vases sprouting everything from ferns to pussy willow sprigs, the decor made her feel she had stepped into the office of the Chinese ambassador to the U.N.

But the guy sitting behind the lacquered desk was no diplomat. And not even a designer suit and a fancy name change could make him classy.

In what Gran would have called, "no account, low-down, good for nothin'" style, his eyes swept over her again, lingering on her full bust line. If she had been wearing a tight sweater, she would have forgiven a guy a fleeting glance. She had to admit, her ample bosom was an eye-catcher. But when she was doing business, wearing business attire, there was no excuse for outright ogling.

"Good morning, Mr. D'Alessandro. Ah . . . Sergio," she said, fixing him with a blue-eyed laser stare that pulled his gaze upward, however reluctantly. She plopped herself down on a white leather chair and opened her purse to take out her notebook. "We have a lot to talk about and not much time. Let's get crackin.'"

"Um, okay." He seemed to snap out of his reverie, but he leaned back in his chair and crossed his arms over his chest. "What have you got? Did you find her?"

She shot him a "get real" look. "Please. If I'd found her, I'd have hauled her in here with me today."

"So, what's the problem? I hired you because you're supposed to be good and—"

"Supposed to be good?" She bristled. "Sugar, I'm *way* better than good. But you didn't give me diddlysquat to work with."

"I gave you the keys to her house."

"And I was there last night, till the wee hours of the morning, working my fingers to the bone." *At least until Ryan and John rescued me*, she thought. *And that's none of ol' Sergio's business.* "But when you won't tell me what I'm looking for, it's a little hard to tell if I've found it."

He sighed and leaned even farther away from her in his chair. "Well, what *did* you find?"

"You tell me," she said. "To start with, does the word *'rosarita'* mean anything to you?"

His eyes widened and his cheeks turned flushed, glowing red even under his tan. "Maybe. Why?"

Savannah's patience snapped. "Don't mess with me, boy. If you want me to find Suzette—and more importantly to you, your money—you'd better smarten up quick and start telling me what's what. What does *'rosarita'* mean to you?"

"It's a hotel between here and Santa Barbara."

"I know that. It's also the brand name of a line of Mexican food, and the name of a couple of hundred young ladies in this county, but I need to know what the word means to you personally and to Suzette."

Sergio groaned and shook his head. For a long time he just sat there, his hand over his mouth, staring down at his desk. Finally, he gave up the mental battle with himself and said, "It's where Suzette and I first made love, years ago."

She studied his face. She had seen the same guarded look on suspects, several thousands of them, as they withheld information. "And?"

"And . . . we had another . . . more recent . . . association with the place."

"How recent?"

"The night before she disappeared."

"That's pretty darned recent. You went there again, for old times sake or . . . ?"

"No, not that. She sort of caught me there."

"With another woman?"

He nodded. "Yeah, it was with another woman. Okay?"

"Who?"

"It's not important."

"It's important. Spit it out, Sergio. Who were you doin' this time at Rosarita's when Suzette caught you?"

"I'm not going to say. I have the lady's reputation to protect and—"

"Then I'll just assume for the time being that it was Devon."

His mouth dropped open. "You know about Devon?"

"Oh, give me a break, Sergio. Do you think I'd know that you graduated 273 in your high school class of 275 and I wouldn't know about Devon? What happened when Suzette found you at Rosarita's with Devon?"

He shrugged. "She was upset."

"How upset?"

"Very."

"Because you were fooling around with Devon or because you were doing it somewhere that was yours and Suzette's 'special' place?"

"Both."

"Does Devon know that Suzette saw you there?"

"Oh yes. Suzette got hold of a passkey somehow and broke in on us there in our room. She slapped Devon across the face and slugged me in the stomach."

For some perverse reason, Savannah's estimation of Suzette

Du Bois rose several notches. She fought down a smile. "And this was the night before she disappeared?"

He nodded.

"You might have mentioned that to me before."

"Like I said, I need to protect the lady's reputation."

"Devon is married?"

"Well, no, but . . ."

"I think the hide you're protecting is your own, Sergio. And if you don't start leveling with me, you can just kiss that money of yours good-bye."

His face darkened, and he clenched his fists in a way that made her mentally check the Beretta in her shoulder holster under her jacket. "Don't say that. I worked hard for that money. I have plans. I need to get it back. Now!"

She put on her calmest face and softened her tone. "Then help me, Sergio. Tell me about the money. How much are we talking about? I'm not being nosy here. I need to know exactly what I'm looking for."

Again, she watched the mental battle registering on his face as he decided whether to trust her or not. Apparently, he thought he had to, because he said, "One and a half million dollars."

Her heart skipped a beat and her breathing stopped. But only for a moment before she recovered herself and replied coolly, "Okay. Now we know what we're working with. And was this money in an account, in cash . . . ?"

"In a bank account."

"Okay."

"And it got stolen."

"How, if it was in a bank?"

"It was transferred out of my account."

"Without your knowledge?"

"Yeah. Somebody got hold of my password somehow."

"You must have contacted the bank. What did they say?"

He slammed his fist down on the desktop. A nerve in his jaw was twitching as if it were being zapped by a Taser. "They say that I'm out one and a half million dollars. There's nothing they can do about it, or so they say. They were happy to inform me that I was the one responsible for keeping my password safe and if I didn't, tough luck. They told me to tell my story to the cops, not them."

"And did you . . . go to the cops?" Savannah knew the answer to that one even before he replied.

"No. I want to keep the cops out of this. That's why I hired you. How could she have gotten my password? That's what I want to know. I never told *anybody* that! Nobody!"

Savannah glanced down at the slender notebook computer lying on his desk. "Do you conduct business with that bank there on your computer?"

"Sure. That's the best way to—" A sick look dawned in his eyes. "Do you think Suzette could have gotten my password out of my computer?"

"I have an assistant, a computer whiz-kid, who could have gotten it in about ten minutes. Is Suzette computer savvy?"

"Enough," he said. "Enough to figure out when I was visiting porn sites and dating services while we were living together."

"It's possible then."

"Oh, man. You think your money's safe because it's in a bank and look at what can happen."

Savannah studied Sergio and speculated on the ways he might have accumulated one and a half million dollars of unaccounted-for funds. None were good ones. Especially for a guy who had served time for embezzlement.

Sergio wiped one hand wearily across his face. "Why were you asking me about Rosarita?" he said, suddenly curious.

"Don't you know?" she asked.

"No. Why?"

"It wasn't your password on your account?"

"No. It wasn't. Why would you think it was?"

Savannah's mental gears whirred. *Don't tell all you know*, she told herself. *Not to a guy with half a dozen aliases, a prison record, a missing—and possibly murdered—business partner.*

"I found a scrap of paper in her house. The word was written on it."

"Why would you think it was a password?"

"The notes said, 'Password, *rosarita.*' That's why."

Okay, so Granny Reid wouldn't be proud. But what Gran didn't know wouldn't earn Savannah a trip behind the woodshed.

"So, that's probably the password for the account where she transferred my money," Sergio said, excited. "Do you think you can find that number for me? With that and the password, I could get my money back."

Savannah thought of Tammy back at the office. Tam probably had those numbers memorized by now as she tried to find the bank they belonged to.

"I don't know. We'll keep shaking the tree and see what falls out." With a sly grin she added, "These things have a way of working out. If the good Lord thinks you deserve that money, I'm sure you'll get it back."

His eyes narrowed. He looked about as comforted as she had intended him to be. "But," he said, "you think she used the word '*rosarita*' as the password for the account where she stuck my money?"

"I reckon she did." Again, she couldn't hide a smile. Suzette was a corker; Savannah's kind of gal. "I figure Miss Suzette chose that particular password to make a point."

"Yeah, she made her point all right." He sighed. For a moment Leonard/Sergio looked much older than his age, in spite of all the plastic surgery. "I screwed Devon at 'our' hotel, and now I'm screwed."

Savannah nodded. "That's about it . . . in a pe-can shell."

Chapter

8

After Savannah finished speaking with Sergio D'Alessandro, she was more than eager to leave Emerge. As lovely as the establishment might be, architecturally speaking, the place felt creepy to her. A few too many dark secrets seemed to cast a gloom over even the most beautifully decorated and sunlit interiors.

She was walking across the parking lot to her Mustang when she spotted Devon Wright, who was approaching her Corvette. Before the younger woman climbed into the convertible, she glanced around, as if to see whether anyone was watching her. Fortunately, she didn't look Savannah's way, or she would have seen that, indeed, she was being observed.

What's with the paranoia, girlie? Savannah thought. *What are you up to that you don't want anyone to know about?*

As Savannah got into her own car and started the engine, she decided to follow the publicist and find out.

She would have to tail her at a distance; the bright red Mustang wasn't exactly a low-profile vehicle. More than once Savannah had considered trading it in for something less conspicuous. Something that got more than nine miles to a gallon of gasoline, had air bags, and didn't need a carburetor tune-up every month to run smoothly. Ah, the joys of owning a classic.

But just thinking of getting rid of the 'stang broke her heart. Years ago, she had made the mistake of selling the Camaro she'd had since high school. The loss had plunged her into a depression so deep that only those who owned a collectable muscle car and were continually challenged to race while sitting at stoplights could possibly understand.

No, the Mustang was here to stay. She'd just have to stay a couple of blocks behind anyone she wanted to tail. And fortunately, she knew every street, alley, nook, and cranny of San Carmelita, so it was fairly simple keeping track of her quarry.

Devon drove along the edge of the foothills, then headed toward the downtown area. Lined with palm trees, mission-style boutiques, antique shops, and souvenir stores that sold what Savannah affectionately called "that glued-together seashell crap" to the Los Angeles tourists, Main Street was picturesque and quaint.

But Devon Wright drove right through the picturesque part, past the quaint section and into the grungy side of town. Here the cute shops gave way to X-rated video stores, tattoo parlors, strip clubs, and pawn establishments.

It was in front of one of those hock shops that Devon parked her convertible. Savannah was more than a little surprised that she would leave such a nice vehicle in that sort of neighborhood, especially with the top down.

But there was no accounting for naiveté.

Savannah watched from a block away as Devon and her black leather miniskirt disappeared into the store. Fifteen minutes later, she emerged, a satisfied look on her face. Apparently, her business had been accomplished.

As Savannah watched her get into the Corvette and drive

away, she considered what she should do—continue to follow her, or go into that store and find out what the publicist had been up to.

Fortunately, Savannah knew the owner of the store, a sweet old Jewish fellow named Saul, who had helped her and Dirk a number of times on other cases. Once he had even helped them solve a murder, so he was high on her list of favorite citizens.

She decided to scoot inside and find out what Devon Wright had pawned. She could always tail that gal some other time if she ran out of other leads and needed an excuse to stay away from home and sweet Cousin Abigail.

"Saulie," she exclaimed as she entered the front door, setting the string of silver bells hanging from the ceiling tinkling. "What's shakin', sugar?"

Saul rounded the corner, his arms outstretched. "Savannah, my dear! How have you been? Where have you been? I thought you and I had something special, and then I don't see you for months! My heart, it's broken, broken, I tell you."

For effect he clasped both hands to his chest and shook his head, gazing mournfully heavenward.

"Oh, Saul, don't give me that. You've got a harem of women, bringing you food, doing your laundry, picking out ties for you, and god knows what. You're the most eligible bachelor in town."

Saul's wizened face split with a wide grin. "That's true," he said. "The women, they flock to Saul's store, his house. They think I'll give them some of my treasures here." He waved an arm, indicating the glass counters filled with both new and estate jewelry.

"And tell me, Saul," she said, lowering her voice to a conspiratorial whisper, "do you barter favors from the fairer sex with all of these shiny baubles of yours? Come on, you can tell *me*."

The old fellow laughed so hard she thought he might fall

down. "Ah, Savannah, you do me good. I'm flattered that you think I would still benefit from such 'favors,' as you call them. But I'm past all that."

"No man is ever truly past all that, until he's six feet under. So don't give me that line of hooey. Don't tell me you didn't enjoy the legs on that gal who was just in here. The one in the leather miniskirt."

He giggled again. "I looked, yes. I enjoyed, true. But beyond that . . . ?" He shrugged. "What can I do for you today, dear Savannah? You want something sparkly for yourself? I'll give you a good deal. I have a pendant, a London blue topaz, the exact color of your beautiful eyes. Let me get it for you. You look and see, and you won't be able to live without it."

He shuffled over to a counter, slipped behind it, slid the door in the back of the display open and reached inside.

"No, no, no, Saul. I can't afford any of your pretties, so don't even tempt me. I came in to ask you a question."

His bottom lip protruded, but his eyes twinkled. "And here I thought you came into my shop to see me and ask me to run away with you to Acapulco."

"If I ever get a yen to run away to Acapulco, Saulie, I promise it will be with you and no other. But meanwhile, would you mind terribly telling me why that young woman was in here?"

"The one in the miniskirt with the great ankles?"

"That's the one. Did she buy something or hock something?"

He stroked his scraggly beard with one hand and his smile faded slightly. "Neither one. She sold me something. And you'd better not tell me that it wasn't hers to sell. I checked the sheets the policemen give me, the lists of things that have been stolen. There was nothing on there about sapphire and diamond earrings. Nothing at all."

Sapphire and diamond earrings?

A bell went off in Savannah's head. And it sounded very, very sweet. Rather like the bells of the old mission in town when they rang on Christmas Eve and Easter morning.

"Would you mind if I took a look at those earrings, Saul? Pretty please with whipped cream and chocolate sprinkles on top?"

Reluctantly, he reached behind him and took a small black velvet box from the top of a desk. He slid it across the counter to her.

She could feel the shot of adrenaline hit her bloodstream as she opened the lid. It made her knees weak, the ultimate high for a junkie like her. These were the moments she lived for.

Yes. There, nestled against the black velvet were a pair of exquisite earrings. At least two carats each of emerald-cut sapphires, surrounded by diamonds, set in white gold.

Marilyn Monroe had owned a pair just like this.

And more importantly, so had Dr. Suzette Du Bois.

"Saulie," she said, trying not to be too happy, considering the kindly old fellow's misfortune. "I hate to tell you this, honey, but you need to hold on tight to these earrings. Don't sell them, don't even touch them until I get Sergeant Coulter over here to look at them."

Saul looked bewildered. "But that young lady. She seemed nice, like a good girl. You don't think she stole these, do you?"

Savannah lifted one eyebrow. "At the moment, Saul, my man . . . I don't know *what* that girl's capable of, but I intend to find out."

As Savannah and her new-found girlfriend sat across from each other in a booth at Cache, Savannah wondered why Myrna, a woman in her sixties, would have chosen this glorified ladies' strip joint as a place to meet for a drink.

All around them, women in their twenties and thirties strutted their far more youthful "stuff" for the equally young—or as Savannah preferred to think of them, "immature"—men who were waiting on them, wearing only black spandex pants and black bow ties.

Either the strutting ladies didn't mind the fact that most of the mega-muscled, gorgeous waiters were gay, or they just preferred not to think about the fact that they wouldn't have a chance with them, no matter how charming their "stuff" might be.

Savannah didn't mind the fact that she was old enough to have mothered some of these gals. She had done more than her share of strutting in her day. Now it was their turn. And while she might miss the excitement and vanity boost of donning a sexy outfit, sashaying around, and having people notice, she wouldn't go back to that era in her life for anything.

Young and bouncy was fun. But she wouldn't have given up the life lessons she'd learned in the past ten to twenty years for any amount of perkiness.

Myrna, on the other hand, didn't appear to realize that it was no longer her turn.

Her two-sizes-too-small skirt and midriff-baring top looked ludicrous on a woman her age. But she didn't seem to notice the disparaging glances the younger women shot her way as they passed by. And when she batted her eyes at the waiter and made an overt pass at him, she didn't appear to register the look of disgust that flitted across his handsome face as he placed her gin and tonic in front of her.

"Do you have a boyfriend, Savannah?" Myrna asked as she twirled her fingertip in her drink, then made a show of licking a few drops from the end of her bright red fingernail in what was, no doubt, intended to be a sultry gesture. "You must have, a pretty girl like you."

"No boyfriend," Savannah replied, sipping at her own cola. "I have men friends, but no romantic entanglements at the moment."

Myrna looked shocked and mortified. "How sad!"

Savannah shrugged. "Not really. I don't have the time or energy for all that rigmarole right now anyway."

"But don't you get lonely?"

"Don't have time for that either."

Myrna shook her head, still bewildered. "But at night, when you're sleeping all alone, surely that must bother you."

"Oh, I may not have a boyfriend, but I never sleep alone."

Myrna's eyes widened. "Oh, you mean you . . ."

"Yes, I have two cats. If I shut them out of the bedroom, they sit outside my door and howl all night. Sleeping alone is a luxury I'll never have as long as Diamante and Cleopatra are alive."

"Oh."

Savannah could tell she had just lost some major points in Myrna's estimation. Nobody worth anything slept alone if they could help it. Not in Myrna's world.

"Do you have a boyfriend, Myrna?"

A look of profound sadness crossed the woman's face. "Not anymore. He left me for . . . well . . . someone else."

"I'm sorry to hear that. Had you been together long?"

"Six years."

"That's long enough. More like a divorce than a breakup at that point."

Myrna nodded. "We were doing fine, getting along really good. I thought he was even thinking about marrying me. But then, I made a big mistake. I treated him to having some work done at Mystic Twilight last year. Suzette did a great job on him. When she was finished with him, he looked ten or fifteen years younger. Ran off with a girl half his age."

"Ouch. That must have really hurt. Especially considering the expense of your 'treat.' That sort of gift doesn't come cheap."

"Suzette let me work it off. I work off all of my . . . procedures."

Savannah wondered how long it had been since Myrna had gotten a full paycheck, if ever.

"Speaking of Suzette," Savannah said, eager to get away from romantic gossip and on to the case, "can you tell me about Suzette and Sergio?"

"What's to say? They're off and on, together then apart, year after year."

"And why would you say that is?"

"Simple enough. Suzette loves Sergio. Always has. He uses her, then dumps her, then takes her back, then dumps her. It's ridiculous how much nonsense she takes from him. She could do a lot better than him, but she doesn't realize that, so . . ."

"And how about Devon?"

"Devon is nothing to Sergio. She's this month's fling. Nothing more."

"How about Devon and Suzette? How do they get along, considering . . . ?"

"They hate each other, of course. Suzette tried to fire her when she found about the two of them, but Sergio wouldn't hear of it."

"And he's the boss when it comes to that sort of thing?"

Myrna snorted with disgust. "Sergio is the boss when it comes to anything. And why that is, I'll never know. Suzette is the surgeon, the one with the skill and the credentials. He does nothing but sit in that office of his and pretend to manage things. Suzette could replace him in a heartbeat, but he's having a heck of a time filling her shoes."

Savannah set her drink down abruptly. "What? He's trying to replace her already?"

"Oh, he's been trying to pull in another surgeon since the day she went missing. Making calls all over Beverly Hills, Malibu, Santa Monica, even talking to New York doctors, trying to sell them on the idea of a practice in sunny California. Right now,

Emerge doesn't have a surgeon. We're out of business until we do."

Savannah toyed with her straw and waited for a group of young women to pass by their booth and out of earshot. Then she leaned across the table and lowered her voice. "Myrna," she said. "What do you think has happened to Suzette? What's your best guess?"

Myrna looked sad and thought for a long time before answering. "I don't want it to be in your paper that I said this, okay?"

Savannah nodded. "I promise that absolutely nothing you say to me will wind up in any paper."

"I'm not sure what's happened to Suzette," Myrna said. "Either she got fed up with Sergio, once and for all, and just took off somewhere. Like a mini-nervous breakdown, and she's sitting in some hotel somewhere sobbing her eyes out and letting him worry. Or . . . worse."

"And by worse, you mean . . . ?"

"Foul play. Someone has hurt her . . . or worse."

"And who would have hurt her? Could you make a guess? Just between us girls, of course."

Again, Myrna considered her answer carefully, then said, "If I had to guess who might murder her—and that's what we're talking about here, murder, right?—I'd say that Devon is the most likely to have done it. After all, she threatened to kill Suzette. Maybe she did."

Savannah froze, her glass half way to her lips. "Devon threatened to kill Suzette? When? Where?"

"In the parking lot, the night before Suzette went missing. They were screaming at each other because Suzette had caught Devon and Sergio together at some hotel. And Devon told Suzette to back off or she'd be sorry. When Suzette asked her what she meant by that, Devon said, 'Back off or you'll find out. I know people who would take care of you for fifty bucks and as far as I'm concerned, it would be money well spent.'" Myrna paused and took a breath. "That sounds like a threat to me. How about you?"

Savannah recalled the sapphire and diamond earrings in Saul's pawn shop and the satisfied smile on Miss Devon Prissy Pants's face when she had strolled into his place that morning.

"Yeap," she said with a thoughtful nod. "Sure as shootin' . . . sounds like a threat to me, too."

"Hey, this rabbit food ain't too bad," Dirk said as he buried his face in the toasted pita sandwich that Tammy had prepared for them. "Considering that a bimbo made it," he added.

"It is good, Tam," Savannah said. "I didn't know you could cook . . . other than cutting up celery and carrot sticks and pouring mineral water, that is."

From the other end of the table, Tammy beamed as she passed a bowl of salad to Abigail, who sat silently beside her, staring at her plate with open disgust. "Why, thank y'all," Tammy said in a fairly dreadful imitation of Savannah's southern drawl. "I figured you'd cooked for me plenty of times, and since Abby's here, I should make dinner for a change."

"I like Savannah's cooking better," Abigail said.

Everyone paused, momentarily stunned by the blunt comment. Then Savannah shook her head and said, "What's the matter with you Yankees? You don't have the good manners that God gave a jackass."

"I don't eat crap like this," Abigail replied nudging the pita on her plate with one finger, like a kid would a dead bug to see if it would wiggle.

"It's good," Dirk said. "There's little shrimps and some kind of melted cheese in there with all that green grass-stuff. It ain't half bad."

"I could make you something else, Abby," Tammy said, her feelings obviously wounded.

"Don't bother." Abigail turned to Savannah. "Do you have any of that fried chicken that you made last night left over?"

Savannah thought of the drumstick and thigh securely locked away in a plastic bag in her refrigerator. "Nope," she said. "We ate it all. Nothing left. Your dinner's there in front of you. Eat it or wear it."

Again, everyone at the table froze.

Abigail just glared at her for a long moment, and even Savannah considered the wisdom of making a threat that had always worked fine for Granny Reid, but . . .

To everyone's surprise, Abigail picked up the sandwich and bit into it. After a moment of chewing, the frown disappeared from her face and she attacked it with gusto.

"So, Tammy," Savannah said, "how far did you get with that account number and password I gave you?"

Tammy gave Abigail a wary look, then replied, "Not far. Nothing yet. Sorry. I worked on it for hours, but couldn't get it to work with any of the online banking sites. I haven't gotten through the list yet. So I might find something."

Savannah turned to Dirk, "And how's your drive-by case?"

"Wrapped it up," he said between chews. "Wasn't hard. You lean on those wanna-be gangsters, and they give each other up for a thin dime. No honor among punks."

"Good. Then you can get back to business on this Du Bois case."

"What case? Is she still missing?"

"Yes, and it's been 72 hours since Suzette Du Bois was last seen. And besides that . . ." Savannah glanced over at Abigail, who was contentedly munching away.

Abby stopped in mid-chew. "What? You're afraid to talk in

front of the fat girl? You think I might have killed that stupid doctor, just because she promotes the harassment, degradation, and humiliation of people of size? You think I bumped her off the other night when I said I was out shopping for souvenirs?" She stood and picked up her plate from the table. "Fine. I'll go out in the backyard so that you can talk about me all you want."

"Oh, Abby," Savannah said, "sit yourself down there and eat your meal. I'm pretty sure I know who killed Suzette Du Bois, and it wasn't you. I just want you to keep anything you hear at this table to yourself. Don't go spreading it when you're there at Emerge."

Tammy perked up. "You know who killed her? You know that she's been killed?"

"I'm pretty sure she's dead," Savannah said. "And I think Devon Wright, their publicist either did it or had someone do it. She's fooling around with Sir Sergio Full of Himself, and Suzette caught them together. The gals got into a catfight and someone overheard them arguing in the parking lot three nights ago . . . the night Suzette was last seen."

"That's not a lot to go on," Dirk said.

"How about if Miss Devon pawned a pair of Suzette's earrings this morning?"

"That's better," he said. "You sure?"

"Pretty darned sure. I told Saul to hold onto them until you can get over there to look at them. And there's a picture of Suzette wearing them in her nightstand drawer."

He actually looked interested . . . as interested as Dirk ever got. "That's much better. As soon as we're finished eating here, let's go get that picture."

"Don't rush off," Tammy said. "I made dessert!"

Savannah gasped. "You made a *dessert*? No way! Not with sugar or flour, I'll bet."

"I made watermelon sorbet. And don't make a face, Savannah. It's good, even without sugar or flour."

"I'm sure it's delicious," Savannah said through only slightly gritted teeth. She had to be a good example for Abigail . . . even if she would have much preferred a dish full of Ben and Jerry's Chunky Monkey ice cream smothered with hot fudge.

"Great! I'll dish some up now." Tammy jumped up from the table and danced over to the refrigerator.

A rude buzzing sound came from Dirk's shirt pocket. He reached in and took out his cell phone. "Coulter," he barked. "Yeah. Oh? Where? Okay."

He returned the phone to his pocket and gave Savannah a loaded look across the table. "Gotta go," he said. "And you're gonna wanna come with me."

"What is it?"

"DB."

"Oh."

"What's a DB?" Abby asked.

Savannah swallowed hard. "A dead body." To Dirk she said, "Is it Suzette?"

"Nope."

"Who then?"

Dirk suddenly looked tired and a little bewildered. "You gonna come with me or ask questions?"

"I'll get my purse and weapon."

Chapter

9

By the time Savannah and Dirk arrived at Emerge, half a dozen radio cars were already there, forming a barricade in the driveway in front of the entrance with red and blue lights flashing. Across the front door was a strip of yellow crime scene tape . . . the very sight of which could give Savannah an adrenaline jolt.

They piled out of Dirk's Buick and hurried up to the door. A young, uniformed cop stepped aside to let them pass.

"Where is it?" Dirk asked him.

"Down there . . . at the end of the hall," the patrolman replied.

As they strode down the hallway, toward a knot of still more policemen standing in a circle around a figure lying on the floor, Savannah could hear a woman sobbing hysterically in one of the offices that they passed.

It was a sound she had never gotten used to. The pure, gut-wrenching sound of human sadness at its deepest. Sometimes she could hardly stand it.

As they approached, some of the cops recognized them and moved away from the body to make room for them.

"Sergeant," one of the oldest ones said, "Jake and I were the first ones here. We've started a log."

"Good," Dirk replied. "Who called it in?"

"The janitor lady. Said she practically tripped over it when she came in to clean. Jake's talking to her there in one of the offices. She's really upset."

Savannah joined Dirk beside the corpse, and they knelt beside the body to study it closer.

This was something else that, no matter how many times she saw it, she never grew accustomed to it. The difference in "alive" and "dead."

When the soul left a person and only the shell of a body remained, the contrast was deeply shocking. It hit her hard every time she witnessed the phenomenon.

Only hours before she had been talking to this man, watching his every movement, hanging on his every word. And now he was gone. Completely, absolutely gone.

But in spite of her shock, the cool, trained, professional part of her brain took over, scanning the body in a methodical manner.

Sergio D'Alessandro's corpse showed no obvious signs of trauma. Since he was lying on his side, they had a pretty clear view of the front and the back of the body. There was no blood on the exposed skin or clothing. At least, nothing visible to the naked eye, although every inch of his garments and body would be painstakingly examined before that was officially concluded.

His eyes were open, and his mouth, as well. His expression was mostly blank—maybe slightly worried. There were no bruises or signs of violence on his face or hands.

"How do you figure he died?" Dirk asked Savannah.

"Don't know. Maybe a heart attack or something?"

"Could be." Dirk turned to the cop who had been first on the scene. "Did the maid say if she saw anything unusual, suspicious?"

"She said everything was just the way it always was. Door locked. Nobody around. His car is in the parking lot. She saw it and figured he was working late."

"Did you search the building?"

"We did," one of the other patrolmen said. "Me and my partner, Jack Pierce. There's no one else here. No sign of any struggle or anything out of the ordinary."

"Help me turn him over," Dirk said.

Two of them assisted him in rolling the body onto its other side. The left side was as benign as the right.

"Maybe it's natural causes or a drug overdose or something," Dirk said. "We won't know anything for sure until Dr. Liu gets him on her table tomorrow morning."

Dr. Liu's autopsy table, Savannah thought. *That's one place I never want to end up.*

No, an autopsy table was where they sent you when society didn't know who or what the hell had killed you.

And suspected the worst.

Savannah and Dirk waited until Dr. Jennifer Liu and her entire coroner's crime scene investigation crew had come and gone. And by the time the white van, emblazoned with the Great Seal of the State of California on its side, drove away, Sergio D'Alessandro's remains in the back, it was nearly nine o'clock in the evening.

As they walked back to Dirk's Buick, he glanced at his watch. "It's not too late to call on your buddy, that Devon gal, is it?"

"Well, her lover has just been found dead, of god knows what cause. I should think she'd want to be informed, if nothing else."

"How much do you want to bet she already knows that? I'll bet you pizza next Saturday night at your house and the heavyweight championship fight on your HBO."

"Against?"

"Dinner out with me. You pick the place."

"No way. Any restaurant? Like Chez Antoine?"

"Get real. I'm talking McDonald's, Burger King, or Burger Bonanza."

"Gee," she said dryly. "Think you can handle that?"

"Yeah, I can handle it. As long as you don't go wild and order the most expensive burger on the menu."

Savannah shook her head. "Dirk, you're so cheap you could squeeze an Indian head nickel until the buffalo poops."

"Thank you."

Devon Wright lived in Two Oaks, a small community inland from San Carmelita, and it was nearly half past nine by the time Savannah and Dirk arrived at her modest house. The place wasn't easy to find, sitting at the end of a long dirt road that bisected a large avocado grove.

As they left the Buick and walked up to the house, a security light flipped on and Savannah saw some sort of critter skedaddle into the nearby brush.

"I don't like running around in the dark on these farms at night," she told Dirk. "I haven't ever since that night that we nearly ran head-on into that mountain lion. Remember him?"

Dirk knocked on the front door. Inside they could hear the television blaring. "Uh, yeah," he said. "I'm not likely to forget that guy. I think I wet my pants when we came running around the back of that house and practically tripped over him. Scared me so bad I let the perp get away."

She cast a quick look into the weeds that grew thick and high on either side of the house. "The occasional opossum I can handle," she said. "But the big cats I can do without."

When no one answered, he knocked again, louder and longer.

Savannah shifted from one foot to the other and tried to peek through the lace curtains that covered the door's upper half window. "Did I ever tell you about the time when Gran's old hound dog, Colonel Beauregard, treed a bobcat right there in her backyard?"

"Yes, at least a dozen times," he replied. "When two people have spent as much time together as we have, they've heard all of the other one's good stories."

"Well, I pretend to listen to your reruns with bated breath. You could do the same, you know."

"That's because you're a better person than me, Van. I'm not ashamed to admit it." He pounded with his fist on the door and shouted, "San Carmelita Police Department! Open up this door right now before I break it down!"

The woman who finally opened the door bore little resemblance to the publicist Savannah had followed only that morning to the pawn shop. She looked like Devon Wright's disheveled and depressed twin, wearing a ratty bathrobe, no makeup, and a pair of men's house slippers.

"What do you want?" she demanded, a cigarette dangling from the corner of her mouth. "Bust my damn door down, will you?! What's the matter with you? I got a kid in here!"

"Well, answer your door next time," Dirk snapped back. "I knocked three times and—"

"Allan, turn that friggen TV down!" she screamed over her shoulder. "And go to bed. I told you to go to bed half an hour ago, young man! Get going! Move it!"

A thin, pale little boy, about seven years old, sulked over to the television and turned it off. An equally dejected, scruffy terrier trailed after the child as he meandered down the hall to bed.

"I need to speak to you," Dirk told her, his tone as irritable as hers.

"Well, it's a little late, and I'm not in the mood to talk to you anymore about that stupid Suzette. I keep telling you, she'll show up sooner or later. She's just messing with our heads, disappearing like this. She loves to do that kind of thing."

"We aren't here to talk to you about Suzette," Savannah told her.

"Yeah, and what are *you* doing here? What's a magazine reporter doing, hanging out with a cop?"

"I'm not a magazine reporter," she admitted. "I'm a private investigator. I'm . . . I was working for Mr. D'Alessandro, trying to find Suzette for him."

"He never told me he hired a private investigator."

"I believe he wanted to keep it confidential," Savannah said. "But that's not really important now. May we come inside? We really do have something to tell you. Something you need to hear."

"And it can't wait until morning?"

"No," Dirk said, brushing by her and entering the house. "It can't. Go sit over there on the couch, and brace yourself. I've got some unpleasant news for you."

Twenty minutes later, Devon was still crying, wringing her hands, and wiping her nose on the sleeve of her robe, in spite of the fact that Savannah kept shoving handfuls of tissues at her.

"I can't believe it!" she said for the seventh time. "He was so healthy! So energetic! That guy could go all night and frequently did!"

The thought of Sergio "going" at all, let alone all night, made Savannah want to go scrub her mind's eye with a steel wool pad and bleach. But considering the depth of Devon's apparent grief, it was clear that his smarminess held a certain appeal for some females.

There was no accounting for taste, or the lack thereof.

Savannah was already mentally celebrating the fact that she had won the bet with Dirk and would be dining in splendid repast at Burger Bonanza soon.

Devon might be a jerk, and she may have killed Suzette and robbed her of her earrings. But there was no way that she had murdered her lover. Her shock at hearing of his passing was genuine; no doubt about it.

"How?" she kept saying. "How did he die?"

"We'll find out tomorrow," Savannah told her. "After the autopsy."

"And until we do find out," Dirk added, "there's not much more to talk about concerning that topic. I've got something else to discuss with you tonight."

Devon's red, swollen eyes narrowed even more. "What? I told you, it's late, and now that I've gotten this awful news . . ."

"And you're about to get some more." Dirk gave her an ugly smile. "I'd like you to know that I'm seriously thinking of arresting you for murder."

"Murder?" Devon choked and sputtered. "How can you even think I'd kill Sergio? I loved him! And besides, you just said you don't even know how or why he died. It could have been natural causes and—"

"Not D'Alessandro," he said, "Suzette Du Bois."

"That's just stupid!" She threw the handful of tissues at him, but they fluttered to the floor midway between them. "You don't even have a body. How can you be sure she's dead, let alone that I did it?"

He gave her his most intimidating look, the one he reserved for his least favorite suspects. "You pawned her earrings this morning."

"I did *not*!"

"We have the earrings. We have your fingerprints on the earrings. We have Suzette's thumbprint on the earrings and her DNA. We've traced the earrings back to the jeweler where they were purchased . . . by Suzette Du Bois. They're hers. You pawned them. In other words. *We* have *you*."

Savannah gave Dirk a sideways glance and had to suppress a giggle. Not having been raised by Granny Reid, Dirk had no qualms about lying until his tongue turned black and fell out. Considering that he hadn't even heard about the earrings until little more than an hour ago, he had just told a string of whoppers. DNA, indeed.

But it worked. Which proved, contrary to Granny's teaching, bad guys *did* occasionally win.

Devon dissolved into hysterical sobs. Hands over her face, she spilled it, just as Dirk had intended her to. "Okay, okay, I had her earrings. I took them out of her dresser the other night when Sergio and I were searching her house."

"You and Sergio were searching Suzette's place?" Dirk asked.

"For what?" Savannah added. She knew already, but she wasn't sure how much Sergio had told his girlfriend.

"For the money that Suzette stole from Sergio. And when we didn't find it, he told me to go ahead and treat myself to something. He said that, considering how badly she'd ripped him off, we deserved to take a little of it back. So, I took those diamond and sapphire earrings."

"What did he take?" Savannah asked.

"A couple of the rings he'd given her, and a bracelet, and a pendant, and some silver candlesticks from Tiffany, and some Waterford crystal, and Sammy's diamond collar."

"A dog collar?" Dirk frowned and shook his head. "A diamond dog collar?"

"Yeah. He said he'd pry the diamonds out and sell them. He was always jealous of Sammy, said she cared more about that stupid dog than she did about him. But now..." She began to choke again. "Now he's... he's... he's dea-a-a-ad!"

Dirk turned to Savannah. "A diamond *dog* collar? Is she serious?"

Savannah shrugged. "Sure. Why not? I'd buy a couple for my kitties if I had the bucks."

"You women are nuts."

As Dirk maneuvered the Buick around the dark road with its sharp curves, Savannah couldn't help thinking that the way home seemed a lot longer than the way to Devon's house.

Deep, heavy, depression of the soul could cause that.

"We've got nothing," she said. "Not a blamed thing."

"So? I've barely started on the case," he replied. "It's too soon."

"*You've* barely started. I've been working on it for thirty-six hours, and I've got squat, zip, nada. You know as well as I do that if you don't solve a homicide in the first forty-eight hours, your chances are cut in half."

"That's just because most murders are obvious. You arrive at the house, you see the body on the floor and the body's brother standing over it with a bloody steak knife. You ask the other relatives what happened, and they tell you the two of them were drunk and fighting over who got the biggest steak. Case solved. The other kind take longer."

"Which kind?"

"The kind where it ain't so obvious."

Savannah sighed. "That's probably wise and profound, but I'm way too tired to appreciate your sapience right now. I just want to go home and go to bed."

"Did you just call me a sap?"

"No."

"Good. Then I'll offer to take you home and even tuck you into bed myself. Maybe I'll throw in a little backrub, a little all-over, hot oil, body massage. What do you say?"

"Eh, bite me."

"Okay. Never mind."

Chapter

10

Years ago, Savannah had promised herself that, someday, she would treat herself to one homicide. Just one.

She intended to murder Officer Kenny Bates. And she was sure that if there was even one woman on the jury, she'd get away with it.

Kenny served the fine citizens of San Carmelita by guarding the front desk in the medical examiner's complex. You had to get by him to see Dr. Liu or any of her assistants.

Getting past him wasn't difficult. He was a worthless guard. But signing in without being highly offended and grossly insulted was impossible. Kenny was living proof that not all pigs had snouts. Some of them just had body odor, bad breath, and manners to match.

"Savannah! Hey, babe!" His ugly face split with a smile the moment she walked through the doors. "Long time no see!"

"Long time no bathe," she replied as she approached his desk and tried to breathe through her ears. Experience had taught her that breathing was a bad idea within an eight-foot radius of Kenny Bates.

Dirk walked through the door behind her and growled under his breath. "Back off, Bates and slide that clipboard over here."

Bates pushed the board with its attached pen toward Savannah and leaned over the counter as far as he could, straining to see down the front of her blouse.

She caught a whiff of something that smelled like egg salad and nacho cheese chips as he said, "I was wondering when you were going to come see me. I've been meaning to tell you . . . after you solved that last big case, I saw your picture in the paper. I cut it out and taped it to my ceiling, right over my bed, next to Miss December."

"Hey!" Dirk barked. "Watch your mouth or you'll be eating your teeth, jackass!"

Savannah held up one hand. "That's okay, Dirk. Bates and I have an understanding. He stays on that side of the counter, and I don't give him a karate kick in the groin."

She grabbed the sign-in board and scribbled a name on it— P.H. Cue. Then she pushed it back at him and said in a low, menacing voice, "Get that picture off your ceiling, Bates. I mean it. If you don't, I'll find out. I'll wait for you in a dark alley. And I'll blow your brains out. You won't even see me coming. You'll just be hanging around one minute and the next, you're in pervert hell. Got it?"

He snickered, but looked uncomfortable.

She leaned closer. "Look into my eyes, Bates, and see if I don't mean it."

Kenny squirmed under the blue lasers like a worm on a hot sidewalk. "All right. I'll take it down."

"And tear it into little pieces and throw it away. I'm a private investigator. I'm going to check in twenty-four hours. I'll know whether you did or not."

"Yeah, okay."

As she and Dirk left the counter and walked down the hallway, she could see Dirk grinning from the corner of her eye.

"Ol' Kenny actually believed you," he said. "Like you would know what was on his bedroom ceiling."

"Like I would go within ten miles of his bedroom . . . wearing a biohazard suit."

As they passed the double doors to the medical examiner's autopsy suite, Dirk pushed one open and looked inside. "Nope," he said. "Nothing going on in there. She must be done with your buddy Sergio."

"Not my buddy. Never my buddy. Sergio was only a few degrees away from Kenny Bates. Better dressed, same lousy attitude toward women."

Dirk turned and gave her an inquisitive look. "I never asked. What do you think of me when it comes to that stuff? My attitude toward broads, that is."

She laughed and punched him in the ribs. "For a guy who calls females 'broads' you're remarkably progressive. Go figure. Did you call Dr. Liu earlier to see if she was finished before we bopped over here bright and early in the morning?"

"Naw, I never call her anymore. She gets mad. Says I'm nudging her; that I need to take patience management classes."

"Patience management? Wouldn't you have to actually *get* some patience before you learn how to manage it? Come on, let's look in her office."

Sure enough, Dr. Liu's door was open, and she was sitting at her desk. When she first laid eyes on Dirk, she gave an exasperated sigh. But when she saw that he had Savannah in tow, she jumped up and hurried to embrace her.

"Hey, sister," she exclaimed. "You still hanging out with this old dinosaur?"

"Somebody's gotta hold his leash." Savannah returned the

hearty hug and marveled that she could have probably wrapped her arms twice around the slender M.E. Tall, willowy, and breathtakingly beautiful, Dr. Jennifer Liu looked more like a lingerie model than a woman who dissected human bodies on a daily basis. Her long black hair was pulled back with a bright red scarf and even a baggy lab coat couldn't totally conceal her womanly curves.

But Savannah liked her anyway. They both loved Godiva chocolate, and that was a powerful bond.

"You should have called first," Dr. Liu told Dirk as he settled onto a chair next to her desk. "I don't have anything to tell you yet."

"Didn't you do the autopsy this morning?" He looked bitterly disappointed. "I figured you'd get right on it, what with me telling you I need it ASAP and all."

Dr. Liu seated Savannah in another chair and returned to her own behind the desk. "You detectives always want everything ASAP," she said, "but *you* are the worst. You must think the world revolves around you. The rest of us live and breathe merely to make your life more convenient."

"And pleasant," he added. "Don't forget pleasant. When are you gonna do my guy?"

She reached for a manila folder on top of a stack on her desk and tossed it toward him. "I *did* your guy. First thing this morning."

He grinned and reached for the folder. "Thanks. You're the best, doc. No matter what anybody says."

"I did it right away *in spite* of the fact that you told me to do it ASAP. I actually had a hole in my schedule. Don't expect that sort of service ever again."

Dirk turned to Savannah. "The good doc here is madly in love with me. Can you tell?"

Savannah nodded. "Oh, it's written all over her face. I think she's about to 'love' you over the head with that paperweight there."

He opened the folder. "I can't read this gobbledygook. It's all Greek to me."

"Actually, it's more likely to be Latin," Dr. Liu said. "But the bottom line translation is: I don't know what killed him."

Dirk glowered. "Well, that's just hunky-dory. What am I supposed to do with that?"

Dr. Liu frowned back. "Not yet."

"Not yet what?"

"I don't know what killed him yet. But I haven't gotten the labs back. When I do, maybe they'll tell me."

Savannah reached over and took the folder from Dirk. She scanned the page, hoping it might make more sense to her than it did to Dirk.

It didn't.

"So," she said, "tell us what he didn't die of."

"He didn't die of heart disease," Dr. Liu said. "Or a stroke. No evidence of any sort of illness, other than a bit of liver cirrhosis, apparently from drinking too much."

"Poisoning?" Savannah asked.

"Maybe, but I saw no signs that he had ingested anything toxic. The stomach lining was normal, not inflamed, and the stomach contents to be expected for a man who had eaten lunch but no dinner yet. My CSI techs said there were no signs of vomiting at the scene. No food or drink either."

"Could he have breathed in something?" Savannah said, thinking of Kenny Bates's toxic breath.

"The nasal passages, bronchial tubes, and lungs were unremarkable. I doubt it. The only thing I noticed was a reasonably fresh injection site on his outer right thigh, about here. . . ." She pointed to a spot on her own leg, several inches above the knee. "And there were a couple of old, healed needle marks there, as well."

"The guy was a junkie?" Dirk asked.

"I doubt it, although we'll know better when the lab results are in. I saw none of the other signs of drug addiction, and his veins were healthy. All he had were the intramuscular injection sites. Not like a chronic, intravenous drug abuser."

"Maybe somebody held him down and forced something on him," Savannah suggested.

"No bruising of any kind," Dr. Liu said. "If he'd been forced, surely there would have been some contusions or defensive wounds."

"You'd sure have to bruise me to get a needle in *my* leg," Dirk said. "I think he shot up with something bad, chronic or not."

"Then we should have found a kit at the scene," Savannah told him. "At least a syringe or something."

"It's a medical clinic," Dr. Liu said. "There are needles and vials of all sorts of things all over the place. You probably wouldn't have noticed, even if there had been something there."

"That's true," Savannah agreed. To Dirk she said, "We ought to go back over there and look around . . . now that we have some idea what to look for."

Dirk sniffed. "A needle and a syringe . . . at a medical clinic. Oh joy. That'll be sorta like looking for a piece of hay in a haystack."

Savannah felt the residue of communal sadness the moment she stepped across the threshold into Emerge's lobby. At the front desk, Myrna sat with her head in her hands, softly crying.

A sobbing Devon stood by the atrium window, her arms around Jeremy, who looked as though he, too, had been weeping.

The only one who wasn't crying was a young, dark-haired

woman in a white nurse's uniform, who stood behind Myrna, rubbing the receptionist's shoulders.

Myrna looked up when Savannah and Dirk approached, her eyes red and swollen. "Hello, Sargent Coulter," she said. "Hi, Savannah. I guess you've heard about our bad news."

Savannah was a little surprised at the apparent depth of Myrna's grief. While having a drink with the woman, she had gotten the idea that Myrna wasn't all that crazy about Sergio. Resented and disliked him, in fact.

But Savannah knew from personal experience that, even if you couldn't stand someone, it was sobering and shocking if they died unexpectedly.

If nothing else, it reminded you of your own mortality, and that alone was enough to ruin your day.

"Yes, I heard," Savannah said. "I'm so sorry for your loss."

"Yeah, me, too," Dirk added with a bit less of a sympathetic tone. "What are you guys doing here? There was crime tape across the front door. Nobody was supposed to be in here."

Devon and Jeremy had left their places by the atrium and strolled over toward the desk area. Jeremy spoke up. "The medical examiner's people removed the tape over the front door just a while ago," he said. "And they said we could be here in the lobby and in some of the rooms on the west side of the building. They left the tape across the hallway there, blocking our way into the east side where Sergio . . . where the body was found. And they told us to stay out of there until you released it."

"Good." Dirk headed toward the cordoned off area with Savannah behind him.

"How come *she* gets to go in there and *we* don't?" Devon objected as Savannah walked past her.

"Because *she's* with *me*," Dirk shot back. "Any more dumb questions?"

Then he paused and looked back over his shoulder at the young woman in the nurse's uniform. "Who are you?" he asked.

"Bridget O'Reilly," she replied.

"You a nurse here?"

She nodded.

"Then you come with us."

As the three of them walked down the hallway toward the recently departed Sergio's office, Dirk asked Nurse Bridget, "What is it you do here, exactly?"

"Everything," she replied. "I draw blood, give shots, dispense meds, assist in the surgeries."

"How long have you worked here?"

"Only about six months."

"Did you like the doctor?" Savannah asked. "And Mr. D'Alessandro?"

"The doctor was good to me. I hate the idea that something might have happened to her."

"What about him?" Dirk said. "Was he good to you, too?"

Bridget's Irish blue eyes suddenly looked a bit guarded. Then she said, "Mr. D'Alessandro and I had a pleasant enough working relationship."

"And that was his idea, I'll bet," Savannah said, quickly scanning the nurse's *pleasant enough* figure.

"What's that?" Bridget asked.

"That your relationship remain professional. I would imagine that was more your idea than Mr. D'Alessandro's."

She looked uncomfortable with Savannah's brand of frankness, but she nodded. "Yes, I suppose you could say it was more my idea than his."

"Do you know of anyone who would want to do either or both of them any harm?" Dirk asked.

"Well . . ." She mulled it over for a moment. "I guess there were some people who weren't all that pleased with the results of their surgeries. Some patients have very high expectations. They think they'll achieve some sort of physical perfection and then their lives will be much happier. And of course, that's an unrealistic expectation."

"Anybody in particular more disappointed than normal?" Dirk asked.

"Maybe a couple."

"Could you give us their names?" Savannah said.

Bridget looked horrified at the very thought. "Oh, we guard our patients' anonymity very carefully at the Mystic Twilight spa. If word got out that we had released their names—"

"Look, Nurse Bridget," Dirk interjected. "I appreciate the fact that you want to protect your patients and all that noble stuff. But we have a dead person, maybe two, and I don't have time to worry about whose face-lift is going to be public knowledge, if you know what I mean. If you can think of anybody who was upset with either Dr. Du Bois or Mr. D'Alessandro, you'd better spit it out."

"I'll make a list for you," she said, "if you promise me that you won't tell where you got it."

"I'll cover you," he said with sudden and unexpected kindness. "Don't worry about it. I like nurses. I have a lot of respect for what they do. They took good care of me when I got shot in the line of duty."

Oh, no, Savannah thought. *Here we go again.* The "Bullet in the Ass" story that she'd heard a few hundred times too many. She liked to think she was as compassionate and empathetic as anyone. But when it came to Dirk's barely-grazed right buttock, she had run out of sympathy in 1999.

"Here we are," she announced brightly as they reached the door to D'Alessandro's office. "Let's check in here first."

They entered the office, and after a quick look around, Savannah decided that it looked just the same as it had when she had last been in here. It had the neat, tidy appearance of a worker who did precious little work. Nothing appeared to be out of place. Not a pen or pencil in sight.

"Let me ask you something bluntly, Nurse Bridget," Dirk said. "To the best of your knowledge, did Mr. D'Alessandro use illegal drugs?"

The nurse looked genuinely shocked at the very idea. "No, not at all. He drank socially." She paused, then added, "And he was . . . well . . . very sociable. But other than that, nothing."

"How about prescription drugs?" Savannah asked. "Was he on any sort of medication that you know of?"

"No, and if he were, I think I would know. I'm in charge of our med inventory and I would know if he was taking anything out of the cabinets." She looked quizzically from Dirk to Savannah and back. "Why do you ask?"

"There were some injection marks on his thigh," Savannah said.

"Oh, those." A light dawned on Bridget's face. "The B_{12} shots."

"What are those?" Dirk asked.

"He gave himself B_{12} shots, claimed they kept his strength up. I gave him a couple when I first started working here, but then he got the nerve to start doing it himself."

"And he did this regularly?"

"Yes. Once a month."

"Did he do this here at work or at home?" Dirk said.

"Here. It's handy. We have the needles and syringes and gauze, and we keep his vials of B_{12} in the drug cabinet."

"Which room is the cabinet in?" Savannah asked.

"Exam Room One, where I draw blood," she replied.

Dirk gave Savannah a quick glance. She knew the look: He was onto something. Or at least he thought he was.

"Let's go there," he said. "Nurse Bridget, you lead the way."

* * *

Exam Room One wasn't much bigger than a closet. In one corner was a chair, the sort that kids sat in at school with a half desk in front of them. A blood pressure machine hung on the wall, and the smell of alcohol hung in the air.

Locked cabinets filled with large bottles and tiny vials lined another wall, and a counter held the supplies, cotton balls and swabs, gauze squares and bandages, all in spotless glass and stainless steel containers.

"So, if he recently injected himself here at the clinic," Dirk said, looking around, "it probably would have been in this room?"

"Most likely," Bridget replied.

"Go through it with us, step by step, how he would have done it."

"Well, he would have opened this drawer and taken out a syringe. One like this," she said, going through the motions. "Laid it over here on this tray. Gotten one of these alcohol wipes and laid it here, too. Then he would have used his key to get into this cabinet and taken out a vial of the B_{12}." She removed one of the small bottles of clear liquid, the one nearest her in the box, closed the cabinet and locked it.

"Then he would have loaded the syringe like this, tapped it to get the air bubbles to rise, pressed the plunger to expel the air and laid the syringe on the tray. He would have rolled up his pant leg, or dropped his trousers and cleaned the spot on his thigh with the alcohol wipe. Then he would have injected it into his thigh, right here in the muscle."

"And what then?" Dirk wanted to know.

"He would have thrown the needle into the biowaste can under the cabinet there."

"And the empty vial?"

"Tossed there, in the regular trash can."

Eagerly, Dirk reached for the can and looked inside. But

Savannah was a step ahead of him. She had already donned a pair of surgical gloves. She took the can from him and began to rummage among the small amount of garbage inside.

In seconds, she had found it—a small vial with printing on the side. "Is this it?" she asked, holding it up for Bridget's inspection.

"Yes, that's it."

Dirk pulled a small brown paper bag from his jacket pocket and held it open for Savannah to drop it inside. He promptly sealed it and began to scribble the date and other pertinent information on what was now an evidence bag.

Savannah continued to scrounge around until she had found the rest of what she was looking for. "Is this the top from that bottle?" she asked, showing it, as well, to their resident nurse.

Bridget studied the top for a moment, then nodded. "That's it."

"Good job, ladies," Dirk said, as he opened a second bag for Savannah.

"Oh, so for now we're ladies and not broads?" Savannah asked teasingly as she watched him seal that one, too.

"Nope," he said. "No broads around here at the moment. You two definitely qualify as ladies in my book. Now, let's see if you dames can help me find that syringe, too."

Chapter
11

"You didn't have to give us a ride over here, Savannah," Tammy said, leaning over Savannah's shoulder from the back seat. "I could have taken Abby myself. My bug's been running better lately."

Savannah decided to be kind and not mention that Tammy's VW Bug was about ready to be swatted and put out of its misery. The car was on its last tire and had been for months. When you had to pour in more oil than gas on a regular basis, it was time to start thinking about trading up to a later model . . . say, from the seventies or eighties. As much as the Moonlight Magnolia team loved their classics, a car that got you places "most" of the time didn't cut it.

"No problem," she said. "I wanted to drop by there and nose around anyway. This gives me a good excuse." She turned to Abigail, who sat glumly in the seat next to her. "Another appointment with that hotty, Jeremy . . . that can't be too dreary a prospect. Huh, Abby?"

To her surprise, a tiny smile appeared on Abigail's lips and a soft look came into her eyes. "I like Jeremy," she replied. "He's kind. He treats me with respect."

"Of course he does," Tammy said. "Why shouldn't he?"

"People don't always do what they should," Abigail replied. "Take that jerk in the car ahead. . . ."

Savannah studied the bomb-mobile in front of them, an old sedan with four different colors of primer instead of paint, and bumper stickers galore that bore witness to the driver's extensive travels. According to the faded, torn banners, he had visited all of the world's great wonders: Old Faithful, the Stardust Casino, the Tuscaloosa Rattlesnake Farm, and Joe's Catfish Shack in the Heart of the Ozarks.

But smack in the middle of all the others, one of the bumper stickers was all the more obvious because it was bright yellow and not as faded. Apparently a new addition to the montage, it read: SAVE A WHALE—HARPOON A FAT CHICK.

Savannah cast a sideways look at Abigail and was surprised to see tears in the woman's eyes. It was a disgusting sentiment, no doubt, but the world was full of such insults. She was taken aback by Abigail's sensitivity to such insensitivity.

"It should be against the law to put something like that on your car," Abby said, her voice shaky. "Don't you agree?"

Savannah shrugged. "I can see why it upsets you, but I've always thought that a body should be able to say whatever's on their mind without it being illegal. How else are we going to be able to tell the assholes from the good folks? That yahoo puts a thing like that on his car, we know he's an idiot from a block away. Forewarned and all that."

But Abigail shook her head vigorously and said, "No, it should be illegal. Can you imagine the uproar if, instead of saying 'Fat Chick' it said 'Lesbian' or 'Black Man?' Somebody would shoot his tires out. Somebody else would sue him for two-hundred and fifty thousand dollars and win. The ACLU would be all over it. Because society has decided not to tolerate that sort of thing. But you can bash a fat woman at home, at work, on late-night talk shows, and people everywhere will laugh."

Tammy spoke up from the backseat, her words soft and hesitant. "I guess it's because society believes that a lesbian is born a lesbian, and a black person is born black. But they think a fat person chooses to be that way."

"Sure they think that," Abby said. "They think we're all a bunch of lazy slobs who do nothing but lie around all day, shoving junk food into our faces. They think a simple change of lifestyle would just fix everything. Eat right and exercise! Yeah, right. That works for most people, but not for all of us. It's a lot more complicated than that."

Savannah wasn't going to argue with her. Years ago, when she had been at war against her own body, she had tried every diet in the world. But after months and months of counting every calorie, exercising herself half to death, eating nothing but "wholesome" food and still gaining weight, or going to bed hungry night after night and losing next to nothing, she had decided her body had other plans.

One morning she looked in the mirror and saw a barely thinner, miserably unhappy, sallow woman whose hair was falling out, who couldn't walk up a flight of stairs without nearly fainting, who hated the world and everybody in it . . . and she had decided to love her body and herself more than that.

She had never dieted again—in spite of the yahoos with insulting bumper stickers, late-night TV comedians and their hurtful jokes, the constant barrage of commercial ads that hawked one weight-loss solution or another, and fashion designers with their stick-thin models.

And she was fine with it.

She only wished that young women like Abigail could be fine with it, too.

"It's too bad," Abigail was saying, "that in this world there are more jerks like that one in front of us than there are people like Jeremy."

"But you're on your way to see Jeremy," Savannah reminded her. "You're choosing to spend your time with someone like him. And that guy in front of us . . . you can just chalk him up as an idiot; give him the mental finger and keep walkin'."

Abigail gave her a long, thoughtful look. "Is that what you do?"

"No, I'm a Southerner. I mentally lop his head off with a great big sword, watch it roll across the ground, kick it into a ditch, and spit on it. *Then* I walk away. Us Georgia gals are a little more mentally violent in the way we deal with people who irritate us."

Abby laughed. "I love it! I think us Yankee gals might have to follow your example. Maybe I'll mentally push him onto a subway track and watch the train run over him."

"Whatever it takes to get the job done," Savannah replied. "As long as you maintain your inner spiritual tranquility."

"You guys are weird," Tammy said from the back seat. "And a little scary."

"And don't you forget it," Savannah reminded her.

"Yeah, don't mess with a fat chick," Abby added. "You never know when we might act out one of those violent fantasies of ours. You could wind up headless *and* under a subway train."

Savannah lifted a militant fist. "Amen, sister."

The moment Savannah pulled into Emerge's parking lot, her cell phone rang.

"You ladies go on in," Savannah told Tammy and Abigail. "I'll take this and follow in a few minutes."

As they got out of the car and headed inside, Savannah answered the call. It was Dirk.

"What's the news?" she asked. It was safe to assume there was some sort of business to discuss; Dirk never called just to shoot the breeze.

"Lab just called me about that bottle and syringe we dropped off," he said. "They found something good."

"Fingerprints?"

"Yeah, but they're just his. No big deal there."

"Anything suspicious in the vial?"

"Nothing. It was clean. Not even residue from the vitamins that should have been in it. Like somebody washed it out really good before they pitched it. Same with the syringe. Nothing but water inside."

"So what's the good word?"

"The cap. It had a trace of something else on the inside."

"Oh yeah? What?"

"The gal at the lab wasn't sure, but she said it looked like botulism."

"Botulism?" Savannah started to grin. "You mean like Botox, the stuff they use at plastic surgeons' clinics?"

"No, she said she checked that and it isn't Botox. Similar, but not the same. She said that Botox is relatively safe. In order to kill somebody with Botox, you'd have to inject them with something like thirty-five vials of the stuff. And at four hundred and fifty bucks a vial, the cost alone would be prohibitive."

"Not to mention trying to hold a victim down long enough to inject them with thirty-five vials of anything."

"Right. But this stuff she found, she said it's a lot more concentrated than Botox. She's not sure what it is."

Savannah looked up at the brass sign and its fancy "Emerge" logo. "Well," she said, "I just happen to be sitting in the clinic's parking lot. Let me go inside and see what I can find. I'll get back to you."

"Thanks, babe. I owe you one."

"Oh, sugar, you owe me *way* more than one."

* * *

Once inside, Savannah found Myrna alone at her desk. She looked tired and bored, but happy to see Savannah.

"Hey, girlfriend," she said as Savannah walked over to her and stuck out her hand. "You about ready to go out for another drink?"

"Any time," Savannah replied, shaking her hand heartily. "For you, any time at all." She looked around at the clean desk, the bottle of red nail polish and file, the hand cream. "Not much going on, huh?"

"Nothing. Nothing at all. But I guess that's to be expected. With one owner missing and the other one dead, what do you expect? I'm just going through the motions. We all are."

"Like having Abigail come in for her meeting with Jeremy?" Savannah asked.

Myrna smiled sweetly. "That was Jeremy's idea. He likes Abby, thinks he can be of help to her. He asked me to call her this morning and have her come in for a stylist consult."

"Where are they?"

"He just took her and Tammy out to the patio for a nice lunch. You can join them if you like."

"No, I'd rather talk to you."

Myrna seemed pleased. Savannah got the idea that the receptionist might not have a lot of friends. The woman had an air of loneliness about her.

"Good. Pull up a chair and let's chat."

Savannah settled herself in the offered chair and glanced around to see if they were alone. There was no one in earshot except the butterflies.

"How much do you know about the medicines they use here?" she asked.

Myrna looked a bit sad. "Probably more than I should . . . personal experience and all. Why? Which meds do you want to know about?"

"Botox."

"Botox? Why? Are you considering some injections for those forehead wrinkles of yours?"

"No. I like my wrinkles. I earned every one of them. I was just wondering if they use Botox here . . . or something like it."

"They used to use Botox. But lately Suzette had switched to something else, a new product she was raving about."

"Do you know the name of it?"

"No, but I can look it up for you." She turned to the computer on her desk. "I'm sure it's listed in our inventory."

After a minute or so of searching, she found it. "Here you go. That's right; I remember now. It's called Bot-Avanti. It's the latest thing on the market."

"And why would Suzette have switched to it, if you know?"

Myrna gave a little sniff. "It's cheaper."

"It costs less per bottle?"

"Well, no. It's actually expensive initially. But it's much more concentrated."

Savannah nodded. She couldn't wait to get back to Dirk with this little tidbit. "And they keep a good stock of it here at Emerge?"

Myrna squinted at the screen. "Actually, there's only a few bottles of it here. Most of it is at Mystic Twilight, our old spa. That's where Suzette did most of her work."

"What's going on there these days?"

"Not much there either. It's as dead as here." She lowered her voice. "Between you and me . . . Mystic hasn't had a real client in months now. Suzette and Sergio had pretty much turned their backs on the old place and invested all of their time, energies, and money in this new one. That's why we were so hoping this opening would make a big splash." She sighed. "I guess now it's more like a belly flop. We're all going to have to start looking for jobs around here. It's so sad. We all had such high hopes for the new place."

Savannah studied the receptionist, her face with its overworked, windblown look, her swollen lips that looked like she'd had an allergic reaction to a new lipstick. She thought how hard it must be to live Myrna Cooper's life, even without losing one's job.

"Are you going to be okay?" Savannah asked her.

Myrna's eyes sparkled. She smiled and it occurred to Savannah that, in that moment, Myrna was a lot prettier than any plastic surgeon could make her. "Oh, don't you worry about me," she replied with a toss of her head. "I'm like a cat. I always land on my feet. Always."

Savannah laughed and patted her shoulder as she stood to leave. "Glad to hear it. And when I'm finished with this whole Suzette/Sergio business, we'll go out again and since I won't be 'working,' I'll have a margarita."

"One big enough to take a jacuzzi in. My treat."

"It's a date."

"I thought it was supposed to be warm all year here in Southern California," Abigail said as she wrapped her sweater more tightly around her and covered her bare feet with the edge of the beach towel.

On a larger blanket next to her, Savannah and Tammy were busy setting out a picnic that Savannah had thrown together at the last moment. She and Tammy had a frequent ritual of packing a dinner and bringing it down to the beach to watch the sunset. Thinking Abigail would enjoy this west coast experience, they had suggested it when she had given a thumbs down on fajitas at Casa Madre.

But at the moment, the beach picnic wasn't going over all that well either.

"What is that stuff you've got there?" Abby wanted to know as she peered into the crock pot that Savannah had pulled from a box.

"It's southern style pulled pork," she told her. "And, girl, you haven't lived 'til you've sunk your chompers into some of this."

Abby looked doubtfully into the pot. "Looks like somebody already ate it."

Tammy cringed and Savannah counted to ten before saying, "That's because the pork was cooked for hours in a sweet and spicy barbecue sauce until the meat fell all apart. It's very tender and tasty."

Abby wrinkled her nose. "I don't think I'm going to eat any of it. What else do you have?"

"Onion buns to put the meat on, coleslaw and corn on the cob. So if you don't eat the pork, it's gonna be slim pickins for you, kiddo."

When Abby grunted in reply, Tammy said, "Let me make you a sandwich of this and if you don't like it, I'll eat it."

Abby looked surprised. "You? I thought Miss Vegetarian never ate anything like that. Where's your tofu burger?"

Tammy laughed. "When it comes to Savannah's pulled pork sandwiches, even I fall off the wagon."

Abby seemed satisfied with that and settled back on her towel to take in the scenery while Tammy and Savannah assembled their sandwiches.

"I guess it's pretty nice here," Abby said, as she studied the horizon. The sky, deep turquoise blue, was tinged with gold and a delicate shade of peach around the sun, which had dipped halfway into the water.

Far in the distance off to their right a long, dark irregular shape stretched between the water and the sky. "What's that?" Abby asked. "Some sort of island?"

"That's Santa Tesla Island," Savannah told her. "It's quite a ways out there. You can't usually see it unless it's a clear day, like today."

"Do people live out there?"

"Sure they do," Tammy said. "There are some beautiful homes there, a couple of luxury hotels, a nice little town with shops and—"

"A lighthouse!" Suddenly Abigail shot up off her towel, pointing toward the end of the island. "I saw a flash of light! I'm pretty sure it was a lighthouse beam!"

Savannah chuckled, pleased to see Abigail animated over something. Anything at all. "It *is* a lighthouse," she told her. "It's been there forever, even before people settled the island. There are some treacherous rocks out there, and the light's there to warn ships away."

"I *love* lighthouses," Abigail said dreamily. "I mean I really, really love them. In fact, I was talking about lighthouses today with Jeremy."

"You and Jeremy were discussing lighthouses?" Tammy asked. "How did that come up in casual conversation?"

"He was asking me what I like. What really inspires me on a deep level."

"And you told him lighthouses?" Savannah said, marveling at this new insight into what made Abigail tick.

"Yes, I do love them. The whole idea of them. There's a purity about them. They were built strictly to help people, to save human life. And throughout the ages, lighthouse keepers lived solitary, lonely lives in those barren, inhospitable places, just waiting for the chance to go down and rescue people who had run into trouble on the rocks. And no matter what, the lighthouse keepers and their families kept those lights lit, even when they were sick or dying themselves, they wouldn't let the lights go out, because they considered it their solemn, sacred duty. It's a beautiful thing, really, when you think about it."

Savannah looked across the water and saw the tiny white blink of light, then a pause and two more. "I guess I never thought about it that way," she said. "But I can see why it's one of your passions. Why did Jeremy ask about things like that?"

"Because he's helping me get in touch with who I really am. It's the first step in creating a style that's uniquely mine alone. How can I express myself if I don't know who I am?"

"What other sorts of things do you like?" Tammy asked.

Abigail gave her a quick, guarded look and crossed her arms over her chest. "Just . . . stuff."

Tammy handed her a glass of iced tea. "What kind of stuff?"

"Private stuff. I'm not going to tell you."

"Ah, come on. It's just me and Savannah, and we won't tell anybody."

Abigail thought for a moment, then said, "Belly dancing. I like belly dancing, okay? Happy now? The fat chick likes belly dancing. And you might as well go ahead and say it, 'I've certainly got enough of it . . . belly, that is.'"

"I wasn't going to say anything like that," Tammy objected. "I would never—"

"No, but you thought it. What's somebody who looks like me doing even thinking about something like that? Nobody would want to see *my* body doing any kind of dance, let alone something sexy and graceful like that."

"Here, Abby," Savannah said softly. "Here's your sandwich. Take a bite and tell me what you think."

As she handed the plate to her, Savannah thought of the beautiful, sensual woman swaying in her living room the other night. But the anger in Abigail's eyes warned her not to say anything. Abigail had been dancing for herself alone, not for anyone else to see. And Savannah suspected it was one of the woman's sacred secrets.

Abigail bit into the sandwich. Her face lit up. "Not bad," she said.

"You think that's good . . . slap a little of this coleslaw on there and you'll be in pure tastebud heaven."

The threesome sat down on the blanket and began their meal. For awhile, no one spoke as they took the edge off their hunger.

Finally, Tammy broke the companionable silence. "So, you like that Jeremy guy, huh? He *is* really cute and seemed nice."

"He's more than cute or nice," Abigail replied. "He's a genius. Those places of theirs, the Mystic Twilight Spa and Emerge . . . those were his ideas. He thought up the whole concept, designed the facilities. He even decorated Suzette's house and Sergio's condo. He's brilliant, the brains behind the whole operation. And they never gave him credit for it, not at all. And they ripped him off in the money department, too. He's probably going to start his own place, as soon as he finds the backers and another surgeon, of course."

Savannah tried not to sound too interested when she said, "Oh? Did he tell you all that himself?"

"Most of it, and the rest I read between the lines. He's gotten a bum deal from those people. But with Suzette missing and Sergio dead, maybe it'll work out to his advantage in the end."

As Savannah continued her dinner, she thought about the beautiful, brilliant young man who had gotten the short end of a stick, or at least, thought he had. Just how bitter was he?

She thought of Devon Wright, who, for all her salesman-style cunning, didn't seem to be all that sharp. And the person who had made Suzette Du Bois disappear and had killed Sergio D'Alessandro with nothing more than a tiny pin-prick of a mark on his body . . . it wasn't likely to be a dimwit.

It had to be someone who was relatively bright, not to mention resourceful.

And when it came to murder . . . "bitter" could be a potent ingredient, too.

Maybe it was time to look elsewhere.

And even though Savannah had instantly taken a liking to Jeremy Lawrence and had heard only good things about the talented young man, perhaps it was time to look in his direction.

Chapter

12

Later that evening, Dirk dropped by Savannah's house with a small satchel under his arm. Savannah ushered him inside and offered him a seat and a cold beer.

"Nope, I'm sorta still working," he said as he collapsed wearily onto the sofa. He glanced into the kitchen where Tammy and Abigail were sitting at the table, playing a game of cards.

"Yeah, me, too." Savannah nodded toward a piece of foam core board she had propped next to her easy chair. On the board was stuck a series of sticky post-it notes, some with names written on them, some with dates.

"Messing with that board of yours, huh?" he said. "Got anything?"

Savannah sat in her chair, picked up the board and looked at it. "No. I've been shuffling these people, places, and things all around, trying to make sense of this case. And so far, I've got a whole lot of nothing."

"I hear you." He leaned closer, peering at the board. "I see you've got that ditzo Devon gal at the top of your suspect list."

"At the moment, but I think she's about to get demoted."

"I never did take her that seriously as a suspect. Too much of a fluff-head," he said. "The only reason you really considered her was because you didn't like her personally."

"What gave you the idea I didn't like her?"

He shrugged. "I don't know. She's just the sort of gal that women don't like, so I figured you didn't."

"And guys? Do they like a woman like Devon Wright?"

A lecherous little grin appeared on his face. "Only for about ten or fifteen minutes."

"Ten or fifteen, huh? Mmmm . . . a real Casanova."

"Hey, there's something to be said for efficiency." He glanced back down at the board. "So, who takes her place when she gets demoted?"

Savannah looked into the kitchen, but Tammy and Abby were deep in conversation over their cards. "I'm thinking Jeremy, the stylist," she whispered.

"Oh really? Any special reason?"

"Just that Abby said he sort of made Du Bois and D'Alessandro what they were and didn't get enough credit—or money—along the way. Apparently, he's looking for investors and a surgeon right now to open his own place."

"Okay, that's good. I'll run a check on him and—"

"Tammy already did. Online."

He gave a little sniff. "Boy, she's quite the whiz kid these days. You don't even need cops around anymore, as long as you've got a computer and know how to use it. Which reminds me . . ."

He reached down and picked up the black satchel, which he had placed on the floor. "I have a favor to ask." As he unzipped the case and reached inside, he nodded toward the kitchen and whispered, "Doesn't the kid there have her own apartment anymore? Seems like ever since that grumpy cousin of hers came to town, she's been practically living here with you."

"I think she's afraid to be alone with her," Savannah replied softly. "Strength in numbers and all that. What's that you've got there?"

"Sergio D'Alessandro's computer. They say that a personal computer is a treasure trove of forensic goodies, but . . . well . . . I couldn't even find the on/off button on this thing, so . . ."

"And you brought it to me?" Savannah shook her head. "You've got to be kidding. You could write what I know about computers on a peach pit."

"Well, actually, I wasn't going to ask you. I was gonna ask the kid if she'd do it for me."

"And considering all the sweet, uplifting, soul-affirming compliments you've given her lately, I'm just sure she'd be thrilled to do you a favor . . . to spend hours of tedious labor, pouring through the maze of a dead man's computer . . . all for the love of you."

"She'll do it," Dirk said as he hauled the thin, lightweight notebook computer out of the case and laid it gently on her coffee table. And she'll do it, not because I asked her to or because she loves me so much." He smiled confidently. "She'll do it because she's just like you."

"Meaning?"

"She's nosy."

"Sure. I'd be happy to," Tammy said as Dirk handed her the computer. "Especially for real money. But if it's full of porn, which most guys' computers are, I'm charging you extra. And the grosser the pictures, the more it's going to cost you. I'm not looking at close up pictures of body parts that I'm not aroused by for minimum wage, you know."

"Hey, I'm not responsible for what some other guy looks at. The captain said I could pay you a hundred bucks. That's it; that's all. Take it or leave it."

Tammy hugged the computer to her chest. "Heck," she said, "I would have done it for free, but since you've got an expense account, fork over the cash up front, big boy. I've got clothes to buy, shoes to purchase."

He stuck two twenties and a ten into her outstretched hand. "Make me proud," he said. "And I'll give you the rest the next time I see you. The captain's a tightwad, and he's gonna want to know what he got for his money."

"Yeah, yeah," she said. "And we know how much he loves *you*, Dirko. Wouldn't want to sully that sparkling reputation of yours."

Savannah snickered. While she adored Dirk and considered him easily the best detective she'd ever known, the rest of the San Carmelita Police Department didn't hold him quite so dear. Good detective or not, most of them—including his superiors—considered him little more than a major bum pain.

"That's right," he said. "My reputation is riding on this, so do a good job and find something."

"I'll do my best," Tammy said as she sat on the end of the sofa, opened the computer, and clicked it on.

"And one more thing," Dirk added.

"What's that?"

"If you could get it done right away, that would be great."

Tammy sighed. "I see you and Savannah are working on the same timetable. Yesterday is good, last week even better."

"You got it. And thanks, kiddo."

"No sweat, Dirko."

He turned to Savannah. "What are you doing with the rest of the evening?"

She shrugged. "Looking at my board here. Going to bed a little early. Getting some sleep for a change."

"Boring," he said.

"You got a better idea?"

"I'm just full of ideas."

"I'm afraid to ask."

He patted his jacket pocket. "Guess what I've got here."

"Hm-m-m-m . . . let me guess. Tickets to the opera? An invitation to a black tie ball?"

"Search warrant for Sergio D'Alessandro's condo on the water."

She grinned. "Who needs to sleep? I can snooze any time. Let's go snoop."

"Yuck."

"Wow!"

Savannah turned to Dirk, a horrified look on her face. "You actually *like* this?"

"Like it? I *love* it. I'd move in here tomorrow if I could!"

She shook her head. "I never thought I'd hear the word 'love' in a sentence coming out of you in connection with home décor."

"But this place is great! Just look around you."

Savannah was looking around, and what she was seeing left her cold. Colder than cold.

Sergio D'Alessandro's waterfront condo was ultramodern and white. Glossy white walls, white-washed wooden floors, white leather furniture.

Except for the bright red leather sofa and one oversized black lacquered vase filled with some sort of tree branches . . . sprayed white. Even the baby grand piano in the corner of the living room was white.

Savannah felt like Thanksgiving leftovers, hanging out in a giant refrigerator.

"How could anybody possibly like this?" she said. "It's stark, sterile, soulless—"

"Clean," he said. "It's clean. Sophisticated, clean lines."

She sniffed. "Oh, give me a break. Clean, my butt. There's just less to dust here. No knick-knacks. That's why *you* like it."

"Hey, it's a bummer having to dust all that house decorating crap. This is way better. One swipe with a dirty tee-shirt, you're done."

"Oh, yeah, you just about kill yourself dusting all those Clint Eastwood video tapes, empty beer bottles, and piles of laundry. You slave over that trailer of yours, boy . . . *sla-a-ave!*"

"Shut up. I can like this if I want to."

She softened and gave him a smile. "Yes, of course you can. Bloomers, boxers, briefs . . . different britches for different hineys, right?"

"Something like that."

Savannah walked into the kitchen and found the same lack of ornamentation there. The marble-topped counters had absolutely nothing on them: not a toaster, blender, not even a coffeepot.

"Hey, check it out in here," Dirk called to her from another room.

She found him in the bedroom, which was similar to the living room in color scheme, although she had to admit, the one red wall and the other black one was interesting. So was the bed, which was spread with a coverlet—red, white, and black-checked.

Interesting. But she still wouldn't have wanted to sleep on it.

She could, however, see right away what had Dirk so excited.

Boxes. Cardboard boxes, sealed with packing tape and labeled with a black marker: bedroom, bath, living room, or kitchen.

Dirk had an excited grin on his face. "The guy was moving! He was packing up and moving! That tells us a lot!"

Savannah thought, fast and furiously. She didn't want to be outdone here. The truth had to be obvious. But . . .

"What?" she finally asked. "What does it tell us?"

His smile faded. "Hell, I don't know. But it's gotta tell us *something.*"

"Yeah, well . . . when you figure out what, you let me know."

"Me? Why do you think I brought you along, woman?"

"To do your thinking for you?"

"Exactly."

It wasn't until four-thirty in the morning that it came to her. And Savannah figured that if she had been lying there awake for hours, Dirk probably had been, too. And if he wasn't awake, he should be. After all, he was the one who'd started the whole thing.

She sat up in bed, moved Cleopatra off her right arm, and reached for the phone.

He was number one on her speed dial.

"What?" he answered, far grumpier than usual.

Oops. "You asleep?"

"Are you kidding me? Of course I was." Then he uttered a couple of expletives that definitely would have gotten him a hide tanning from Granny Reid.

"Now, now," she said. "Is that any way to talk to a lady?"

"One who wakes me up in the middle of the first night's sleep I've had in a week? Yes."

She felt a stab of guilt. Actually, it was more like a prick. A very small prick.

"I know why he was packed. At least, I think I do."

"Oh yeah?" He perked up considerably. "Why?"

"I think he was going to join Suzette. I think she's somewhere waiting for him."

He was silent for a long time, mulling it over. Then he said, "Even if she was ready to kill him and his squeeze doll at Rosarita's the other day?"

It was her time to mull.

"I hadn't thought of that," she replied.

"And if he was getting ready to go join her, why did he hire you to find her?"

"Um . . . maybe not then."

"Van," he said with a tired sigh. "Do me a favor, babe."

"What?"

"Promise me something. The next time you get one of these bright ideas in the middle of the night and think I want to hear about it, remember: it's probably a stupid idea and I don't give a rat's ass. Don't call me. Just roll over and go back to sleep."

"Okay."

He hung up. Dirk had always been a man of few words . . . and most of them curt.

She replaced the phone on its base, turned out the light, and reached for the recently displaced Cleopatra. Diamante moved up from her feet and nuzzled under her other hand, demanding her half of the petting.

"What do you girls think? Was Sergio getting ready to fly the coop and go join Suzette?"

Cleo purred.

"Yeah, I think so, too. But why would he hire me to find her, if he'd already made plans to skip town with her?"

Diamante had nothing to add to the conversation.

"Maybe Dirk's right. Maybe these middle-of-the-night revelations aren't all that reliable. But Granny Reid says we're more intuitive in the moonlight than when the sun's shining."

She stared at the window, at the winter moonlight shining through the lace curtains and painting silver patterns on her bedspread, her arms, her hands, and the cats.

Intuition, or the musings of an exhausted, perimenopausal woman?

She decided to wait until the morning light to make the call.

Chapter

13

Tammy sat at Savannah's rolltop desk, Sergio's computer in front of her, a scowl on her face. Savannah stood over her shoulder, staring at the screen, looking just as irritated.

She didn't know exactly why she was irritated. But Tammy was out of sorts, and when Lady Sunshine and Light was in a funk, things had to be bad.

"No luck so far, huh?" she asked her.

"Not really. Sergio was a pretty boring and predictable guy, judging from his files here," Tammy replied. "Lots of porn—as I suspected there would be. He had . . . uh . . . exotic tastes. A lot of matchmaking services of the sleazier variety."

"Searching for his soul mate?"

"More like trying to connect with somebody—or bodies—with equally exotic tastes in the bedroom."

Tammy clicked a couple of times and a picture popped up on the screen. Savannah stared at it a few seconds, turning her head to the right, then the left several times, before she could finally decipher what the threesome were doing to each other and themselves. She thought that after working a stint in vice in West Hollywood, she'd seen it all.

She hadn't.

"Well, isn't that lovely," she said. "People are just so . . . re-sourceful . . . when it comes to that sort of nonsense. What else was ol' Sergio into?"

"Sports cars, luxury boats, home movie theaters—the usual big-ticket boy toys," Tammy replied. "Quite a bit of stock market research, although he obviously didn't know what he was doing. And . . . wait a minute . . ."

"What? What is it?"

"A whole folder here full of info off the net about how to create a new identity."

Both women went from grouchy to excited in two seconds.

Across the room, Abigail sat on the sofa, watching the news on television. Both cats were in her lap, begging for petting with a degree of enthusiasm that they usually reserved for Savannah alone.

"Did you hear this?" she said, pointing to the TV. "Now they're saying that the government grossly overestimated the effects of extra weight on a person's overall health."

"What sort of things are in that folder?" Savannah asked, pulling up a chair so that she could sit next to Tammy.

"How to get a fake birth certificate, for one thing," Tammy told her. "It's shockingly easy in some states. All you have to do is supply the basic information by phone and order it, and you get it in the mail in a couple of weeks."

"They're even saying here on TV that it's actually better for you to be moderately overweight than to be as thin as those stupid charts say you're supposed to be!" Abigail laughed—a chuckle that sounded like it was right out of an old Vincent Price horror film. "Wait 'til I tell some of those bony-assed friends of mine about that!"

"And there's info here," Tammy continued, "about how to set up anonymous bank accounts."

"Anonymous accounts? Like in Switzerland, where you don't even have to give them a name when you open the account?"

Tammy nodded and laughed out loud. "Aha! That's why I couldn't find his account! I was looking at all the mainstream banks' websites. I swear, I'd tried to log into them all with that stupid number and password. Dead ends everywhere."

She reached for a sheet of paper in a stack on the desk and showed it to Savannah. It had at least fifty bank names and their Web sites listed. Every one of them had been scratched off.

"Hey, get a load of *that*!" Abigail interjected. "This reporter says that the research behind those previous claims was funded by companies selling weight-loss products. Figures. I hate those people. They suck."

"I didn't even think about the anonymous banks." Tammy crumpled the paper and tossed it into the wastebasket under the desk.

"But that makes perfect sense," Savannah said. "If he was going to stash ill-gotten gains, especially in that big a sum, it wouldn't be at a run-of-the-mill, local bank. They report deposits of over ten thousand dollars to the IRS."

"If they want to do some helpful research," Abigail continued from the sofa, "how about some studies on how many people have ruined their health by buying all those stupid products and starving themselves?"

"But I can't imagine Sergio travelling to Switzerland with that kind of cash," Savannah mused. "With airline security as tight as it is today, they'd have a lot of questions if your suitcases were stuffed with that kind of money."

"He wouldn't have to go all the way to Switzerland," Tammy said. "I know there are banks like that in the Cayman Islands in the Caribbean."

"Did you know," Abigail persisted, in spite of having no audience, "that the average dieting woman in America consumes fewer calories a day than one who's literally starving to death in a famine-plagued, third-world country?"

"But even the Cayman Islands would present the same problem," Savannah told her. "You'd have to go through customs, and you can't stuff a mil and a half in your shorts."

"Let me go online here," Tammy said. "And I'll see if I can find any other banks with anonymous accounts. Maybe there's one closer to home."

"And all this crap about eating right and exercising to keep the weight off." Abby shook her head. "Do you know that a person has to walk thirty-five miles to work off one pound of fat! Thirty-five miles! One pound! And yet our society just assumes that if you're heavy, you're lazy. The big people I know work a lot harder at exercising than the skinny ones I know. You have to exercise if you're heavy, if for no other reason, just to keep your self-righteous, buttinsky friends off your back."

"You get on that anonymous bank angle, Tam," Savannah said. "That sounds promising."

"And," Abigail continued, "I hate how they just assume that if you're thin, you're physically fit. I can't even tell you how many women keep their weight down by smoking, purging, or taking uppers. And the minute they quit, here come the pounds, stacking on, so they go back to smoking, taking laxatives, and barfing. Tell me how healthy *that* is! And yet, they're the first ones in line to tell their bigger friends how they need to lose weight for *health* reasons. It's not a matter of vanity, on no, it's for *health*! Health, my ass. It's a way for them to make other people feel inferior, that's all."

Savannah could see Tammy sinking lower and lower in her chair, and she wondered how she must be feeling. Abigail's words must sting a bit, since Tammy was apparently a slender "them" on her cousin's list of offenders.

Savannah turned to Abby and with the softest tone she could

muster, she said, "I hear you, Abby. And I even agree with a lot of what you're saying. But there just *have* to be a few slender people in this world who actually stay that way by eating right and being active, who don't smoke, purge, or take drugs."

Abigail scowled. "Well, maybe a few, but . . ."

"And some of them may actually mean well when they express concern for their loved ones' health. They might be worried about diabetes—"

"My blood sugar is perfectly normal."

"And high cholesterol—"

"180."

"Heart disease—"

"Had a stress test two months ago. Just fine."

"Blood pressure and—"

"Low, unless I'm getting pissed off, arguing with somebody about *my* health and *my* weight, which is *my* business!"

Savannah took a long deep breath, then said, "You're absolutely right, Abby. All of that is your own business, and it sounds to me like you're healthy as a hor—I mean, as healthy as anyone could hope to be. God bless you, darlin'." She turned to Tammy. "You ladies excuse me for a minute. I'm going to call Dirk and see if he's heard anything from—"

The phone in the kitchen rang.

"That's probably him now," she said. "Hopefully we'll have some word from Dr. Liu's office."

She looked at the caller identification and picked up the phone. "Hi, turkey butt," she said. "What's the word?"

"Turkey butt?" Dirk sounded only slightly offended. She had called him worse. Much worse. "Do you answer the phone that way when Ryan and John call you?"

"Of course not. Ryan and John bring me lavender roses. They take me to the finest French restaurants. They tango with me and—"

"Yeah, yeah, yeah. But I've been on stakeouts with you when you had the stomach flu, and I didn't even complain. Now that's *true* romance."

Savannah smiled. "It is. It is. You're quite the Romeo."

"You wanna hear what I've got or not?"

"Absolutely. Go."

"Liu says it was that stuff. That super bot-whatever medicine that the receptionist told you about. It showed up in D'Alessandro's tox screen."

"Enough to kill him?"

"Oh yeah, a couple of times over."

"Wow. Okay, that narrows our list of suspects a bit," she said. "It wasn't someone who just walked in off the streets. Somebody had to have a key to their medicine cabinet."

"Yeah, I was gonna go over there to Emerge this afternoon and ask around about that. But right now I'm on my way to Santa Barbara to talk to Du Bois's sister. They're estranged, but I wanna shake the family tree and see if anything like rotten apples fall out."

"Okay, Tammy and I are working here at home on Sergio's computer. And she's trying to get a hit on that bank account number and password."

She heard a click on the line and glanced at the ID screen. "Hey, somebody's calling here from Emerge," she told him. "Let me see what they want, and I'll get back to you."

She punched the "Flash" button. "Hello?"

"Hi, is this Savannah?"

She recognized the husky, tobacco-and-bourbon-roughened voice on the other end instantly.

"Yes. Hi, Myrna. What's up?"

"Is Abigail there with you?"

Savannah glanced into the living room, where Abby was still

lecturing away to the cats and herself as Tammy continued to work at the desk. "Yes, she is. Did you want to speak to her?"

"That isn't necessary. If you would just give her a message. Tell her we feel bad about what's happened with her. How she traveled all the way here from the East coast and isn't getting her complete Emerge experience. So, we want to give her a make-over anyway, at least as much as we can without a surgeon. Hair, makeup, wardrobe, all of that."

"That's very sweet of you. I'm sure she'll enjoy that." *Maybe she'll enjoy it,* Savannah added mentally. *Or she might just spit in your face. You just never know with Miss Abby.*

"Great!" Myrna said. "If you could bring her over right away, we can get started."

Sure. I didn't have anything else to do today, Savannah thought. *Just cart Abby around and listen to her ranting and . . .*

Then she remembered the medicine cabinet and the fact that Sergio had died as a result of injected Bot-Avanti.

"You betcha," she said. "I'll get her over there right away."

As soon as she had said good-bye to Myrna, Savannah went back to Dirk, who was, surprisingly, still on the line. "You just take care of interviewing the Du Bois family members," she told him. "I'll check out Emerge for you."

"Wow, thanks, Van. I appreciate it. Especially since you aren't even getting paid anymore, now that your client's gone toes-up. Making a special trip and all just for me. That's so sweet."

"Hey, what are friends for? You can make it up to me someday soon."

There was a long silence on the other end, then a dubious, "Oh, yeah? How?"

"Oh, I don't know. The oil in my Mustang needs changing, the seal on my downstairs toilet is leaking, a couple of tiles on my roof are loose."

"Hurrumph."

He hung up. Dirk was never one for long, sentimental fare-wells. Especially after home and auto repairs had been men-tioned.

Smiling, she replaced the phone and walked into the living room. "Get out of those pajamas," she told Abigail. "And put your ridin' britches on, girl."

Abigail looked skeptical. "Why?"

"Cause you're on your way to Emerge. You're gonna go get all prettied up. A whole day of be-e-e-auty."

"No."

"Yes."

"Hey, I'll take it!" Tammy piped up. "I'd love a day of beauty at a spa! Besides, it would be worth it just to hang out with that hotty Jeremy."

"I'll go. I'll go." Abigail didn't exactly shoot off the sofa, but the cats had to scramble to keep from hitting the floor when she dumped them off her lap.

As she headed up the stairs, Savannah walked over and slapped Tammy on the back. "I didn't know you had a thing for Jeremy Lawrence."

"I don't. But *she* does, and that's all that matters."

"Deception. I didn't know you had it in you, Tam."

She chuckled. "I didn't, but I've been hanging out with you. It's contagious and you're a carrier."

"That's true. If liars' pants really did catch on fire, I'd be buy-ing new drawers five times a week."

Chapter

14

The ride to Emerge with Abigail was a bit more pleasant than usual for Savannah. Abigail had brightened considerably at the prospect of spending time with Jeremy Lawrence. She was somewhat less morose, and considering it was Abigail, "less morose" qualified as "darned near giddy" in Savannah's book.

And the moment they arrived and entered the building, a swarm of friendly Emerge employees, including Jeremy Lawrence, descended on Abigail and rushed her away into the luxurious and mysterious recesses of the spa.

In less than two minutes, they disappeared and Savannah found herself alone in the lobby with only Myrna for company.

And Myrna wasn't all that sociable. In fact, she was downright standoffish.

She returned to her desk and busied herself there, shuffling papers, sticking them into a folder, and ignoring Savannah entirely.

Savannah followed her and sat, unbidden, on one of the chairs next to her desk. "That was so sweet of you guys, arranging this whole day of beauty for Abigail. I think it'll do her a world of good."

Myrna didn't reply, just continued to mess with her papers, a look of anger mixed with hurt on her face.

Savannah wondered what might have happened to change the climate so quickly. When they had spoken on the phone less than an hour ago, Myrna had been her usual warm and friendly self. Now things had gone from warm to frosty and Savannah had to find out why.

"Is everything okay, Myrna?" she asked. "Have I upset or offended you in some way?"

"You mean, by lying to me, telling me you're a reporter when you're really a private investigator?"

Oh, that. Savannah cursed herself for not telling Myrna herself. It was always worse if they heard it from someone else.

"I'm sorry, Myrna. Sometimes in my line of work, I'm not always honest with people. It's a part of the job that I'm uncomfortable with. Especially when I'm dealing with someone I like, I'd rather be forthcoming."

Myrna stared down at a folder on her desk. "You could have told me. If you could tell somebody like Devon, you could have told me. I thought you and I were girlfriends."

"I didn't confide in Devon as a buddy," Savannah said. "I had to tell her because I was with Sergeant Coulter when he went out to inform her of Sergio's death. And I'd still like to be friends with you, if you can forgive me for that deception."

Myrna looked up at her, the anger in her eyes softening. "Is there anything else you need to tell me? Anything else you might have lied . . . or been deceptive about?"

"No. That's it. Really."

"Okay." She took a deep breath. "Then let's start over."

"Done!" Savannah glanced down at Myrna's desk, at the one and only folder there. It had Abigail's name on it. "Not a lot going on, I guess," she said.

"Next to nothing. We're going to close the doors for good to-morrow. With Suzette gone and Sergio dead, there doesn't seem to be any reason to go through the motions anymore. That's why we figured we'd go all out for Abigail today. Might as well start and finish Emerge with panache."

"And how about Mystic Twilight? What's going to happen to that spa?"

"Same thing. It was about to fold anyway. Closing will just be a formality at this point. It's all very sad."

"Do you have any leads on another job?"

"No," Myrna said sadly. "Everybody wants nineteen-year-olds at the front desk at these clinics. Maybe I'll retire. Move to Florida and spend my time lying in the sun."

"There are worse ways to spend the rest of your life, that's for sure."

Myrna reached beneath her desk and took out a small box. "I just need to pack up a few things here," she said, "and then I'm off to . . . well . . . the rest of my life, as you say."

She opened a drawer and began to load personal items into the box: nail polish, makeup, sugarless gum and mints, some costume jewelry, and a few pictures.

Savannah reached for one of the snapshots. "May I?"

"Sure."

It was a picture of a white poodle, holding a small black teddy bear in his teeth. The teddy bear was wearing a bright red and green plaid vest and looked a bit ragged around the edges. Savannah could swear that the dog was grinning.

"That's Sammy," Myrna said, "and Baby."

"Baby?"

"The teddy bear's name is Baby. I taught Sammy the cutest trick with it. You say, 'Sammy go get your baby,' and he'll run and get it. Then you say, 'Sam, love your baby,' and he growls and shakes it like it's a rat. It's hysterical. Sammy lo-o-oves Baby."

Myrna collapsed into giggles, but Savannah continued to stare at the picture. "He's really attached to it, huh?"

"Oh yes. Suzette always took Sammy with her, everywhere she went. Everywhere! And wherever Sam went, Baby went. If she tried to leave the house without the bear, Sam would stand by the door and bark until she brought it, too."

Savannah mentally retraced her steps when she had searched Suzette's house. Both times. She was pretty sure she would have remembered a teddy bear wearing a red and green plaid vest.

So, Suzette wasn't allowed to leave the house without Baby, huh? Interesting. One more reason to consider that maybe Suzette had staged her own disappearance after all. Leave the dog's collar out in a conspicuous place, but take his favorite toy.

She'd have to mention that to Dirk when she checked with him next.

Thoughts of Dirk brought her back to the business at hand. "Myrna, I need to ask you about something."

"As a reporter, or a private investigator?"

"Touché. As a plain old P.I. who's no longer technically on the job, but eternally curious."

"Okay. Ask away."

"Who has keys to the medicine cabinet? The one there in Exam Room One, where Nurse Bridget takes blood samples."

"Keys? Well, let me see. Sergio and Suzette, of course. And Bridget. And Yasmina."

"Who's Yasmina?"

"Our anesthesiologist."

"Why haven't I seen her around?"

"She hasn't been here because we haven't had any surgeries scheduled."

"Who else?"

"Well, I have a key that I keep here in my desk." She opened the bottom drawer and pointed to a small key that was fastened to the side of the drawer with a piece of cellophane tape. "We keep one here, just in case somebody loses or forgets theirs and needs to get something out of the cabinet."

"And who knows that one is there?"

"Pretty much everybody, I guess."

Savannah sighed. *Everybody*, she thought. *Boy, that narrows the list—not at all.*

"So, tell me more about this anesthesiologist, Yasmina."

"She's fantastic at what she does. *She* won't have a problem getting work at another clinic. A bunch of Beverly Hills surgeons have been after her for years, trying to lure her away from Suzette."

"Do you suppose I could speak to her sometime soon?"

"You could talk to her today, but as I said before, she isn't here. She's at Mystic Twilight, also packing up her things."

Mystic Twilight, Savannah thought. *I need to check that place out anyway.* "Could we maybe call her there? See if she'll talk to me and if she'll hang around long enough for me to get out there."

"Sure. I'll give her a call right now and you can ask her." She gave Savannah a funny little smile. "Anything for a girlfriend."

Dr. Yasmina La Rue sounded like a sweetheart over the phone, with a soft, Caribbean accent and a chuckle in her voice. But she also sounded like she meant it when she told Savannah, "I'd be happy to talk to you, dear, but once I'm packed, I'm leaving Mystic Twilight for good. You'd better hurry."

So Savannah didn't dawdle about getting into the Mustang and heading into the foothills east of town. She called Dirk on her cell phone and gave him the news.

"Where are you?" she asked him.

"Just approaching the city limits. I got done in Santa Barbara a little early. Why?"

"I'm headed for the Mystic Twilight spa in Hidden Canyon. I

have a personal invitation from Suzette's anesthesiologist, a lady named Yasmina La Rue. Have you been there yet?" she asked him.

"No. The staff there at Emerge told me that nobody has been around there for a couple of weeks now, so I didn't bother. Did you check out the keys there at Emerge . . . who had them, who didn't?"

"They all had one or had access to one. Everybody and their uncle's dog's first cousin. Nothing there."

"All right. You want me to come out there with you?"

"Not particularly. I'm just going to poke around. If I see anything interesting, I'll give you a buzz."

"Okay. I'm going to go back to the morgue and see if Dr. Liu has anything else for me."

"Give Kenny Slug Breath my regards."

"A one-finger salute?"

"Exactly."

"Will do."

Savannah was upon Mystic Twilight before she knew it. Rounding a sharp curve about a mile into the canyon, she saw the entrance, a paved road with a discreet sign with a fancy, intertwined M and T.

She turned onto the road and traveled another half mile or more between old gnarled oaks in a park-like setting.

As always, when venturing into one of these canyons that were scattered among the hills of Southern California, Savannah felt a strange mixture of peace and unease. With her car window rolled down, she experienced the place with all of her senses. The ancient oaks, the smell of wild sage in the air, the taste of dust, the feel of the hot sun and dry wind on her skin, the sounds of birds, frogs, and crickets, along with a distant rush of a creek over its rocky bed; she felt she had stepped back in time.

The Native Americans had considered these valleys sacred, forbidden ground. And when she was there, she felt like a careless interloper . . . as though the land itself was somehow aware of her. Aware, and not particularly hospitable toward her.

She always breathed a sigh of relief when she left the valleys and returned to her own stomping grounds by the sea.

Rounding yet another corner, she saw the spa, a large, square, flat-roofed building that looked like it belonged in Morocco, not sunny California.

The exterior walls were stucco, painted a dark, terra-cotta. Mature palm trees planted all around the building added to the feeling that it was some sort of desert oasis.

As she pulled up in front, she saw that a man-made stream crossed in front of the edifice, styled to look like the natural creek beds in the area.

The front door was an elaborate, arched, wrought iron affair, surrounded by colorful tiles of deep blue and gold . . . more of the Moroccan influence.

She left the Mustang and walked up to the door. She hurt her knuckles knocking on the door, and no one answered. Gingerly, she gave it a push, and it creaked open with a spookiness that she might have found delicious under other circumstances. But having just seen a dead guy and knowing that a woman was missing, she wasn't in the mood for "creepy."

"Hello?" she shouted. "Anybody here? Yasmina? It's Savannah Reid. Yoo-hoo."

As her eyes adjusted from the bright sunlight outside to the dark interior, she saw that the entrance was at least two stories tall, as well as wide and deep. More of the blue and gold tiles covered the walls and were arranged in ornate patterns on the floor. In the center of the room was a massive fountain, but it was dry and looked as though it hadn't run for a long time.

Three hallways branched off from the entry, heading in numerous directions. And each hall was even darker than the entrance.

Savannah wasn't eager to go roaming and exploring, even if that was the job description.

Mentally, she checked her weapon, chose one of the hallways, and headed down it.

Big girls aren't afraid of the dark, she told herself.

Well, Sergio probably wasn't afraid of the dark either, and look at where that got him. He's in a drawer in Dr. Liu's morgue with an autopsy "Y" incision on his chest, her self replied.

"Anybody here?" she called again.

Her voice echoed off the tiles and came back to her, sounding a bit less confident than she wanted to feel. In fact, she sounded scared . . . and she wasn't sure why.

It wasn't just the dark. The dark felt ominous somehow. And the building didn't feel empty.

She felt as though someone . . . someone in the dark . . . was watching her.

Stopping in the middle of the hallway, she looked back at the entry and its other corridors and said, "If you've got something to say to me, come out and say it. Don't hide in the shadows like a coward."

She felt stupid. There was probably no one there, but—

Then she heard it: a movement. It sounded like something had brushed against a wall. Softly. Barely. But there.

She reached for her gun and pulled it from its holster.

"Come on out," she said. "I mean it. Come out now and put your hands up or I'll shoot you."

Her adrenaline was pumping, her heart racing.

She could almost hear someone breathing, there in the darkness where she had just stood. Whoever it was, was following her. At least trying to. But she wouldn't stand for it.

"I can see you," she lied. "Come on out now with your hands up! Do it!"

Then she heard it, unmistakable this time. Someone was running down the opposite hallway, in the other direction. And running hard.

Gun in hand, but pointed at the ceiling, she ran after them.

If somebody was going to spy on her, she was going to know "who" and "why."

Ahead, at the end of the hallway, she saw a door open and bright sunlight stream in, but only for a moment. Then it slammed closed.

She raced to the door and carefully, cautiously opened it.

The sunshine was blinding, but she saw a figure directly in front of her. She lifted the gun and pointed it. "Freeze!" she shouted. "Hold it right there. Hands up and don't you even twitch!"

"They're up!" the figure said. "I'm not moving. Don't shoot!"

Her eyes adjusted, and she realized she was aiming her gun at Jeremy Lawrence.

He was standing there, six feet in front of her, his hands and arms raised, a look of alarm on his face.

"Why were you spying on me?" she demanded.

"What? Spying? I don't know what you're talking about."

"Don't lie to me. You were back there in the entry area. You were watching me. I chased you out here, so don't act like you don't know what's up here."

"I was over there . . ." He lowered one hand long enough to point at a smaller building across a large patio area. ". . . saying goodbye to Yasmina. I was coming over here to the main building to lock up. I think I saw somebody run out just now, before you, but I didn't get a good look at them."

She studied his perfect, beautiful face and saw absolutely no expression. His pale blue eyes gave nothing away, nothing at all.

He was remarkably cool for a guy who was on the receiving end of a big bad Beretta.

And that could mean that he was innocent. Or very, very good at being guilty.

She scanned his figure quickly, but saw no outline of a weapon beneath his thin silk shirt or in his twill slacks.

Lowering her gun, she said, "You must have seen something. Was it a man or woman?"

He dropped his hands. "I don't know. I just caught a glimpse and—"

"Big or small?"

He shrugged. "Really, Savannah. I didn't even get a look, just a blur of movement and that was all."

"I thought you were supposed to be at Emerge, helping with Abigail's makeover," she said as she reholstered the gun. "I just left you there."

"I probably left a few minutes before you did. I heard that Yasmina was here, packing and getting ready to go. I had to say good-bye to her. I'm heading back to Emerge right now. They're coloring and cutting Abigail's hair. That'll take a while."

Savannah felt the war inside herself . . . the trusting, kind, loving person whom Granny Reid had raised to always be fair and never accuse an innocent person of wrongdoing . . . versus the cop who had been punched, spit on, shot at, and lied to twenty times in one evening.

She decided to let Granny's girl come forward and deal with Jeremy Lawrence. At least for the moment.

She offered him her hand. "I'm sorry about the gun, Jeremy. I hope you understand. I'm investigating a murder here and a possible kidnapping."

His blue eyes widened. "A murder? Sergio was murdered?"

"Yes. The lab reports are in and the M.E. is ruling it a homicide."

"Oh, no! That's horrible." He shook his head as though in disbelief. "It's bad enough that he died. But we figured it was natural causes. Murder? Who would want to kill him?"

"You tell me, Jeremy. You tell me."

"I don't know. I really don't. He wasn't exactly a gentleman where women were concerned . . . or, I hate to say, an especially good businessman. But to have someone deliberately kill him! Are you sure?"

Savannah nodded. "Yes, but if you could keep that to yourself . . ."

"Sure. I understand. You don't want the person who did it to know that you know what they did."

"Right."

"I need to get back to Emerge now," he said, "if you're finished with me, that is."

"I am. Thanks, and sorry about the gun business."

He smiled his soft, peaceful, ethereal smile. "It's forgotten. Just catch whoever did that to Sergio and help find Suzette. That's all we want right now, Savannah."

"I'm trying. I'm trying."

Savannah watched the young man walk into the building and close the door behind him. And she wondered. He was so perfect. Perfectly handsome. Perfectly poised. Perfectly mannered and perfectly groomed.

Yes, she'd definitely have to keep a closer eye on Jeremy Lawrence.

Nobody on God's green earth was *that* perfect.

Chapter

15

Savannah found Dr. La Rue in the small building across the patio, where Jeremy Lawrence had indicated he had just spoken to her. The tiny black woman had an enormous smile for Savannah when they met in the middle of a hallway. She was struggling to carry a cardboard box that looked nearly as big as she was.

"Dr. La Rue, I presume. I'm Savannah. Thank you for waiting for me," she said. "Here, let me take that."

"I've got it. I've got it," Yasmina said between huffs and puffs.

"More like *it's* got *you*. Gimme that thing."

Savannah took the box from her and instantly realized why the doctor was having a difficult time. The box was not only large but extremely heavy.

"What do you have in here? Lead? Water? A dead body?"

Yasmina threw back her head and laughed heartily. The sound went through Savannah and gave her the same warm feeling that she got from hugging Granny Reid.

"A bit of all three, my dear," the doctor replied as she opened a door and ushered Savannah back outside. "How kind you are to give an old woman some help."

Savannah studied the doctor over the top of the box as they headed toward a parking lot and a beautiful, navy blue Jaguar. Dr. La Rue could have been any age, from late thirties to sixty. It was difficult to tell. Her skin was a delicious shade of bronze and glowed with health; her eyes were bright with intelligence and warm with kindness. She couldn't have been more than five feet tall, and Savannah was sure that her own right thigh weighed more than the whole of the other woman.

"You don't look that old to me," Savannah said as Yasmina opened the trunk of the Jaguar and motioned for her to place the box inside.

"I'm older than these hills," she replied, gesturing to the mountains around them. "Older than trees and dirt. And so are you. Don't you believe that? Can't you feel it in your bones, child?"

Savannah jostled the box until it fit and closed the trunk. "Oh yeah," she replied. "And some days these bones feel even older than that, depending on what I've been up to."

"And what are you up to on this fine day?" Yasmina dusted her hands off on the bright blue and purple tunic she wore over dark blue pants. Her ears and neckline sparkled with blue and purple beaded jewelry that might have been considered by some to be too large for such a small person. But Dr. Yasmina's personality easily carried such a bold statement.

"Like I mentioned on the phone, I'm a private investigator and—"

"And what are you investigating?"

"The disappearance of Suzette Du Bois."

"I figured as much."

"And the murder of Sergio D'Alessandro."

Dr. La Rue gasped and put her hand over her mouth. She staggered backward and leaned on the Jaguar's trunk. "Murder? His *murder*, you say?"

"Yes, I'm sorry to say so, but it appears now that he was a victim of homicide."

"How? How was he killed?"

"Apparently with an overdose of Bot-Avanti, that new botulism drug the clinic has been using instead of Botox. Someone put a lethal amount into the B_{12} solution he normally takes."

The doctor was obviously, deeply affected by the news. She shook her head several times, as though denying the information. Then tears sprang to her eyes.

Savannah cursed herself for not telling Yasmina more gently. How many years had she been informing people of horrible, heartbreaking things. She should have known better.

"Are you all right?" She reached for the doctor's arm. She could feel her trembling and was afraid she might faint. "Why don't we open the car door so that you can sit down?" she suggested.

"No, I'll be okay. I just . . . oh, this is so terrible."

She covered her face with her hands and began to sob.

Savannah fumbled in her purse and brought out a handful of tissues.

She stood silently by, allowing the woman time to cry and then to partially compose herself. Finally she said, "I can see that you and he were very close. I'm sorry for your loss . . . and for the awful circumstances of his death."

Yasmina took a deep, shuddering breath. "Sergio and I weren't close," she said. "I don't believe Sergio was close to anyone in his entire life. He just didn't have it in him. But murder. Murder is such a deep, horrible evil. It upsets . . ." She waved her arms, indicating the mountains, the trees, that surrounded them. " . . . it upsets the balance, the harmony of nature. It is a wickedness that damages us all."

Savannah could agree with that, absolutely and completely. In her years of experience she had seen the ripple effect caused by a homicide that was more like a tsunami. The taking of a human life could destroy not only the victim, but entire families. Even communities were deeply damaged by the act of homicide, taking generations to heal.

"It *does* damage us all," Savannah said. "That's why I feel so strongly about bringing a murderer to justice. For the victim, for the family, for all of us."

Yasmina wiped her eyes and straightened her back. "How can I help you, Savannah? Tell me what you need from me."

"I need to know if he had any enemies, anyone who may have threatened to do him harm recently."

"Other than Suzette . . . and the women he's thrown aside when he was finished with them . . . and the husbands of the women he's seduced . . . and the patients who weren't happy with their results . . . and the people who have lost the fortunes they invested in his dubious business ventures . . . the professionals whose careers he has destroyed through his lies and incompetence . . . people like that?"

Savannah's jaw dropped. Then she recovered herself and nodded. "Yes. Exactly. People like that."

"Come inside," Yasmina said, heading back to the building. "We might as well get comfortable. This could take a while."

An hour later, Savannah's brain and her notebook were filled with the names of people who were everything from disgruntled to furious with Sergio D'Alessandro. She didn't know whether to feel grateful or overwhelmed.

"It's been ages since I've had a list of suspects this long," she said, flipping through the pages. "I must admit, I didn't care for Mr. D'Alessandro when I met him, and I think even less of him now."

Yasmina sighed and took another sip of hot herbal tea. "I hate to speak ill of the dead. But under these terrible circumstances, we must also tell the truth, even if it's ugly."

"I appreciate that."

When the doctor had first brought Savannah into her office, she had made them each a cup and offered her some coconut macaroons from an antique tin. Savannah had settled into a comfortable chair next to her desk and allowed herself the luxury of temporarily basking in the peaceful ambiance the woman seemed to create around her.

Some people had an air of spirituality about them, an aura of otherworldliness that calmed and nourished those fortunate enough to spend time in their presence. Savannah's grandmother was one such soul. And Dr. La Rue was another.

Savannah was reluctant to leave her, but she had work to do— processing this list, among other things.

She looked around the office with its pictures of tranquil island scenes on the walls, candles and fresh flowers floating in sparkling, cut glass bowls, the sweet, exotic scent of lemongrass in the air. "So, you're moving out of here, huh?" she said.

"I am. This part of my life has been dying for a long time. And that's fine. All things die sooner or later."

"A sad thought."

Yasmina smiled. "Not at all. The leaves die and fall in a blaze of glory, and they feed the hungry saplings that grow and flourish. Everything in its time."

Savannah offered her hand and wondered at the power that radiated from the other woman's touch. "Thank you, doctor," she said humbly, "for all your help. I'm so glad we met."

"Me, too, Savannah. Do stay in contact. I'd like to hear from you from time to time, and I'd be pleased to get to know you better."

"Absolutely. It would be my pleasure."

The two women walked out together, as Savannah took yet another box to the Jaguar.

It was when Savannah was saying good-bye that she glanced back at the main building—the back door in particular—and she thought of one more question she wanted to ask Dr. La Rue.

"By the way," she said, "did you speak to Jeremy Lawrence a while ago, before I arrived."

"Indeed I did. Jeremy rushed over here from Emerge to say good-bye and wish me well."

"And how long was it, would you guess, from the time you said good-bye to him and I met you there in the hallway?"

Yasmina shrugged. "I don't know, a few minutes. I was involved, packing all those books into that box. I really can't say."

"Okay." Savannah thought for a moment. "And one more thing. Did you see anyone else here today, other than Jeremy and me?"

Yasmina nodded. "Just one other person, someone else who came by to say farewell, right before Jeremy arrived."

Savannah had a feeling she knew the answer even before she asked. "And who was that, Dr. La Rue?"

"Someone else who, like Sergio, needs to find and love herself better. Then she could love others better. It was Devon. My other visitor today was Devon Wright. Now there is a troubled soul."

Sitting at a table in Chez Antoine was one of Savannah's most enjoyable sensual experiences. The food, the wine, the crisp, white linens, the classic French decor and the hospitable, solicitous Antoine, who hovered and pampered his guests, all combined to create the perfect dining experience.

But the reason Savannah loved the place most was because

when she was here, she was always the guest of Ryan Stone and John Gibson. And they were, hands down, the best dates a gal could have . . . if a gal was satisfied with having chocolate mousse for dessert, and not a serving of hunk *á la mode*.

And tonight the experience was even richer, because she could share it all with two young women who were enjoying every moment.

Across the table from Savannah sat Tammy—relaxed and happy for the first time since her cousin had arrived—chatting away with John, discussing the finer points of breaching online security systems.

Next to her sat Abigail . . . a transformed Abigail, thanks to the talents and efforts of the Emerge staff. Savannah had decided, the moment she saw Abigail at the spa, that maybe this idea of a metamorphosis wasn't just hype, after all.

Abigail Simpson had, indeed, unfurled like a beautiful butterfly.

Her hair had been cut, and although it was still well past her shoulders, it fell in soft waves around her, with feminine layers framing her face. And they had colored it a stunning shade of golden red that brought out the peach tones of her complexion.

Before the makeover, her brows had been bushy and well-knit in the middle. Now they were shaped and gracefully arched, setting off her big eyes to perfection.

Her new makeup was a mixture of golden and bronze tones, expertly applied to look glamorous, yet natural.

The blouse they had chosen for her was an elegant copper silk affair, and her chocolate velvet skirt had a split that showed off her nicely shaped calves and ankles.

Even Dirk had commented upon seeing her earlier, "Gee, Cousin Abby's got great gams. Who would've thought it?"

High-heeled sandals of bronze-metallic leather and a matching handbag completed the ensemble, along with a necklace, earrings, and bracelet that featured mystic twilight topazes—the perfect final touch.

But it wasn't the hair, the makeup, the clothes, or the jewelry that had transformed Abigail and made her shine. It was the un-accustomed attention she had received at the hands of the staff and now from her friends, the interest in her concerns and pref-erences, the pure pampering—being treated like a lady.

And a lady she had become.

Tonight her expression was softer, her gestures more feminine, her whole demeanor more gracious. The difference was simply amazing.

And underlying all that womanly pulchritude was a purely fe-male strength, born of newfound confidence. The sort of female strength that, in another era, could have led armies of chariots against enemy troops or ruled the civilized world from a queen's throne.

"Abby," Savannah said, "I just can't stop staring at you, girl. You're gorgeous!"

"Isn't she though?" Ryan said, giving their guest of honor the benefit of his heart-stopping smile. "You're absolutely glowing."

Abigail blushed under the compliments, but for once, no self-deprecating comments came out of her mouth.

"What do you like best about your makeover?" Savannah asked her.

Abby tossed her head and ran her fingers through her hair. "I like being a redhead. I was when I was a kid, but then it turned dark."

"And now you're a redhead again. Come to think of it," Tammy said, "you've always been a redhead . . . temper-wise, that is."

"Now, now . . . you aren't buying into any old stereotypes, are you?" Savannah cautioned.

"Stereotypes?" Tammy cleared her throat and grinned. "Tell

me the truth now . . . have you ever known a boring, passive red-head?"

The guys at the table laughed heartily. "She's got you there, Savannah," Ryan said. "I have to admit that every redhead I've known could be classified as feisty, to say the least."

"Absolutely," John agreed. "And here's to feisty redheads! May they rule the world!"

"I think we already do," Abby replied.

"To Queen Abigail," Tammy said, lifting her glass. "Long may she reign!"

"Here, here!" John raised his own glass and they clinked all around.

"And now," Abby said, "if you two could solve this murder case, we'd have even more reason to celebrate."

"Oh, talk about popping somebody's bubble." Savannah visibly deflated. "You had to bring that up?"

"Yeah, really," Tammy added. "Just when we're celebrating your 'coming out' you have to remind me of my wasted hours, sitting there, messing with that stupid computer."

Ryan leaned closer to Tammy and lowered his voice, "Actually, we brought you a little present tonight to help you with that."

Tammy's eyes lit up. "Really?"

"Oh yeah. You're going to love us after you see this."

"I already love you."

"Okay, then we'll be adored. I borrowed a little something for you from a friend of ours at the Bureau."

"The FBI?" Abigail said, instantly all ears.

"Sh-h-h," Ryan replied, giving her a discreet nod.

"What is it?"

"Software," John said. "Forensic software."

Ryan pulled a square envelope from his pocket and slid it across the table to Tammy. "You use that, you're going to be able to find everything in that computer . . . even the stuff your poor, dead buddy thought he had deleted."

"Really?"

"Would I lie to one of my girls?"

"Sweet!" Tammy clutched the envelope to her chest, a look of pure rapture on her face. "Oh, this is so-o-oo sweet!"

"Speaking of sweets," Savannah said, eyeing an overladen dessert tray that was passing her by. "I think we should all have crêpes suzette tonight. It just seems appropriate somehow."

Chapter

16

"Isn't there a song that says, 'It never rains in California'?" Abigail asked as they all stood huddled in a sodden lump, trying to ignore the fact that their umbrellas weren't doing a bit of good. Umbrellas only worked when the rain was falling vertically. Thanks to an unseasonable and particularly fierce, onshore storm, the horizontal precipitation was drenching everyone present and making them generally miserable.

But it was the perfect setting for a funeral.

Savannah, Tammy, and Dirk had insisted on being present when the mortal remains of one Leonard Roy Hoffman of Bakersfield, California, aka Sergio D'Alessandro, were laid to rest.

Abigail had come along because she didn't want to sit at home alone. And not even the previous day's Emerge experience was going to lift her dampened spirits as she stood there in the cemetery in the pouring rain, shivering with the other mourners.

"Sh-h-h-h, it'll be over soon," Savannah admonished her, seeing a couple of heads turn their way at the sound of Abby's complaining.

She, too, wanted nothing more than to go home, peel off the

cold, wet clothes, and get into a warm robe. But she wasn't there just to pay her respects. Especially since she had precious little respect for ol' Sergio. She was working.

She, Tammy, and Dirk were all working, as they scanned the faces of the crowd and accounted for everyone.

It was commonly known among the members of law enforcement that murderers were frequently nearby after a killing, hanging about the crime scene, helping with a search if one was conducted, and attending funerals.

What was the fun of causing a horrific hullabaloo if you couldn't be around to appreciate it and watch its effect on others?

So the Moonlight Magnolia team was at the funeral in full force, studying the attendees and the interactions between them, looking for anything out of the ordinary or suspicious.

Savannah squinted against the cold, driving rain, shivering, listening to the minister go on and on about how loved Leonard had been, such a fine son, a dear friend, an accomplished businessman, and what a contribution he had made to his community. The clergyman made ol' Sergio sound like a real peach.

Savannah wondered if the preacher had ever met him.

The coffin was suspended over the freshly dug grave on straps, waiting to be lowered. A temporary pavilion had been stretched over the site, and a ring of folding chairs placed around it.

Unfortunately, only those seated in the chairs were sheltered by the covering. Everyone else had to stand outside it and be pelted.

Savannah kept repeating the mantra, "Hot chocolate. Hot chocolate," to herself to keep her teeth from chattering as she studied the small, intimate gathering.

The elderly woman sitting nearest the head of the coffin had to be his mother. An elderly and frail woman, dressed in black with the traditional veil over her face, she wept softly into a lace handkerchief. The minister seemed to be addressing his parting words to her alone. Savannah speculated that he might be her minister, rather than Sergio's . . . or Leonard, as he was being called today.

She appeared to be the only one genuinely, deeply distressed at Leonard's untimely passing. Except, perhaps, for Devon Wright.

From her spot at the foot of the grave, Devon was wailing, eyes heavenward in what certainly appeared to be a display of wrenching, soulful agony. Except for the fact that there didn't appear to be a tear in sight.

Directly behind her stood her son, the little boy that Savannah and Dirk had seen that night at her house. He was just far enough outside the canopy to receive absolutely none of its protection and he was being soaked to the skin. Shivering violently, he was staring at his mother in alarm.

It took all the self-control Savannah could muster not to go grab the boy and rescue him from the scene. The kid didn't need to be standing in a cold rain at the funeral of some guy who was nothing more than his nitwit mother's Bang of the Month. The boy needed some hugs, a change of warm, dry clothes, and a hot fudge sundae with a cherry on the top.

At least, according to Basic Savannah Reid Child-Rearing 101.

In the crowd, someone else was watching the interplay between Devon and her boy. It was Dr. Yasmina La Rue who watched for a moment, then locked eyes with Savannah and shook her head sadly.

Savannah thought of what Dr. La Rue had said—that Devon needed to love herself more so that she could love those around her.

Savannah supposed that was true. But she also decided that Yasmina was a better person than she was. The good doctor saw

Devon as a lost soul who needed to find herself, someone who needed to be loved, understood, and upheld.

But Savannah was just as quick to admit she, personally, just wasn't that virtuous. She'd much prefer to just push Devon Wright off the end of the San Carmelita pier and find out later whether she could swim or not.

She decided to pray about it and ask the Lord to make her a better, more loving, understanding, and tolerant person. But she'd prayed that quite a few times before and hadn't noticed any great changes in her personality. So she wasn't overly optimistic that it would take this time either.

Jeremy Lawrence stood about twenty feet away from them, wearing a somber, dove-gray suit and an even more somber expression on his handsome face. He was holding an oversized umbrella, trying to keep himself and Myrna Cooper dry. She stood stoically beside him, clinging to his arm. And for all of the water soaking the lower halves of their bodies, neither of them had even a hint of moisture in their eyes.

From time to time Myrna shot an angry, hurt look at a man who sat beside the coffin under the canopy. The object of her disdain looked to be in his early fifties. A relatively handsome man, he was holding the hand of a woman young enough to be his daughter, but who bore no resemblance.

Savannah would have bet her detective agency's petty cash that the guy was Myrna's former honey who had dumped her for a younger woman after she had paid for his face-lift.

And she didn't blame Myrna for the nasty looks either. If a guy had done that to *her*, he wouldn't have been able to walk straight for months, and the last thing he'd need was another girlfriend.

Behind them, Nurse Bridget stood quietly, clutching a rosary, her head bowed and eyes closed. She was mumbling under her breath. Next to her stood a man, who had one arm around her shoulders and held in his other arm a little girl who looked exactly like Bridget.

A few other faces were vaguely familiar to Savannah, employees of Emerge, like the maid who had discovered the deceased's body, a young woman who had been Abigail's hair stylist and another who had been introduced to Savannah earlier as the spa's manicurist.

Apparently, Sergio had no other close friends or family.

Savannah wasn't particularly surprised.

"Anybody here you don't know?" Dirk whispered, leaning close to her.

"Just the older woman, who I think is his mom," Savannah replied. "And that gal over there with the platinum blond hair and the big sunglasses."

"The older lady is his mom. I've talked to her already. She's a real mess over him dying so young. And the blonde is Suzette's sister, the one I interviewed in Santa Barbara."

"You'll have to tell me about her later," Savannah whispered.

"Nothing to tell. She thought her sister was a nutcase for caring about this guy. That's it."

"How much longer are we going to stay?" Abby said, nudging Savannah in the ribs with her elbow. "I'm about to freeze to death here."

"I hate to say it, but I'm really cold, too," Tammy added. Savannah could see that she was turning a little blue under her perpetual tan.

The mourners were beginning to throw roses on top of the coffin. And the minister had gotten to the "dust to dust" part of his eulogy.

"Let's go home," Savannah said. "I think we all need to thaw out. How's about some double fudge hot chocolate?"

"With a shot of Bailey's?" Dirk asked, "Savannah style?"

"Of course. Let's let the dead rest in peace."

Dirk groaned and wiped a hand wearily across his wet face. "Rest? God knows, somebody needs to."

As Savannah heated milk in a pan and melted some chocolate chips in her microwave, she looked across the kitchen to the table where Dirk sat, his elbows propped on the table, his head in his hands.

"Dirko doesn't look so good," Tammy whispered in her ear. "I'm worried about him."

Savannah nodded. "I know. He just can't burn the candle at both ends like he used to. When he tries it, he fizzles like a defunct Fourth of July bottle rocket."

"I heard that," he said, raising his head and glaring at them with bloodshot eyes. "I may be tired, but I'm not deaf, and I'm sure as hell not old. So watch it over there."

"Yeah, yeah, we's tremblin' here. Shakin' in our boots," Savannah replied. "That's us. Did you eat good today? Want me to scramble you up some eggs? Make you a bowl of chicken noodle soup or something?"

"Naw, I'll perk up in a minute. I just need to rest my eyes."

Savannah poked Tammy. "You just wait. He'll be snoring in thirty seconds. Happens every time he 'rests his eyes.' He closes those peepers and a second later, he's making zz-zz-zz's like a cartoon bear."

Savannah and Tammy left him alone and continued to make the hot chocolate and, as Savannah had predicted, it was less than a minute before he started to snore. When the cocoa was finally ready, steaming hot mugs topped with peaks of whipped cream and sprinkled with shaved dark chocolate, Savannah was reluctant to wake him.

"Leave him alone for now," she told Tammy. "Let him get a few winks. That'll do him a world of good. Perk him right up."

Tammy snickered. "I don't think the words 'Dirk' and 'perk' even belong in the same sentence."

"Sh-h-h." Savannah took the tray with its bounty and tiptoed past Dirk and into the living room.

Ryan and John sat with Abigail, who had changed out of her wet clothes and into a dark green Georgette skirt and matching blouse. The color accented her new hair color and even though the outfit was a bit bohemian with its flouncy layers, the monochromatic scheme was an enormous improvement over her previous mixture of paisley and plaid.

She still had multiple bangles on her arms and gypsy hoops in her ears, but the look was more elegant than eccentric. No more Bag Lady Abby.

"I love this new look of yours, love," John was telling her. "It's still you, but more sophisticated."

She beamed and blushed. For a moment, she looked more to Savannah like a demure Southern belle than a tough gal from New York City. But then, John and Ryan had a way of making any woman melt.

"Jeremy helped me pick out everything," she told them. "He talked to me a long time about what I liked, and I admitted to him that I've always thought I must be part gypsy. I love stories about them, their mysticism, their travels. I always dressed up like a gypsy at Halloween and pretended to tell everyone's fortunes. Jeremy encouraged me to embrace my passions, to express myself through my clothes and accessories. So . . . this was the result."

"And a charming outcome it was," John said. "That Jeremy chap seems to have captured more than just your style. He seems to have snared your fancy just a bit . . . or is that my own romantic imagination working overtime?"

Her blush deepened. "I like him, sure," she said. "Who wouldn't? He's really sweet, not to mention gorgeous. He actually told me that he might move to New York someday. He's already found a surgeon in Manhattan who may be interested in what he has to offer. I told him that I'd do everything I can to help him make the move and get settled, if he decides to try the East Coast for a change."

Savannah set the tray on the coffee table and began to hand out the mugs. "Well, he certainly did a good job for Suzette and Sergio. He's a highly creative, resourceful young man. And I can see why you would like him, Abby. It might be nice for you if he did move to New York."

But even as she spoke the words, Savannah thought back on her visit to Mystic Twilight the day before and the person in the shadows who had watched her and then run from her.

In the past twenty-four hours she had replayed her conversation with Jeremy Lawrence outside the back door of the place, and she still wondered . . . had he been the one watching her?

Or if he hadn't been the one following her, spying on her, had he seen Devon Wright run out that door and then covered for her?

And if so, why?

Nothing in his behavior today at the funeral told her anything. He had been stoic. Moderately attentive to Myrna. That was about all.

And now he was actively seeking employment or business opportunities elsewhere. That could be suspicious. With Suzette still missing, it might seem a bit premature to assume that she wasn't coming back, that he needed another place to work. Unless, of course, he knew something that others didn't.

Tammy took a mug of cocoa, walked over to the desk and sat down. Turning on Sergio's laptop, she motioned to John. "You should come look at what I found," she said, "thanks to that awesome forensic software you loaned me."

Both John and Ryan hurried over to the desk and leaned over her shoulders.

"What did you find?" Savannah asked. "I didn't know you found something."

"Well, it isn't a 7.6 on the Richter scale, but I thought it was interesting." Tammy typed away on the keyboard for a minute or so, then said, "*Voila!* There it is."

Savannah squeezed into a spot beside Ryan. "What? What is it?"

"Ah!" John said. "I see!"

"Wow, look at that!" Ryan added.

"I thought you'd like it." Tammy beamed up at them, terribly proud of herself.

"What in Sam Hill are you guys talking about?" Savannah said, staring at the screen. All she could see was a long list of words, abbreviations, and symbols that made no sense at all to her.

"Oh, I'm sorry, Savannah," John said. "We computer nerds forget that not everyone is as savvy about this foolishness as we might be, because—"

"What is it, plee-ease?" Savannah held in a scream. "Speak to me in English! Now!"

"Simply put, someone was messing with Sergio's computer behind his back," Ryan told her. "They installed a special program into his notebook here, probably without his knowledge, that would record every single keystroke he made when he used it. At a later time, the person who placed the program there in the first place could retrace his keystrokes, see everything he'd typed, every online site he visited, etcetera."

John nodded. "It's a program that's used by parents who want to see what their children are looking at online; who they're talking to."

"And," Tammy added, "it can be used by employers who want to know what their employees are doing on company time: if they're working, playing video games, or looking at naughty pictures."

Ryan said, "Many a cheating spouse has been caught by these, emailing their honeys, setting up dates or whatever. Or maybe a hubby has sworn off his pornography addiction and his wife wants to know if he's fallen off the wagon or not."

"Can you tell who put the program in there?" Savannah asked.

"Not who, but when," Tammy told her. "It was installed about a year ago."

"If it was a year ago, I'd vote for the wife . . . or perhaps I should I say 'girlfriend.' That's about the time Suzette kicked Sergio out of the house. I'll bet you it had something to do with this program. She probably nailed him with other women, using that program."

"And get this," Tammy added. "It was uninstalled. That's why I couldn't find it before. It was uninstalled and all files relating to it deleted. With this new program of yours I was able to dig it out. This thing rules!"

"I'm so glad it's helping," John said. "And you'll find as you work with it, you'll be able to uncover even more. It's the equivalent of going through someone's personal garbage."

"Without getting potato peels, tomato sauce, and kitty litter all over you," Savannah said, recalling some of her less favorite searches.

"Hey," Tammy said, leaning forward and studying the screen. "I just noticed something else. Something that could be important."

"What's that?" Savannah asked.

"As I said, the snooper's program was uninstalled and all the pertaining files deleted. I can see right here when that was done."

"When?"

Tammy looked up at Savannah. She lifted one eyebrow. "It was done three days ago."

Savannah caught her breath for a moment, then nodded. "Yeap, three days ago was the day our old buddy Sergio kicked the bucket."

Chapter

17

When Savannah hurried into the kitchen to tell Dirk about the snooper software on Sergio's computer, she found him exactly where and how she'd left him, his arms folded on the table, his head on them. He looked like an over-sized kindergartner taking a "rest break."

And while Dirk might be a bit lazy from time to time when it came to domestic chores like cleaning or microwaving a TV dinner, he never slacked on the job. He lived for his work, and he tended to be a pit bull when it came to never letting go until the job was done.

He had to be sick.

She walked over to him and put her hand on his shoulder. Giving him a gentle shake, she said, "Hey, buddy. You asleep?"

His only response was a muffled groan.

"Dirk?" She ran her fingers though his hair. "Sugar, you okay?"

He raised his head slightly and looked up at her with glassy eyes. "I don't think so," he muttered. "To be honest, I feel like shit."

"To be honest, you look a bit like dog poo, too. Here, let me feel your head."

She laid her hand across his forehead and was not surprised at how hot he was. "You've got a fever, big boy," she told him. "You're sick."

"I don't get sick when I'm on a case, and especially not a homicide."

"Oh, yeah? Well, you'd better revise that motto of yours, 'cause you're burnin' up with fever there."

"I'm just tired and run down. I'll be all right."

"Yes, I'm sure you will be, once Dr. Savannah has taken care of you. I'm going to get you some aspirin to bring that fever down and put you in bed."

Dirk squinted at his watch. "It's six o'clock. I ain't going to bed at six. I was going to go back over to Du Bois's place and—"

"I was going myself anyway," Savannah said. "I'll go for both of us, and you're staying home. I reckon you caught your death o' cold, standing out in that rain today. You're not going out in it again."

"Yes, I am."

"Over my dead body, boy."

He started to rise from his chair, but she put one hand on his shoulder and shoved him back down. She was surprised at how easily he complied.

Dirk was many things. Compliant wasn't one of them.

"What's going on in here?" Ryan asked as he and John walked into the room just in time to see the mini-skirmish.

"Dirk's sick," she said. "He's been running himself ragged, and he's plumb worn out. He's got a fever. I'm going to give him some aspirin and put him to bed."

"So she says," Dirk mumbled.

John leaned over Dirk, studying him closely. "Any other symptoms?" he asked Savannah.

"Other than general cussedness and standard orneriness... just fatigue and fever."

"I've known several people who've come down with something like this lately," Ryan said. "It'll knock you off your feet for weeks if you don't nip it in the bud early."

He looked at John, and they both nodded.

"Fix him up, John, like you did me," he said.

Dirk scowled. "What? What are you talking about? Fix me up how?"

John left the table and walked over to the kitchen counter where Savannah kept a perpetually full bowl of fresh fruit. He picked out a large orange.

"Savannah," he said, "be a dear and get me some whole cloves, your sugar bowl, and your finest Irish whiskey. I'm going to make the lad a hot toddy."

"I ain't drinkin' when I'm on the job," Dirk said, but he was scowling a bit less and his bleary eyes reflected more than a passing interest.

"I'm making you an Irish toddy, and by god, you'll drink it and like it," John replied.

As Savannah searched her relatively sparse liquor cabinet for whiskey, John set to work, heating water on the stove and cutting the orange crosswise, then studding the thin slices with the cloves.

He dissolved a couple of spoonfuls of sugar in a cup of steaming water and floated a few of the orange slices on the top, then added an obscene amount of the whiskey to the mixture.

He took it to Dirk and set the mug in front of him on the table. "Drink up, old chap," he said. "It's the cure for the common cold. Works in twelve hours. You'll be a new man by tomorrow morning, I assure you."

Dirk lifted the mug and sniffed it. "Really?"

"Well," Ryan said, "let's put it this way: If it doesn't cure what ails you, at least you won't mind being sick half as much."

Dirk took a sip, grimaced, and looked up at John, who was

leaning over him with a parental, no nonsense expression on his face.

"Drink it down," John said. "Now."

Dirk did as he was told, and even licked his lips afterward. "It's not really all that bad," he said. "In fact, it's pretty kickass."

Ryan laughed and turned to Savannah. "We'd better get him upstairs and in bed right away," he told her. "That stuff's going to kick *his* ass any second now, and then he'll be dead weight."

And Ryan wasn't exaggerating. By the time the three of them had Dirk up the stairs, peeled down to his skivvies, and tucked between Savannah's pink satin sheets, he was too looped to even resist.

But, being Dirk, he managed to complain at least a little during the process. "I don't want no gay guys undressing me," he said as Ryan removed his shoes and Savannah tugged his jeans off.

"Oh, hush up," Savannah told him. "Ain't nobody here interested in what you've got. And you're not getting into my clean bed in those dirty, damp clothes."

John grabbed the hem of Dirk's Harley tee-shirt and yanked it over his head. "Not to worry, Dirk, old lad. Ryan and I can resist ravishing such a fine model of manhood as yourself." He chuckled. "'Tis a hardship, to be sure, but we'll bear up."

True to her word, Savannah wasted no time once dinner was finished and hurried over to Suzette Du Bois's house. In her hand she had a checklist of the things Dirk had wanted her to cover: numbers on her phone's caller ID, last number dialed, and numbers programmed for speed dial. She also needed to pick up Suzette's address book and look again for any sort of diary or journal.

To satisfy her own curiosity, she intended also to look for a certain black teddy bear wearing a green and red plaid vest . . . the toy named "Baby" without which Sammy Du Bois never left the house.

It was still pouring rain when she pulled up in front of the house, and she made a dash for the front door. The feel of the cold rain on her skin brought back less-than-fond memories of the funeral earlier in the day. No wonder Dirk had gotten sick. "Depressing" and "cold" were a bad combination, especially when mixed with "exhausted."

She was a little worried about him. But his fever had broken before she left, and Tammy had promised to check on him every hour or so until she returned, so she wasn't overly concerned.

She unlocked the door with the house keys she had nabbed out of Dirk's leather jacket pocket and let herself into the house. This time she went ahead and flipped on the foyer lights. With Dirk's expressed permission, she wasn't exactly breaking and entering this time.

And while convenient, she had to admit it was a little less exciting.

Until she saw the light on in the living room and heard someone stirring in there.

Instinctively, she reached inside her raincoat and unsnapped her Beretta's holster.

A moment later, a woman walked out of the living room and into the foyer. She looked Savannah up and down, then said, "May I help you?"

Savannah recognized the platinum blonde, even without the big sunglasses she had been wearing at the funeral. She was Suzette Du Bois's sister.

Savannah took her hand out of her raincoat and held it out to the woman. "My name is Savannah Reid," she told her. "I'm investigating your sister's disappearance with Sergeant Coulter. He asked me to drop by over here and check a couple of things. I hope I'm not disturbing you."

"I'm Clare Du Bois," the woman replied, accepting Savannah's outstretched hand and giving it a brief shake. "No, you aren't disturbing me. I was just..." Her voice broke as she waved a hand toward the living room. "... looking at some family pictures."

"I'm so sorry... about your sister," Savannah said, avoiding the customary words *for your loss*. Her loss wasn't exactly established just yet, although Savannah figured it was probably only a matter of time.

Clare's eyes misted with tears, and she nodded graciously. "Thank you. I'm sure she'll turn up, but it's hard waiting."

"I'm sure it must be just awful." Savannah thought of her own sisters in Georgia. While some of them could be a major ache in the rump from time to time, she would be beside herself if any of them went missing for any length of time. "Is there anything I can do for you?"

"Just find her for me."

"We're trying. Really, we are."

Clare turned and walked back into the living room. Savannah followed her.

She noticed that the clutter on the coffee table had been swept aside and several photo albums were lying open on it.

It occurred to her that, under the circumstances, she might be able to get more out of Suzette's sister than Dirk had been able to do earlier. There was nothing quite like old family photos to open the memory floodgates.

"May I sit with you for a moment?" Savannah asked her. "I'm tired myself, after the funeral today, what with the rain and all. You must be exhausted."

"I am," Clare said. "I hate funerals. Even if I'm not all that..." Her voice trailed away as though she had reconsidered the wisdom of such candor. She sat down on the sofa and crossed her hands demurely in her lap.

Savannah took a moment to glance over the woman, taking in her expensive and beautifully tailored suit. A cream-colored wool, it set off her blond hair and ivory skin to perfection. Her jewelry was one simple gold circle pin and button earrings. She wore an enormous diamond ring, but it was on her right hand. Her left was bare.

She was a pretty woman, probably in her late forties, which would have made her a few years older than Suzette. Her eyes were red and swollen from crying, and Savannah wondered if the tears had been for Sergio or Suzette or both.

Savannah searched her face for any resemblance to either the Marilyn-Monroe-look-alike photo she had seen in the bedroom or DMV photo of Suzette that Dirk had shown her. The basic facial structure was the same: high cheekbones, a strong yet feminine jawline. But there, the similarities ended.

"May I get you a glass of water?" Savannah asked. "Or maybe make you a cup of coffee or tea?"

Clare shook her head. "No, thank you. I wouldn't ask anyone to go into that kitchen. My sister, she's a wonderful person, but housekeeping has never been her forte. I was going to clean it up, but I started looking at these . . ." she pointed to the photo albums, ". . . and I got waylaid."

"It's probably just as well," Savannah said. "I think Detective Coulter would prefer if we just leave things as they are, for the time being."

Clare's eyes widened. "Oh, it's okay that I came in, isn't it? There wasn't any of that yellow tape the police use across the door, saying I shouldn't."

"No, it isn't cordoned off," Savannah said. "There's no evidence that it's a crime scene." *At the moment*, she added silently. "So, if it's all right with your sister that you're in her house, it's okay with him, I'm sure."

Clare looked even sadder. "I don't know if it's all right with her or not. I know where she keeps her extra key . . . under the big brown rock in the petunia bed, but I don't know if I'm really welcome to be here or not."

Savannah nodded. "Detective Coulter mentioned that the two of you have been estranged for a while."

"It's been a little over a year now since I saw her," Clare said. She reached over and picked up the largest of the albums. Taking out one of the snapshots, she looked at it with a sweet, sad, loving expression on her face. "I miss her. Suzette and I were always very close."

"If you don't mind me asking . . . what happened?"

"*He* happened." Suddenly, Clare's face went hard and her eyes cold. "That piece of crap that we buried today. *He* happened."

"Oh. I see." Of course, she didn't see, and Savannah wasn't sure exactly what to say in the face of such sudden vehemence. But this was definitely a conversational road she wanted to travel. "I was no big fan of Sergio's," she said choosing her words carefully. "And I can understand that you might not be either."

"I went to his funeral today just to make sure that he's dead. That's the only reason I was there today in the rain, listening to all those lies about what a great human being he was. I wanted to see that he's dead and buried, once and for all."

"If you were close to your sister and he came between you—"

"I was, and he did. I'll never forgive him for that. Suzette is the only family I have left."

"I realize this is probably a painful topic, but may I ask how it happened? Your estrangement, that is."

Clare handed Savannah the photograph. It was of the two sisters, arms around each other's shoulders, goofy, happy smiles on their faces. Behind them was a large neon sign that read, "Diamond Bill's Casino."

"That was us," Clare said, "my sister and I on our last outing.

Sergio took Suzette, Jeremy, Myrna, and me out on his cabin cruiser for the day. We went to Santa Tesla Island, like we often did, to hang out in the casinos there, rent some mopeds and bop around the island, have a nice dinner, and then come home."

"Casinos?"

"Yes, there are a couple of nice ones there and it's a lot closer than Vegas. Plus Suzette loves the lighthouse. We always had to rent bikes and ride out to the lighthouse. She's a nut about lighthouses."

"Some people are," Savannah said. "And then . . . ?"

"And then we were on our way back home. Jeremy was at the helm. Myrna and Suzette were knocking back margaritas. So was I, to tell the truth. And I had one . . . or maybe even two . . . too many. I got a little sick and went below to wash my face and lie down out of the sun."

Clare paused, took a deep breath, and continued, "And that's when Sergio came down, said he was checking on me to make sure his shipmates were all okay."

Savannah had a feeling what was coming, but she waited quietly for Clare to tell her story.

"I was lying on one of the berths, still wearing my bathing suit, a cold, wet washcloth over my eyes. And the next thing I know, he's sitting on the bed beside me, leaning over me, his hands . . ." She gulped, and Savannah could see she was trembling.

"He started touching me inappropriately," Clare said. "I couldn't believe that he would do that. Not that he was above it. I knew he was a jerk where women were concerned. I always figured he fooled around on Suzette. But to try it with *me*! He should have known I'd never go for it. And with her right there on the boat with us! I still can't believe he was that stupid."

"Oh, it's pretty amazing how stupid men can be when their brains get deprived of oxygen. Did he stop when you told him to?"

"I did more than tell him," she said proudly. "I hit him. I slugged him in the face and bloodied his nose."

Savannah laughed. "My kind of girl. How did he explain that to the others?"

"I got out of there, joined the girls on deck and didn't say any-thing . . . at least, not then. He washed up and came up later, after he got the bleeding stopped. Needless to say, he didn't mention it either."

Clare took the picture back from Savannah and looked at it for a long time, running her fingertip over it, as though caressing her sister's face. "I agonized over telling her for three days after that," she said. "Finally, I decided that I had to. These days, a promiscuous partner can cost you your life. And I figured if she had to find out, it would be better if it came from me. So, I dropped by here unexpectedly that Saturday morning, and I told her what he'd done."

"How did she take it?"

"She told me that he had already told her that I had come on to him, thrown myself at him."

"And she believed him?"

"Yes, she did." Clare began to cry. She reached into her pocket and brought out a lacy-edged handkerchief. "At least, at that mo-ment she did. She threw me out, said she never wanted to see me again. I called her several times after that, left messages on her machine, but she never returned my calls."

The two women sat quietly for a moment, as Savannah al-lowed Clare a moment to compose herself.

Finally, Savannah said, "This was a year ago, you say?"

She nodded.

"Are you aware that she *did* break up with him, toss him out on his ear, just about that time?"

"I heard that they had split. I didn't know when. But it doesn't matter anyway, because if Suzette threw him out ten times, she would take him back eleven. He was some kind of sick addiction for her. I'll never understand why."

"Me either," Savannah said. She thought of her own sister, Marietta, in Georgia, who changed men constantly and just as frequently made terrible choices. "There's just no accounting for taste or judgment."

"And Suzette's smart, too. Not just in the obvious way, as a doctor with a thriving practice. She's wise and kind. She can give you the best advice in the world when it comes to your own problems. She's savvy in every area of her life, except with men."

"That's a big 'except.'"

"Isn't it though?" She shook her head in disgust. "I got over that ridiculous 'bad-boy appeal' business when I was in high school. Some women never learn."

Savannah thought of Dirk, and how—for all of his foibles—he was reliable, sensible, and loyal. Long ago, Savannah had come to realize just how sexy "responsible" could be.

"You're absolutely right," she replied. "'Predictable' is highly underrated in a man."

"And that isn't all," Clare said. "That isn't the only reason I hated Sergio or Leonard Roy, or whatever his name was. He hit my sister. She denied it, but I know he did. I saw her with more than one black eye and other bruises on her face, not to mention the fingertip bruises on her upper arms where he'd grabbed her. I know he abused her. And she tolerated that, too. She was way too smart for that! In her career she's repaired several women's faces, pro bono, after their husbands messed them up. She knows how dangerous domestic violence can be, and yet she kept going back to him. I'll just never, ever understand her."

Savannah reached for one of the photo albums and began to flip through the pages, getting to know Suzette Du Bois better with each page. Her childhood, her adolescence. And on each page, memories shared with her sister.

"Where do you think she is?" Savannah asked softly, hating the fact that she had to hurt this graceful woman even more.

But Clare's answer surprised her. "Oh, who knows? She's hiding out somewhere, I'm sure. She'll come back when she's good and ready."

Savannah didn't want to alarm the woman or even rob her of what might be a self-protecting state of denial. But she needed to get to the truth. "If she's just hiding out, wouldn't she have come to Sergio's funeral today?"

"If she knew about it. Usually she heads for the hills, someplace she can commune with nature, far away from phones and newspapers and televisions."

"Usually? She's done this before?"

"Oh, many times. When she was a teenager, she drove our mom crazy, running away any time she didn't get her way or didn't like what was going on around her. She'd just walk out, then come back a few days later, sunburned from lying on the beach somewhere, and relaxed, after making the rest of us nuts worrying ourselves sick about her. She spent most of her high school years grounded . . . at least theoretically. Enforcing it was a bit difficult. She could always climb out her bedroom window and shinny down Mom's garden lattice."

"She sounds like a corker."

"Oh, you don't know the half of it."

"So, do you think she's lying on a beach somewhere, soaking up some sun?"

"I'm sure she is."

"But her new spa, Emerge, was scheduled to open. The promotion was at its peak—press ready and public interest high."

Clare shrugged. "That's my sister for you. When things are the busiest, the stakes the highest, that's when she freaks out and splits."

Savannah wasn't going to sit and argue with a woman who

knew Suzette Du Bois probably better than anyone on earth. And if Clare wasn't worried, maybe they had no reason to be either.

Perhaps it was just a weird coincidence that one partner in a business went missing and then another got himself murdered.

But, of course, Savannah didn't believe that for a moment.

"I have two more things to ask you, Clare," she said. "And please don't take offense. Investigators have to ask these types of questions."

Clare looked wary, but she said, "Okay. What is it?"

"You've mentioned about half a dozen reasons just now why you would hate Sergio D'Alessandro. And I wouldn't blame you one bit if you did . . . but did you kill the guy yourself?"

"No. But I'd like to thank the person who did when you find them."

"Okay. And the second thing is, do you believe your sister might have staged her own disappearance and murdered him herself?"

Clare said nothing for a long, long time as she stared down at the picture in her hand. Then she raised her eyes to Savannah's and said with calm conviction, "She may have. If she had decided to take him back, to try to trust him one more time, and then she found him with another woman, she might have killed him. Suzette's a proud woman. She doesn't take betrayal lightly. Look at what she did to me, and she only suspected that I had betrayed her. I'd like to think she'd be even harder on him."

Later, after Savannah had done what she had come for, she left the house hoping that Clare was right.

She liked Clare and hoped that her sister truly was somewhere, sunning herself after murdering a guy who, as some Southerners might phrase it, "needed killin'."

Of course, she still intended to find Suzette Du Bois, and if that was indeed the case, bring her to justice. You couldn't just go around murdering everybody who needed killin' just because you had a mind to.

But for Clare Du Bois's sake, she sincerely hoped her sister was still in the land of the living.

And maybe she was.

Savannah had searched high and low, and there hadn't been a trace of a black teddy bear named "Baby" anywhere in that house, plaid vest or otherwise.

Chapter

18

By the time Savannah had finished at Suzette Du Bois's house and returned home, it was late in the evening. She wasn't expecting to see Tammy's car in the driveway when she pulled up. Tammy was an early to bed, early to rise sort of girl. She had to be. Being Miss Perky took a lot of energy and recuperation time.

But Savannah was a little surprised to see Dirk's Buick there. Surprised, but pleased.

She had figured he would sober up after a couple of hours and be on his way. But she was happy he hadn't. He could use all the TLC his stubborn, male pride would allow him to absorb.

Of course, that meant that sleeping arrangements might be a bit strained. With him in her bed and Abigail occupying the guest room, it had suddenly become a little crowded at Savannah's Bed-and-Breakfast Hostelry.

When she walked through the front door, she heard a stirring in the living room and found Abigail stretched out on her sofa, a cat under each arm, a pillow under her head, a blanket pulled up to her waist.

"Hi," Savannah said. "How nice of you to wait up for me."

"No problem," she said, scratching under Diamante's chin.

"Tammy was tired and wanted to go home, but she asked me to stay up and keep checking Dirk until you got back."

"Thanks a lot. How is he?"

"Same as when you left. He hasn't moved an inch. Just lying there like a rock."

"Good. That's what he needs. How's his fever?"

"Tammy checked him before she left, about forty-five minutes ago, and it was still down."

"That's great. Boy, John's toddies must really be potent! I'll have to ask him to make one of those for me sometime, whether I'm sick or not."

"It did look and smell really good, with the oranges and spices."

Savannah sank into her easy chair and kicked off her loafers. "What are you doing there on the sofa? You should be in bed, too, by now."

"I am. This is my bed for tonight. I took the sheets off, washed them, and put them back on, so they're nice and fresh for you and—"

"No. You're my guest. You go sleep in the guest room like you're supposed to."

"And let you sleep on the sofa? No way. Unless, of course, you're sleeping with Dirk."

"Banish the thought."

Abby snickered. "That's what I figured. So, here I am, and you're in the guest room and that's the end of *that* conversation."

Savannah nodded in acquiescence. "As you say, Lady Abigail." She noticed that instead of a man's sweatshirt and sweatpants—Abigail's former sleep attire—she was wearing a lovely white cotton nightgown with tiny pink roses embroidered on the bodice and lace trimming the sleeve edges.

"What a pretty nightgown," she commented. "It looks Victorian."

"I bought it yesterday when the Emerge staff took me shopping. Jeremy says I should allow the feminine side of my nature to have expression as well as all other sides. I saw this gown and loved it, although, without his encouragement, I never would have allowed myself to wear anything like this."

"It's most becoming. A good change from the sweatpants."

"The kitties like it," Abby said, hugging the cats to her chest.

Savannah half expected them to jump up and run away from her. Like her, they couldn't stand any form of restraint. She blamed it on having handcuffed so many people over the years and maybe feeling a bit guilty about some of them. Not a lot. Just a few.

But the cats stayed put. And Cleo even reached up and gave Abby a slurp with a wet, kitty sandpaper tongue on the left ear.

"They like *you*, is more like it," Savannah said. "What did you do? Feed them tuna from a can?"

"Half and half, from the fridge."

"Oh, no wonder."

"And I gave Cleo her methimazole tonight. I figured you'd be too tired to mess with it."

"You gave Cleo a pill . . . and you lived to tell about it? Boy, now I *am* impressed! Any bleeding involved?"

"Nope. I'm unscathed." She held up both hands, turning them this way and that for inspection.

Savannah smiled and wasn't all that shocked when Abigail returned it. Abby grew on you. Once you got past that extremely thick crust, there was a sweet woman underneath. Way underneath.

"If you're sure I can't talk you into trading places," Savannah said, "I think I'll go check on Dirk and then hit the sack myself."

"I'm sure. Good night."

Savannah stood, kissed the tip of her forefinger, then reached down and touched it to Abby's forehead. "Sleep tight, kiddo," she said.

"You, too."

Savannah started up the stairs and for the first time since she could ever remember, the cats didn't follow her.

They say kids and animals can tell a good person from a bad one, she thought. *I guess Miss Abby's a goodie after all.*

She crept into her own bedroom and saw that, just as Abby had said, Dirk hadn't moved a hair. He was still under her silk sheet and satin comforter, only his head sticking out, snoring like a buzz saw.

Softly she pressed her hand to his forehead. It was cool and dry. A good sign.

She repeated the kiss to her fingertip and placed it on his cheek. To her surprise, he turned his face against her hand and for a moment pressed his lips into her palm.

"Thanks, Van," he whispered.

"You're welcome, darlin'," she replied. "Go back to sleep. Feel better."

He nodded and ten seconds later resumed his snoring.

Cowboy Dirk Coulter was a tough-hided buzzard. He'd survive that gunshot/rattlesnake bite/Indian arrow attack/buffalo stampede, after all.

Yeap, it took a whole lot more than that to kill an old gunslinger/lawman like Coulter.

The next morning, Savannah was enjoying some of her favorite activities, sitting in her easy chair, sipping a cup of coffee and nibbling a pastry, watching while Tammy worked away at the desk in the corner and Abigail snoozed, head covered with her pillow, on the sofa.

Life just didn't get much better than that.

If there was anything more pleasant than enjoying one of the seven deadly sins at a time, it was doubling up. And Savannah had found that Gluttony and Sloth went particularly well together . . . sort of like a cinnamon pecan Danish and Sumatra dark roast.

And just when she thought things couldn't get any better, Dirk came downstairs. He practically bounced downstairs. And Savannah hadn't seen Dirk bounce since 1993, when they had busted the guy who had broken into his house trailer and stolen his eight-track tape player and his Johnny Cash collection.

"Wow," she said, "look at you! You're pert nigh perky!"

His hair was standing on end and his eyes a bit puffy, but he had a definite spring to his step and a smile on his face. "I feel great!" he said. "That thing John whipped up for me last night did the trick! I swear, it really is the cure for the common cold."

Tammy glanced up from her work, looked him up and down, and said, "I think we should make you one of those hot toddy thingies every night, Dirko. You look almost human."

"Personally," Savannah said, "I think it was the solid night's sleep that snatched you from the jaws of the Grim Reaper."

"Jaws? Grim Reaper?" Tammy made a face. "I think the Grim Reaper uses a scythe to—"

"Oh, don't go waxing literary on me this early in the morning," Savannah told her. "I can't stand two perky people when I first get up. One of you has to go, or at least turn down the sunshine of your smile."

"Well, it isn't going to be me," Tammy replied. "I think I'm on to something here."

"I'm happy for you," Savannah told her. "An hour from now I might even be happy for us all, if what you've got is really good. But for now, I'm still waking up and have no measurable brainwave activity. Besides, you're gonna wake up Abby, so keep it down."

"Well, *I'm* wide awake," Dirk said, strutting across the room to stand behind Tammy's chair. "Ignore the grumpy woman in the corner and show me what you've got, kiddo."

"Oh, Lord, I can't stand it," Savannah groaned, biting into the Danish. "Sugar, caffeine, do your stuff."

"I've been playing with this software that Ryan and John gave me, and I've found all sorts of skullduggery."

Skullduggery? Savannah shook her head. That girl was going to have to go off Nancy Drew books, cold turkey.

"Like what?" Dirk asked.

"Like major embezzlement . . . from the Mystic Twilight spa for starters."

"Really?" Dirk leaned over her shoulder. "How much and when?"

"Beginning about a year ago."

Savannah couldn't help responding. "A year ago is when Suzette threw him out of her house."

"Well, he got her back, big-time," Tammy said. "He started siphoning off Mystic Twilight's assets. And he was really good at it, too. He got a lot and he did it in ways that would have made it hard to tell he was doing it."

"How much is a lot?" Dirk asked.

"A mil and a half," Savannah offered.

"More," Tammy said.

"More?" Savannah raised one eyebrow. "How much more?"

"From what I can see here, about three million more."

Savannah and Dirk both gasped.

Even Abigail stirred briefly, readjusting the pillow over her head.

"Do you mean he pulled four and a half million dollars out of that business in only a year?" Savannah said. "Wow, he was good!"

"But he got caught." Tammy typed away and produced another file on the screen. "The person who installed the keystroke spyware pulled up his files . . . recently."

"Recently?" Dirk asked. "How recently?"

Tammy grinned up at him. "Would you believe a week before he died?"

Dirk grunted. "I would have killed the guy if I found out he stole four and a half million from me."

"You," Savannah added, "would have gladly sent Billy Bob Mason to the gas chamber for stealing your eight track, so we can't go by you. But just for the record, I would have killed him for that, too."

"I'll bet you that Suzette is still alive and kicking somewhere," Tammy said. "And she installed this spyware to see if he was chasing other women, and lo and behold, she found out he was ripping off the business."

"I'll bet you're right," Dirk said. "She found out what he'd done, took the money back somehow and transferred it to an anonymous bank account in Switzerland or the Caribbean, then she grabbed her dog and hid out . . . waited a couple of days and knocked him off, and then left to go join her money in Europe or the Cayman Islands."

"But if she did do that," Savannah said, "how are we ever going to find her? You haven't had much luck finding an anonymous bank online with that sort of an account number, right, Tam?"

"No, not yet. But there are so many. I haven't even worked through all the ones in the Caribbean."

Suddenly, Savannah stood up, nearly spilling her coffee on one of the cats. "Wait a minute," she said, flashing back to her conversation with Clare. "Do you know that they have casinos on Santa Tesla Island?"

Dirk and Tammy both stared at her blankly.

"So?" Dirk said. "We're talking banking here, not gambling."

"I know. But where do they have casinos?" she said.

"Las Vegas, Native American reservations?" Tammy said.

"And cruise ships!" Savannah was practically dancing in her fuzzy penguin house slippers. "Because the ships go out into international waters where it isn't subject to the laws of the U.S. or other countries. . . . This is great!"

"What the hell are you talking about?" Dirk said.

"Gambling. Anonymous banking. Same sort of thing. They have them outside the legal boundaries of countries that might otherwise regulate them. And if there are casinos on Santa Tesla Island—which is plenty far enough away from the California shore to be in international waters—there may be anonymous banks, too."

She ran over to Tammy's desk. "And last night Suzette's sister told me that Suzette likes to go there, to gamble, run around the island and look at the lighthouse. Find out, quick, if there are any anonymous banks on Santa Tesla Island."

Tammy did a quick search. The results popped up on the computer screen.

She beamed up at Savannah. "Bingo! There are six of them. Six!"

Dirk was already heading for the door. "Find the phone numbers of those banks," he said, "and fax me a list of them over to my desk at the station house."

"But . . . but . . ." Tammy sputtered. She looked at Savannah. "Why?"

"Why? Why? I don't know why. I peaked with the Santa Tesla Island idea. That was my flash of brilliance for the morning, maybe for the whole day." She headed for the kitchen, mug in hand. "Now, I have to refill my coffee cup"—she lowered her voice and whispered—"and eat that other Danish before Abigail gets up. I swear, she's almost as bad as I am about coffee and pastries first thing in the morning. Yesterday she ate my last French cruller before I could even . . ."

*　　*　　*

They found out Dirk's "why" less than half an hour later when he called from his desk at the police station.

"We've got a lead," he said the moment Savannah answered the phone. "A real lead. A solid, bonafide lead. You were hot with that Santa Tesla bank business, Savannah, my girl."

Savannah winked at Tammy, who was standing nearby, jumping up and down with excitement. "He says we've got something." Then, to Dirk, she said, "What? What do we have?"

"I'm looking at phone records right now from Emerge."

"Emerge phone records," she told Tammy.

"And there were two phone calls from there to one of the numbers on Tammy's list of anonymous banks."

"Yay! Tam, somebody from Emerge called one of your banks. Twice!"

Tammy went from jumping to a full-fledged cheerleader routine . . . everything but the pom-poms.

Savannah turned away so that she could concentrate on the call.

From the living room they heard a groggy, "Hey, wanna keep it down in there? Person sleeping here!"

"Which bank?" Savannah asked him.

"Lighthouse Security."

Savannah grinned. The adrenaline that was hitting her bloodstream was far more stimulating than any mixture of sugar and caffeine. "I guess you and I are going to do some island hopping very soon. Eh, big boy?"

She heard him chuckle on the other end. It was an evil, nasty chuckle that reminded her why she loved him so much. "Oo-o-oh yes, babe," he said. "Right away."

Chapter
19

"You're the captain of this boat?" Savannah asked, hoping it wasn't true. When she had spoken to this guy earlier on the phone, she had imagined someone who looked a lot more like Russell Crowe, Errol Flynn or, on a good day, one of those hunks with the bulging biceps and a strategically ripped shirt on the cover of a romance novel.

This skinny, slovenly kid—with mustard and ketchup stains on the front of his T-shirt and knobby knees sticking out of cargo shorts that were about to fall off him—just didn't cut it, fantasy-wise.

"I'm captain of this *catamaran*," he told her, squaring his thin shoulders.

"Boat, ship, catamaran . . . what's the difference?"

"Boat." He pointed to a dingy tied at the dock. "Catamaran." He pointed to the deck beneath their feet—the deck of a sizable ferry designed for carrying over one hundred passengers to and from Santa Tesla Island at a high speed.

"Ah," she said, "it's a matter of size." Then under her breath, she muttered, "Ain't it always with you guys."

Docked nearby was a similar vessel, and she could see Dirk

standing on the deck of that one, showing pictures of Suzette Du Bois to the crew. Together, they had interviewed nearly all of the ships that provided passage to and from the San Carmelita harbor and the island, and so far . . . no luck.

She took the two pictures from her inside jacket pocket and shoved them under Captain Dirty Shirt's nose. One was Suzette's driver's license photo, and the other the Marilyn look-alike pose.

"Have you seen this woman lately?" she asked him. "Maybe given her a ride to or from the island? She may have had a white poodle with her and—"

"Named Sammy."

"What?" She nearly swallowed her gum. "Yes! Named Sammy! You saw them when?"

"I've taken her to the island a few times lately. Yesterday morning, bright and early, in fact. Can't forget a gal like that. She looks like a movie star with that blond hair."

"Like Marilyn Monroe?"

"Who?"

Savannah sighed. "Never mind."

"I don't know who that is, but she was sorta like Madonna, only older. She was wearing those big sunglasses like gals used to wear."

"Okay. Can you tell me anything else about her?"

"She said she's moving to the island, had some boxes and stuff that we had to help her with. She gave my guys a good tip."

"Hmm. She can afford to."

"What?"

"Nothing. This was yesterday, you say, when you took her over?"

"Yeah. Yesterday morning on our first run."

"And when does the last boat . . . er . . . catamaran leave the island to bring passengers back here?"

"This time of year, twenty-three hundred hours. That's eleven o'clock at night," he explained with a condescending tone that made her want to slap him stupid.

"So late?" she asked.

He shrugged. "Some people complain that we don't have even later ones. They like to stay, drink, gamble until all hours. As long as they get back home in time to drag themselves to work the next morning, they're happy."

"Hey, whatever spins your bottle." She glanced over at Dirk and saw that he was watching her. She waved him over. "And did this lady say anything else to you?"

"Like what?"

"Anything at all. Did she talk about her new place, where it is . . . ?"

"Said it has a great view of the water."

Savannah wasn't terribly impressed with that gem of knowledge. On a small, narrow island, who *didn't* have a water view?

"When you docked and your guys helped her with the boxes," she said, "how did she leave with them? Did she load them into a taxi, or . . . ?"

"No, somebody was waiting for her in a car."

"Can you describe the person, the car?"

"Another lady. I don't remember what she looked like. Nothing special. She was driving a big black BMW. We loaded the boxes into the trunk for her."

"How many boxes were there?"

"Four or five."

"What size?"

"Big, medium, little. All shapes and sizes. Listen, I gotta get going. I've got a schedule to keep here. Are you coming with us to the island or not? Because, if you are, you gotta buy a ticket."

Savannah could see Dirk hurrying across the deck toward them, a big grin on his face, still chipper from his long night of alcohol-induced coma. "Oh, I'm with you, Captain, and that dude there is footin' the bill."

"I can't believe this has been here all the time, and I never even knew about it," Savannah said as she stepped off the dock and looked around at the island paradise that surrounded them. Lush greenery covered the hills that sloped gracefully to the sea, in sharp contrast to the dry, brown hills they had left on the mainland. The air had a sweet, clean smell with none of the *eau de* Los Angeles that gagged San Carmelitans when the Santa Ana winds blew the city's pollution their way.

Instead of the standard Spanish style of architecture that prevailed in her neighborhood, this place had more of a Polynesian feel about it. The shops that lined the waterfront were little more than rustic huts, primitive but charming structures with palm frond-covered roofs and bamboo walls and supports that blended nicely with the natural scenery.

The waterfront to their right was a luxury marina, filled with all sorts and sizes of pleasure craft. To their left was a pristine beach with fewer sunbathers than Savannah was accustomed to seeing, even in the cooler months, on the California shore.

And far to their left, on the southern end of the island, stood the lighthouse. Sparkling white in the sunlight, lovely in its simplicity, it was the crowning touch to complete the island's exotic beauty.

Yes, Santa Tesla Island was an unspoiled, uncrowded haven, and it fed Savannah's soul just to stand on its soil. She vowed, then and there, that she would find an excuse to come back here, again and again.

And not when she was looking for a killer.

"So, where do you want to start?" she asked Dirk. "The bank?"

He raised his arm to hail one of the taxis that was slowly driving by, looking for fares. "Lighthouse Security, here we come."

Lighthouse Security Bank was quaint and picturesque. When they entered the building, Savannah felt like she was attending some sort of Hawaiian luau rather than stepping into a bank. She half-expected the clerks to be wearing hula skirts.

But the architecture was where the island friendliness stopped.

The woman behind the manager's desk was anything but welcoming.

"We do not release information about our customers to anyone from the States," she told Dirk, her hands on her ample hips, her eyes flashing behind her tortoiseshell glasses.

He held his badge closer to her nose, but she brushed it away with one hand and reiterated, "No information. None. Your authority is not recognized inside this establishment."

Dirk's face darkened, and Savannah cringed. Sergeant Detective Dirk Coulter had worked damned hard for that gold shield, and the last person who had slapped it away had wound up flat on his face on the floor in one and a half seconds.

"Look here, lady," he said. "I'm investigating a homicide, and even out here in international waters, murder is murder, and can land you in some sort of prison somewhere. Now you better reconsider what you just said to me."

"I haven't murdered anyone, and I couldn't release information to you about a customer here even if I wanted to. All of our banking is done with anonymous numbers and customer passwords. We, ourselves, don't know their identities."

Savannah stepped between them and adopted her most solicitous tone and expression. "Of course, you can't," she said. "I understand your position completely. But we're not asking you for their identity. We need a record of their recent transactions. I already have the account number, even the password. Perhaps you could be so kind as to let us know what's been going on with the account."

"No."

Savannah was a bit taken aback. Her down-homey routine almost always worked . . . at least a little. "No?" she asked. "That's it? Just 'no'?"

"No. And that's not all. If you don't leave right now, I'll have security remove you."

Suddenly, a couple of enormous guards materialized behind them. Savannah turned to look at them and was astonished that people even came that big! They were at least a foot taller than Dirk's six feet, two inches, and their uniforms—khaki shirts and shorts with breast pocket insignia badges—showed off their muscular physiques with intimidating clarity.

"Let's go," she told Dirk. "If these folks aren't interested in helping us, they deserve to have a murderer here on their little island, rubbing elbows with them on a daily basis."

She grabbed Dirk's arm and propelled him toward the front door before he could cause any trouble with Goliath and King Kong.

"But, but. . . ." he sputtered.

"Keep walkin,'" she told him. "Make tracks, buddy."

"I ain't afraid of those guys," he said, looking back over his shoulder.

"Well, I am, and you would be too, if you had the sense God gave a goose." She shoved him through the front door and out onto the street. "We'll find out what we need to know some other way."

"How?"

"I don't know, but—"

Her cell phone was buzzing inside her purse. She reached for it and looked at the caller ID. "It's the kid. Hi, Tam. What's shakin', sugar?" She listened for a long time, a smile spreading across her face. Finally, she said, "Darlin', you are worth your weight in gold. You have no idea how timely this little bit of info is. Consider yourself kissed and hugged."

She flipped the phone closed, turned to Dirk and chuckled. "Turns out you didn't need to go fifteen rounds with those heavyweights in there after all. Tammy's better than Miss Grumpy could ever be."

"Why? I thought she was having a hard time trying to access that account info. The password '*rosarita*' wouldn't work or somethin' like that."

"True, but she kept trying other passwords, and she found one that worked. She opened the account info online and discovered that three-hundred and twenty five thousand dollars was withdrawn, in cash, five days ago."

"Five days ago? That's two days after Suzette Du Bois went missing."

"That's right."

They smiled at each other. They could practically smell their prey.

The trail was getting fresher by the minute.

"Good for the kid!" he said. "She's getting better at this stuff all the time. What did the password turn out to be?"

Savannah laughed. "Sammy."

"Of course."

"Of course."

They walked down the street, passing buildings more substantial than the slapdash huts that lined the beachfront areas. Here the businesses and houses resembled some that Savannah had seen in Key West, Florida, on a vacation there years ago. They had a combination of tropical and Victorian flavor, with lots of gingerbread-house details, verandas, and the occasional widow's walk around the roof. Under different circumstances, she might have considered her surroundings romantic.

But strolling alongside Dirk, whose formerly buoyant mood had been replaced by his standard sullen one, thanks to the snippy manager at the bank, it wasn't easy to get into any sort of romantic state of mind.

And that was okay. She was working.

Who needed romance when there was a bad guy—or girl, as the case might be—who needed catching?

Dirk stopped in the middle of the sidewalk, leaned against a palm tree, and took out his cell phone. "I just want to check something," he said. A moment later he barked into the phone, "Coulter here. I'm on Santa Tesla Island . . . yes, all the way out here. Run a check with DMV. I want to know the name and address of everyone on this island who owns a BMW. That's right." He scowled. "What do you mean you can't—"

Savannah elbowed him in the ribs. "Look around you, Dorothy," she said. "You're not in Kansas anymore . . . or California either, for that matter." She pointed to a passing car that had no license plate, only a red sticker in the lower left corner of the rear window. "They're not going to find any of these cars in the California DMV records."

"Oh." He grunted, then said into the phone, "Never mind." Then he turned off the phone and shoved it back into his pocket. "I have to tell you," he said, "I'm feeling a little out of my element here."

"That's because you are out of your element, kinda like wading through Jell-O. But don't fret. This whole island isn't even half the size of little San Carmelita. We'll find the BMW that picked Suzette up at the dock, and we'll find her, too. You wait and see if we don't."

"Yeah, yeah, yeah . . . a friggen' Pollyanna, that's you, Van."

She laughed and laced her arm through his. That was what she loved about Dirk, that sunny disposition, that effervescent personality, and of course, the eternal optimism.

He shook his head and groaned wearily. "Nope, we're never ever gonna find that gal. She's gotten away with cold-blooded murder. Not if we stay on this stupid island for a hundred years, and look for her from one end of it to the other and then fall down dead in our tracks and rot right there. We're just not gonna find her."

Ah, *yes*. Savannah thought as she looked around her at the lush tropical foliage and breathed in the clean, salt-sea scented air. *This is romance at its finest.*

Chapter

20

"**D**id you really think we'd run across somebody with a BMW in one of these swanky bars?" Dirk asked Savannah. "Or is this just a scheme of yours to see how many of those stupid umbrella drinks you can get me to buy for you in one afternoon?"

She sipped her piña colada and twirled the tiny paper umbrella between her fingertips. Around them, a large portion of the island's population, or so it seemed, had congregated to enjoy equally festive beverages and, in general, make merry, here in a place called Coconut Joe's.

If she used even a little bit of imagination, it was easy for her to look around and imagine that she was in a bar somewhere in the Bahamas. The music being piped into the place had a definite Caribbean flavor, as did the bright batik sheets of fabric that hung from the ceiling along with fishing nets and colorful paper lanterns. So many palmettos decorated the place that she felt she was in a jungle.

The patrons were equally exotic, dressed in bright floral sundresses and tie-dyed T-shirts, with more seashell necklaces than she had seen anywhere since the seventies.

"Apparently," she said, "once the sun starts to set here on Santa Tesla, the natives run to the bars and get stinkin' drunk before suppertime."

"Like you?" he said, sipping on his Pepsi.

"I'm not drunk, I'll have you know, boy. I'm only barely buzzed, and after the week I've had, I think I deserve it. So hush and order me another one of these . . . only with just half the rum this time."

"Such self-control," he said, waving to the waitress. "I'm almost impressed."

"Yeah, well, I've had a rum hangover before, and it wasn't pretty. It was the morning after a bridal shower where we sampled half a dozen kinds of daiquiris. I felt like I had a coonskin cap on my tongue and a hive of angry wasps swarming around inside my head. I had to eat a three pound box of Godiva chocolates just to get my blood sugar level up to normal. But then, a self-controlled fellow like yourself wouldn't know about such things."

"I certainly wouldn't. The only thing that gives me a hangover is tequila."

"Yes, seems like I recall you missing work a few May sixths in a row."

"What can I say? Cinco de Mayo's a rough one." He grinned at her. "Hey, you want something to eat?"

"Why? You buying me dinner?"

"Well, not exactly. I think they've got some sort of appetizer things over there at the bar for free. I could nab you a tray of them if you like."

"What a guy! Dirk, you never fail to amaze me."

"Why, thank you." He flushed under the pseudo-compliment. He received so few, pseudo or otherwise. "It wasn't that much, really, just some free hors d'oeuvres."

"My point exactly." She took another sip of the sickeningly

sweet drink and wondered why she had ordered it. The Pink Squirrel at the last bar was much tastier. "What's next?" she asked him. "Where do we go from here?"

"Like I said, I'm a fish out of water here. Nobody pays any attention to my badge, and I'm probably not allowed to wave a gun around and threaten them for information, so . . . I'm stumped."

The waitress walked up to them and asked what they would like.

"Something a little less potent than that last drink," Savannah said. "When I turn my head, it takes my eyes five seconds to catch up, and that's not a good sign."

"How about a virgin seabreeze?" the waitress suggested.

"What's in it?"

"Cranberry juice and grapefruit juice."

"Sounds good. And another Pepsi for my buddy."

Before the woman could walk away, Savannah grabbed her by the sleeve. "By the way, you don't happen to know somebody here on the island who owns a BMW, do you? I'm in the market for one."

The waitress shook her head. "There aren't that many cars on the island. It's expensive to have them ferried over, plus there's only one gas station and it charges a fortune for just a gallon, so . . ."

She disappeared into the throng.

"Let's forget about the BMW for a minute," Savannah said, "and concentrate on other things."

"Like what other things?" he asked

"Like why Suzette withdrew three hundred and twenty-five thousand dollars in cash from the bank. What on earth could you spend that much money on at once?"

"A fancy car."

"That's a guy thing. A chick wouldn't pay that much for a car."

"How come you can call a broad a 'chick' and I can't?"

"For the same reason you can't call a woman a 'broad' either."

"Huh?"

"Think with me. What's got that sort of high price ticket . . . other than real estate."

They both looked at each other and perked up.

"She bought herself a house," Savannah said. "And paid cash for it."

"Or at least plunked down a hefty down payment."

"She told the guys on the boat—"

"Catamaran."

"Whatever . . . that she was moving here. Hence the boxes of stuff she brought with her."

"Maybe the person who picked her up was a realtor. They tend to drive around in spiffy cars."

Savannah grabbed her cell phone and called her house. Tammy answered. "Hi, babycakes," Savannah said. "Go online and see how many real estate agencies there are here on the island. Yeah, I'll wait." She stirred the remainder of her piña colada and slurped the sweet frothiness off the end of the umbrella handle. "Huh?" she said. "No, we're having a miserable time. You'd hate it. The music? I think it's a bar down the street. Yeah, I'm holding. Go ahead and look."

The waitress came over with her seabreeze and Dirk's Pepsi.

"No, we haven't had dinner. Didn't even have a chance to catch lunch." She grinned at Dirk, who had helped her polish off an enormous basket of fish and chips earlier at one of the beachfront stands. They had each downed double-scoop ice cream cones afterward. "Yeap, all work and no play, that's us. Dedicated professionals, all the way."

"That's *me*, is more like it, Miss Piña Colada," Dirk grumbled.

"Yeah, I've got a pen," she said as she dug one out of her purse along with a notebook. "Four of them? Okay, give me the addresses and phone numbers."

After she had written down all the information and said good-bye to Tammy, she tapped her finger on the notebook page. "Get that Pepsi down, buddy boy. You and I have work to do. Come on now, no dawdling. I ain't got all day here you know."

Sitting in the back seat of a taxi that was hurtling around curved, dusty roads, Savannah dug her nails into the upholstery and tried not to look over the edge of the road. She had taken a peek a few minutes ago and had seen a sheer drop of at least one hundred feet to the churning sea. Her piña colada-filled tummy had done a flip and a flop, and she had vowed never to look again.

"You wanna slow this jalopy down, buster?" Dirk said for the third time. "We'd like to get there in one piece."

The dark little man behind the wheel didn't say a word. He didn't slow down either. At this rate they would make it from one side of the island to the other in ten minutes . . . if they made it at all.

"This is the last one," Savannah said, referring to the realtors on her list. "If they don't drive a BMW, we're back to square one."

Dirk shrugged. "So, sometimes I feel like my house trailer is parked at square one. Familiar stomping grounds. All too familiar."

"Whatcha say you let me handle this one?"

"You gonna do better than I've done?"

"Can't do much worse."

"Hey, those last three didn't drive a BMW. Nothing I could have done about that."

"Yes, but if you hadn't been so abrasive with them, if you had just finessed them a bit, they might have told you who, if anyone, does drive one. Then we wouldn't have to be in this cab, hurtling through space with Nascar Joe here."

"They just don't like us mainlanders here. You can tell. The whole island is like a giant clique that hates outsiders."

"Oh, yes. You threatening to sic the Coast Guard, the Marines, and the Navy Seals on them wouldn't have anything to do with their lack of cooperation."

"I didn't threaten them until after they refused to cooperate."

"Anyway, I'm going to handle this next one."

"How?"

"Girl-style."

"You mean sneaky?"

"Exactly."

They arrived at the realtor's office relatively unscathed . . . if shattered nerves and upset stomachs didn't count.

Savannah grabbed Dirk's hand as she got out of the cab and walked up to the door of an establishment that was quite a bit more polished looking than the other three they had visited. A charming Queen Anne-style cottage, the business had an ornate, hand-carved sign in front of it that read, "Elizabeth Fortunato Realty."

"Nice place," she said, "Maybe Elizabeth is the BMW type. Ladies named 'Elizabeth' tend to be classy."

"And that's been proven scientifically?"

"Through empirical evidence."

"Whose?"

"Mine."

They walked through the front door and found a handsome young man sitting at a desk. He was speaking on the phone to someone, discussing rental rates for a vacation property.

After listening for only a few moments, Savannah decided that she probably could never afford to vacation on Santa Tesla Island for longer than ten minutes. And only then if she brought her own tent.

When he hung up, he smiled at them, and ran his fingers though his thick chestnut curls. "How may I help you?"

"We're looking for Elizabeth," Savannah told him. "I met her a couple of days ago and we discussed a vacation rental, a place on the beach." She turned and gazed up at Dirk lovingly. "For our honeymoon."

"Oh, congratulations!" the young man gushed.

Dirk simply nodded, his poker face solidly in place. But he did squeeze her hand a little harder.

"Oh, thank you." She batted her eyelashes at Dirk, then at the kid behind the desk. "We're getting married next month, on Valentine's Day. It was Dirk's idea. We're going to have lots and lots of red roses. Red roses are Dirk's favorite flower."

The pressure on her fingers increased to downright painful. She got the message.

"Anyway," she said, "Elizabeth was telling me about this darling little beach cottage, and I told her I'd think about it, but I lost her card. I was keeping an eye out for her car as we were driving around today—it's quite distinctive."

The young man chuckled. "Yes, there aren't many BMW's on the island; they're not exactly easy on the gas. I think she's starting to wonder if she should have bought something else."

Savannah smiled up at Dirk and this time, it was genuine. "Yes," she said, "but she's just such a BMW kind of girl."

"True. True."

"Do you have any idea where she is now? I realize it's a little late, but I really wanted to talk to her."

"Here, let me see if I can get her on the phone."

The kid dialed a couple of numbers, then said, "Sorry, she's not answering her home phone or her cell. She turns it off sometimes after office hours. There's more to life than work, and all that."

"Good attitude," Dirk said. "And when she's working at living instead of working at working, where does she do that?"

"Huh?"

"Where does she hang out?" Savannah clarified.

"Oh, that's easy. If she's not here or at home, she's at Coconut Joe's."

Chapter
21

"Hey, déjà vu all over again," Dirk said as he and Savannah walked through the swinging doors of Coconut Joe's for the second time that night. "Are you gonna order enough piña coladas again to put me in the poorhouse?"

Savannah put a hand on her abdomen and groaned. "I may never drink again. That seabreeze didn't settle well on top of the other ones. Too much acid, I guess."

"Good."

"Unless you irritate me with your cheapness, son, and then I might order some Dom Perignon just for spite."

"You order something like fancy-ass champagne, you'll be washing glasses until dawn to pay for it. No way the captain's gonna reimburse me out of petty cash for an expenditure like that!"

Savannah stopped and whirled around to face him. "Are you telling me, that after all the bellyaching you've done about buying me donuts and coffee, you've been dipping into the station's petty cash to pay for it?"

"No, of course not. I just . . ."

Dirk was a lousy liar. Not to perps; he could lie to them all day and never break a sweat, but lying on a personal level . . . he couldn't pull it off.

"Your tongue's going to turn black and fall out one of these days, Coulter," she said.

"Yeah, and my nose is going to grow and I won't get my honesty badge in Girl Scouts. I've heard it all before."

They had to duck and dodge through the crowd, which was at least twice as thick as before, just to get to the bar. But fortunately, once they were there, they found two empty stools together at one end.

Sitting down, Dirk motioned to the bartender. "A couple of colas here," he said, "and pass a bowl of those nibble things down here, too."

The barkeep wasn't impressed. He slid their sodas and the pretzel dish in front of them, collected Dirk's six bucks and twenty-five-cent tip, and turned his back on them.

"That's it," Savannah hissed in his ear. "Piss off the bartender, the fount of all local folklore, before we even get started."

"Who needs him now? We know who we're looking for."

"Oh, yeah? What does Elizabeth Fortunato look like? Unless she drives through the front doors in her BMW, we might have a little difficulty picking her out of the crowd."

"Not me. I know exactly what she looks like."

"What?"

"She's a babe."

"A babe? And you know this how?"

"While you were busy making goo-goo eyes and telling that kid all those lies about how you and me are getting hitched and needing a honeymoon cottage, I was looking around the office there."

"And?"

"There was a picture of her hanging on the wall. She was getting handed some sort of award thing by the Santa Tesla Chamber of Commerce or some such nonsense. And she's a babe."

"You want to be a little more specific?"

"Not necessarily. I'll point her out to you."

"She's here?"

"Not yet."

Savannah snorted and popped a couple of mini-pretzels into her mouth. "I hate it when you're smug."

"Now, now, don't insult your bridegroom right before the wedding. It'll sour our honeymoon."

Savannah took a sip from her cola and turned to the guy seated on the stool next to hers. He looked like he had just washed up on the beach with some flotsam. He wore a faded tie-dyed shirt and peace beads around his neck. His hair hung in limp strands down his back and into his eyes, which were suspiciously bloodshot. The distinctive odor of marijuana drifted about him like a cloud.

Some guys just had a hard time finding their way out of the sixties.

"Hi," she said to him. "Come here often?"

He focused on her with an effort, then grinned broadly with yellowed teeth, as though unable to believe his luck. "Yeah," he said. "I do. I practically live here. How about you?"

"I live in a house."

"But you're here tonight."

"How observant of you! And since you're so perceptive, may I ask you if you've seen a friend of mine?"

"Is she as pretty as you?"

"Oh, some say much prettier. On a good day, she looks like Marilyn Monroe."

Mr. Sixties began nodding his head so vigorously she thought he might tumble off his stool. "I *have* seen her! I've seen your friend. She was here."

"When?"

"I don't remember exactly, but not too long ago. Maybe last night or the night before, or . . . I don't know, but she was here. Sat right over there on the other side of the room and drank martinis. We were all checking her out."

"And did anybody talk to her?"

"I didn't. She was with somebody."

Savannah could feel Dirk leaning against her, straining to hear every word. She could even feel his warm breath on her neck.

Now who was working the room, huh?

"Who was she with?"

"This other really good-looking girl. A pretty brunette. I think she sells real estate."

"And the two of them were talking, drinking together?"

"Yeah, for an hour at least. Then they left together."

Savannah turned to Dirk, a smugger than smug look on her face. "And that," she said, "is what you can find out when you don't alienate them in the first five seconds of meeting them."

But he didn't look rebuked, chastised, admonished, or the slightest bit humbled.

He still looked obnoxiously satisfied with himself. "See," he said, "I told you."

"Told me what?"

"Really good-looking girl? A pretty brunette? Your buddy there just confirmed it: Elizabeth's a babe."

He glanced over her shoulder. "And . . . there she is now."

Savannah turned to see a woman walking into the bar, who was, indeed, a babe—if you were attracted to shapely brunettes with stunning smiles.

Not exactly her type, but she could see why Dirk and the old hippie were impressed. She also noticed that at least two dozen of the other male patrons were following the newcomer's every movement as she walked around the bar, greeting almost everyone she passed.

Apparently, Elizabeth Fortunato was a well-known and well-loved citizen of Santa Tesla Island.

Dirk nudged Savannah. "*I'll* handle this one."

"I'm sure you'd love to," she muttered.

They waited until Elizabeth had sidled up to the bar, ordered a drink, and had it in hand before they fought their way through the crowd to her side.

As he wished, Savannah allowed Dirk to take the lead. He tended to get along better with sexy female realtors than he did with grumpy bank managers and their gargantuan guards.

"Ms. Fortunato?" he said. "Could we please have a private word with you?"

Discreetly, he slipped his badge from his pocket, cupped it in his palms and showed it to her. Elizabeth's eyes widened. She nodded and motioned toward the back of the room.

Again they swam, like salmon fighting their way upstream, through the mob until they reached the rear of the bar and a single unoccupied booth. Elizabeth slid into one side and Dirk and Savannah into the other.

"What is this about?" Elizabeth said, obviously worried. "Has something bad happened? My family . . . ?"

"No, nothing like that," Dirk assured her. "It's nothing to do with you personally. We were just hoping you could help us."

"And you are . . . ?"

"Detective Sergeant Dirk Coulter, San Carmelita PD, and this is my friend, Savannah Reid. She's a private investigator who's helping me with a case I'm working on."

Elizabeth reached across the table and shook their hands. "What sort of case?"

"Homicide."

"Oh, wow, that's serious."

"About as serious as it gets," Savannah added.

"Who is the victim?"

"A fellow named Sergio D'Alessandro."

Elizabeth thought for a moment, then nodded. "I think I read about that in the paper a few days ago. Didn't he own some sort of exclusive spa or something?"

"Yes," Savannah said, "the Mystic Twilight spa and another new place called Emerge. You didn't know him?"

"No. Never heard of him until I read that article in the paper. I thought it said he died of natural causes, though. A heart attack or something."

"We thought so at first," Dirk replied. "But now we know differently."

Elizabeth took a sip of her cosmopolitan and said, "So, why did you come to me? What do I have to do with your investigation?"

"We need to get in touch with someone," Dirk said, "just to talk to her about a few things. And we think you might have seen her recently."

"Oh, really? Who?"

"A woman named Suzette Du Bois."

She shook her head. "No, that doesn't ring any bells. Sorry."

Savannah said, "She may have been using another name."

"What does she look like?"

"That's easy," Dirk said. "She's a Marilyn Monroe wanna-be."

Elizabeth caught her breath, reached for her glass and took a long drink before setting it down again.

Savannah watched her carefully. The woman was clearly stalling for time, her mental gears whirring as she considered her answer. "You've seen someone like that recently?" Savannah said. "Maybe had some sort of business dealing with her?"

"I might have." Elizabeth glanced toward the exit door of the bar, then back at them. "Why?"

"Like I said before," Dirk replied, "we need to talk to her. She's not a suspect at this time, just a . . . person of interest."

A person of interest, my eye, Savannah thought. *If Dirk lays hands on the woman she'll be wearing handcuffs for bracelets in a bunny rabbit's heartbeat.*

Elizabeth squirmed in her seat, obviously miserable. "I don't know what to say to you. I own a very successful agency here on the island. I do business with a lot of people."

"Have you done business with the woman we're talking about?" Dirk prodded.

"I may have. But people here trust me. Believe it or not, but even in real estate, some of the business I handle is quite personal. I have a reputation for being a discreet person, and I don't want to damage that by betraying my clients."

"We're not asking you to betray anyone," Savannah told her. "Just give us a hint as to where we might find her."

Dirk was beginning to lose his patience, hotsy-totsy or not. Savannah could feel him tensing beside her and knew that he was about to switch from solicitous to aggressive and cranky.

Elizabeth took another long, deep drink, and Savannah could see that her hand was shaking. "I may have sold her a house recently."

Savannah said, "And did she come up with a substantial down payment for the property?"

She nodded.

"Like maybe over three hundred thousand?"

Again, a reluctant nod.

"Must be nice digs," Dirk said, "if that's just the down payment."

Elizabeth didn't reply.

"And you met her early yesterday morning when she arrived here on the island?" Savannah asked.

"Yes."

"We thought so. You were seen helping her move boxes from the ferry's loading dock into your car." Savannah got a tingling, deep in her belly . . . the kind she got during an interrogation just before a perp confessed or ratted out a no-good buddy. "Did you take her and her stuff to her new house?"

Suddenly, Elizabeth slid out of the booth, nearly spilling the remainder of her drink. "I'm sorry," she said, "but I'm a professional. This—this is a big deal for me. There's a lot of money involved, a large commission that my agency needs right now. And like I said, it's a small community. The last thing I need is to have word get around the island that I turned over one of my clients to the mainland police."

"But—" Dirk reached for her arm, but she brushed his hand aside.

"I've told you all I can," she said. "I'll have to ask you to continue your investigation without me."

Dirk thrust his card into her hand. "Take this," he said, "in case you change your mind. Call me any time."

She wadded the card into a ball in her fist. "I won't change my mind."

A moment later, she was gone.

"I'll betcha she's laying down rubber getting out of that parking lot," Savannah said.

Dirk reached for the half-finished cosmo and sighed. "I'm losin' my touch with the dames, Van. Just ain't as smooth as I used to be."

Savannah thought back over the years, remembering a younger Dirk with a lot more hair, a bit less tummy, bigger biceps. A guy with a big heart, but hardly any manners, precious little sensitivity, and hardly a clue about how to deal with the fairer sex . . . or the rougher one, for that matter. He was just a bear with a Buick, a Smith and Wesson, and a house trailer. That was Dirk Coulter, then and now.

She hugged his arm—which still had pretty nice biceps—leaned over, and kissed his cheek. "Ah," she said, "don't worry, big guy. You're ever' bit as smooth as you ever were."

"Really?"

"Absolutely."

As they left Coconut Joe's and walked out front to catch a taxi, Dirk glanced at his watch. "Oh, shit," he said.

"What now?" she asked, expecting the worst. And with Dirk, "the worst" could be pretty bad.

"It's after eleven. We missed the last ferry home."

"No way!" She looked at her watch. Unfortunately, he was right.

"We're going to have to stay here tonight." He groaned. "And the captain's gonna be madder than hell with me when he finds out he had to pay for a hotel room."

"Two hotel rooms."

"One hotel room with two beds."

"Two hotel rooms. Don't argue with me, boy. Granny Reid raised me to be a lady."

"Does she know you pee behind bushes on a stakeout?"

"Ouch, that hurt!"

"I meant for it to."

"One room with two beds—that's all I've got. Take it or leave it," said the heavily tattooed, multipierced clerk behind the desk at the island's only motel with a "vacancy" sign.

They were sure. The taxi had driven them from one end of Santa Tesla to the other looking.

"Come on, Savannah," Dirk said, tapping his fingers on the

countertop. "What other options do we have? It's after midnight. Everything else is closed. And without a car, it's not like we can even sleep on the beach."

"All right, all right," she said. "But if my Gran ever finds out about this, or any of the guys at the station, you're deader than a hamburger patty. I mean it."

The guy behind the counter chewed on his toothpick thoughtfully and gave Dirk a "You ain't gonna get any, fellow" look.

"Gimme the key," Dirk told him.

"Do you need help with your luggage, sir?" the clerk asked, his voice dripping with sarcasm.

"Do you see any suitcases here, smart mouth? Do you?"

The guy grinned and shrugged. "Just asking."

"This ain't what it looks like." Dirk barked as he snatched up the key.

The clerk snickered. "I never thought it was."

"Hand me your T-shirt, boy, and make it snappy," Savannah called from the bathroom.

"Why?"

"Because I need something to sleep in and needless to say, I didn't pack any pajamas."

"So sleep in the buff."

"I do *not* sleep naked."

"Oh, hell, Van. I won't look. Just come to bed."

"It's not a modesty issue, you nitwit. It's an earthquake thing."

"An earthquake thing?"

"Yeah, I haven't slept nude since the Northridge quake, and I ain't gonna start tonight, so peel off that T-shirt and hand it here."

She heard a big sigh, then some trudging steps. Opening the door a crack, she reached her arm out. He shoved the shirt into her hand.

"There. Happy?"

"Moderately."

She slipped the shirt on and looked around the tiny bathroom, at her panties, bra, and socks drying on the shower rod next to his socks and boxers. She had done the laundry in the sink . . . his, too, which she felt pretty darned virtuous about.

She spit the minty gum she had been chewing in lieu of a tooth-brushing into the toilet. At the moment, she felt a bit like a she-bear, and it was *his* fault for not getting her to the ferry on time.

Okay, she admitted, it might be her own fault, too. She had a watch and had also gotten wrapped up in the case and forgotten. Oh well, it couldn't be helped now.

She turned out the light and stuck her head out of the door. "You decent?"

"I'm in bed and covered up, if that's what you mean."

"Yeah, well, stay that way. I don't want to wake up in the middle of the night and see you traipsing around in the altogether or whatever."

"If I have to go to the bathroom to take a leak, and I frequently do at night, I just might be traipsing, as you call it, so you just better keep your eyes closed all night."

She settled between the sheets of the bed next to his and pulled the blanket up to her chin.

The digital display from the nightstand clock cast a sickly green light around the room, enough for her to see that he was lying on his side, his back turned to her, facing the window.

Every now and then a bright light shone on the other side of the curtain, then disappeared just as quickly.

"That's the lighthouse," she said softly. "Abigail would love this. She's crazy about lighthouses. I can see why. They're really quite romantic when you think about it."

"Eh, the damned thing's gonna keep me awake all night, shinin' in here like that."

She chuckled. Yes, Dirk was a smoothie, no doubt about it.

"Don't you say anything about us sharing a room to Tammy, either," she said. "If you do, I'll never live it down."

He groaned. "I don't know what the big friggin' deal is. We've spent a million nights together, sitting in a cramped car on a stakeout. You've slept with your head in my lap or stretched out on my backseat. What's the difference? People put way too much emphasis on who sleeps where. Sleepin' is just sleepin'. It don't mean nothin'."

She laid there in the semi-darkness for a long time and thought about what he'd said. Of course, he was right. Eating a meal next to another person, watching a TV show beside them, sleeping next to them . . . what was the difference?

But there was a difference.

It was somehow cozy, intimate, being in that room with him, even if they were in separate beds, even if they were dogged tired and neither one interested in doing anything but resting, even if the room did reek of stale cigarette smoke and have a spotlight shining through the window every forty seconds or so.

It was sort of nice.

Although, of course, she'd never tell *him* that.

Old Dirk Bear would laugh at her if she even suggested such a thing.

"You know, Van," he said, his voice jarring her out of her reverie, "I was just lyin' here thinking."

"What about?"

"Last night. I don't want to make a big deal out of it or nothin', but it was sorta nice, layin' there in your bed after John forced me to drink that frog-piss drink he made."

"Oh?"

"Yeah. I mean, I usually sleep in my trailer and it's . . . you know . . . a guy place. But your room . . . with those satin sheets . . . and those foo-foo lacy curtain things on the window and your nightgown was hanging there on the chair in the corner and the whole room sorta smelled like your perfume."

"Yes?"

"And I was sick and feeling like shit and . . . well, it made me feel better. Being there . . . you know . . . in your room."

She gulped. "Oh. That's nice, Dirk."

"Not a big deal. I just wanted to tell you that."

"Thanks, darlin'. Thanks for sharing."

"You're welcome. Goodnight, babe."

"Goodnight."

She reached down, ran her hand over the softness of his T-shirt, which had still been warm from his body when she had slipped it on. She could smell a hint of his Old Spice deodorant.

Wearing it felt a bit like getting a Dirk hug. And she had to admit it was nice—very nice—to be going to sleep with someone else in the room besides the cats.

A second later he began to snore.

Chapter
22

Savannah had always loved the smell of a library. That slightly musty, but delicious aroma of books took her back to Georgia every time she smelled it. One whiff and she was back in that spooky old house in the middle of the tiny, rural town of McGill, where she and her other eight siblings had been raised by their grandmother.

The creaky, decrepit Victorian house had been donated to the town by an equally spooky old lady known as Widder Blalock, who had designated the house be turned into a library after her death.

Savannah spent many a delicious hour combing through the shelves of that library, living the more exciting lives of the people on those pages—far more interesting worlds than that of a poor girl from McGill, Georgia.

Nancy Drew's and the Hardy Boys' adventures were never quite so scary as when read in the cubicle below the staircase in that rickety old house.

So, when she and Dirk walked through the doors of the Santa Tesla Public Library, she paused just a moment to recollect and reminisce.

"You coming?" Dirk barked over his shoulder as he strode away from her and toward the periodicals racks.

"Yeah, I'm coming. And don't you rush me, boy," she said, following close behind. "I'm only half awake."

"I just want to get this business over and done and back home." He jerked a stack of newspapers off a shelf and began to thumb through them. "I don't like being away from American soil."

"Give me some of those and go sit down," she told him, pointing to a pair of easy chairs that had been arranged in front of a floor-to-ceiling window overlooking the ocean.

He did as she told him and even paused to enjoy the view for a moment. "This is a pretty neat library," he said.

"I know a better one," she replied with a sweet, slightly homesick smile.

She joined him in the chairs, and they both searched the papers in their hands, looking for the back pages and the classified ads.

"Not much of a rag, this one," he said. "But then, I guess there's not much news around here."

"Sounds refreshing."

"You mean boring."

"No-o-o, I mean refreshing, restful, peaceful, safe . . . like San Carmelita used to be before the so-called City of Angels moved in." She found some ads and began to peruse the various events and objects for sale on Santa Tesla. "This is a good idea I had," she told him. "Especially since I had it before breakfast."

"Yeah, we'll see how good it was. Don't go tooting your own horn there, girlie."

"I have to toot it or it goes tootless. Why I'm—"

"Sh-h-h-h. Please, no talking in here."

They both turned around and saw a woman who looked frighteningly similar to the bank manager they had sparred with the day before. She was standing behind their chairs, her hands on her hips, her glasses on the tip of her nose, glaring at them.

Savannah couldn't help giggling. "Sorry," she whispered. "Is it okay if we pass notes?"

"Just keep it down."

"Okay, we will. I promise."

As soon as the woman was gone, Dirk said, "If she comes back over here I'll shoot a spit wad into her hair."

"Oh, cool! And can you make fart noises in your armpit, too?"

Then an ad caught her eye and all juvenile delinquencies fled . . . or were at least put on hold. "Here we go," she whispered, looking over her shoulder. She tapped her finger on the page.

"Read it to me."

"Executive home, new split-level ranch, four bedrooms, three baths, formal dining room, fully finished basement, fully landscaped yard, and spectacular ocean view. One-point-two million. Elizabeth Fortunato Realty."

"Well, here's another one," he said. "Similar to that one, only it's five bedrooms, a guest house, and pool. One and a half million."

"Elizabeth's listing?"

"Yeap. And this one has an address. Let's go. It's in the hills up there where our taxi buddy was wringing out the curves yesterday."

"Oh goody."

"This time you won't get so sick," he said reassuringly.

"How do you know?"

"Because this time you aren't plastered on piña coladas."

Again, they heard a rustling behind them. Again the grating voice spoke. "I warned you before not to talk so loudly. Now you're going to have to leave."

Savannah turned to Dirk. "Do you have that address out of there?"

He nodded. "Got it."

She turned back to the librarian. "Not to worry, ma'am. We're leaving. You have a nice day now, you hear?"

The woman eyed them suspiciously until they walked out the door.

Savannah laughed as Dirk called for a cab on his cell phone. "I just love being sweet to cranky people," she said. "It just confounds them somethin' fierce."

Savannah had a strange fluttery feeling in the pit of her stomach. And it had nothing to do with the hairpin curves they had just traveled to arrive at the top of this steep hill.

The scenery was breathtaking from up here: the island spread beneath them, green and lush, the lighthouse nearby, gleaming white in the morning sun, a stretch of the sparkling, blue Pacific between them and home, and to the west of them, the ocean disappearing into the horizon.

"I've got a feeling," she said as the cab pulled up and stopped in front of a beautiful home that looked like an Italian villa.

"Me, too," Dirk replied, pointing to a sign on the front lawn of the property. It was an Elizabeth Fortunato listing sign, and across it had been pasted a bright red banner that read, SOLD.

"Of course, it could still be that other house in the paper," she said, afraid of getting her hopes too high.

"Or she might have sold her some other house entirely—one that wasn't even listed in the paper."

"True, true. So we should prepare ourselves that this is probably just a dead end."

"A dead end. That's all it's going to be," Dirk replied as he paid the cabby and got out. He offered Savannah his hand, and she slid out as well.

But as they hurried up the stone walkway, Savannah couldn't help saying again, "But I've got a feeling."

"Me, too."

"You want me to go around to the back of the house, in case she tries to run out that way?"

Dirk thought about it for a minute, then said, "Naw, let's just knock on the door and see who answers. It's probably not her and even if it is, it's an island. How far can she get?"

"That's what they said about those guys who escaped from Alcatraz."

Dirk knocked on the door. This time he used his nice, gentle, Avon-lady knock, not his usual heavy-duty S.C.P.D. pounding.

When no one answered, he tried again.

They heard a shuffling on the other side of the door, and then the dead bolt turning.

They both tensed.

But it was a lovely young Hispanic woman in a gray and white maid's uniform who pulled it open. "Good morning," she said with a strong Spanish accent. "May I help you?"

At her feet a small white poodle scampered, barking, trying to stick his head out the door for a better look at the visitors.

He was wearing a rhinestone-studded collar.

Savannah gave Dirk a sidewise smile and whispered, "Sammy."

He grinned back. Then to the maid he said in his sweetest sugar-and-spice tone, "I have to talk to your lady. Is she at home?"

The woman nodded. "She is. But she sick. Cannot have visitor."

"I'm sorry she's sick, "Savannah said. "But we must talk to her. Just for one minute. Please. It's very important. *Por favor.*"

Dirk took his badge from his pocket and showed it to her. The woman's dark eyes widened. "What is your lady's name?" Dirk asked.

"Her name? My lady's name, Norma."

"Norma?" Savannah looked at Dirk. "As in Norma Jean Baker?"

"*Sí,*" said the maid, "Norma Baker."

"Okay, that does it," Dirk told Savannah. "We're going in." Then to the maid he said, "I'm sorry. We must talk to your lady. Now. Okay?"

She nodded, opened the door, and stepped back to allow them to enter.

The poodle scampered at their feet, sniffing their shoes and pants legs.

"*Gracias, Señora,*" Savannah said, glancing down at the simple gold wedding band on the woman's finger.

"No trouble, please," the maid said.

Savannah smiled at her. "No, *Señora*, no trouble. Not to worry."

Dirk pressed his finger to his lips, then said softly. "Where is she? Your lady?"

"Miss Baker lie down. She very sick. She have operation."

"Operation?" Savannah gave Dirk a quick sideways look.

"Yes, operation. In afternoon yesterday at clinic. I take care of her last night and today."

"I'm sure you're doing a very good job, too," Savannah said. "Where is she? In the bedroom?"

She nodded. "*Sí.* Sleeping."

"Not for long," Dirk muttered. "Can you show us where? Which room?"

Reluctantly, she lead them through the sun-drenched home, down marble-tiled hallways lit by skylights and massive windows that made the most of the hilltop views. The dog followed alongside, gleeful about having guests. Savannah stopped once to pat him on his woolly head.

"Nice, what four and a half million dollars worth of stolen money can buy," she whispered to Dirk, looking around.

"Oh yeah. It's gonna be a bit of a drop to a six-foot cell."

They found the master suite at the end of one particularly long hallway. And inside, lying on a canopy bed, her face swathed in bandages, was the lady of the house.

The poodle jumped up onto the bed beside her, nuzzling her hand, wanting to be petted.

"I am very sorry, Miss Baker," the maid told her as they walked through the bedroom door. "But this woman and this man, they say they must speak to you. I told them you are sick, but the man . . . I think he is *policía*."

Even though the woman on the bed had her head wrapped like a mummy's in pressure bandages, there was no mistaking the alarm in her eyes.

"No," she whispered through the slit in the bandage that revealed her swollen, bruised lips. "No."

"Oh, yes," Dirk said as he walked over to the bed. "Norma Jean Baker, huh? Didn't it occur to you that one might be a bit on the nose for an alias? I mean, you can only take this Marilyn thing so far."

Savannah looked at the sprigs of blood-matted platinum blonde hair that poked from between the bandages here and there. "What did you do?" she asked, "get more surgery here on the island to make the transformation complete? I've heard of that sort of thing, but wow, talk about a groupie!"

Dirk sat down on the bed beside the woman and showed her his badge. "By the way, allow us to introduce ourselves. This is my friend and fellow investigator, Savannah Reid. And I'm Detective Sergeant Dirk Coulter with the San Carmelita Police Department. And you, Ms. Suzette Du Bois, are under arrest for the murder of your former lover."

Chapter

23

"No, no . . . I didn't hurt anyone," the mummy on the bed protested as Dirk took a pair of handcuffs from his pocket and attached one cuff to her right arm.

Savannah could see the puncture mark and some bruising from an IV in the crook of her elbow. "Be careful with her, Dirk," she warned. "She's just had surgery. We may have to arrange for a Medevac to get her back home. She doesn't look like she's ferry-worthy to me."

"Don't worry," he said. "We'll treat her a lot better than she treated old Sergio, rat that he was."

Savannah shook her head as she studied what she could see of the woman's face. Her eyes were black and blue and swollen nearly to slits. Apparently she had just undergone some major work. "I guess you were hoping to have your face changed so much that no one would ever recognize you, huh, Suzette?"

She just groaned in response.

"And," Savannah continued, "did you even consider your sister, Clare? She told me you weren't dead, but just hiding out somewhere."

Glancing over at the window, Savannah saw that there was a

magnificent view of the lighthouse from the master suite. "She also told me you love the lighthouse. I guess you thought you had it set up pretty nice here, with your view and your new face. Too bad it had to cost someone else his whole life for you to have it."

A buzzing sound made all four of them jump a bit, until Dirk took out his cell phone and answered it. "Yeah, Coulter here."

He looked a bit surprised. "Yes, hi there. I didn't think I'd hear from you."

He mouthed the word, "Elizabeth," to Savannah, then continued. "Actually, we found the house after all. Yes, we're good. And I'm in the process of arresting Ms. Baker even as we speak."

He listened intently for a long time, then said, "Oh, really? That's very interesting. Yes, I understand now why you were reluctant to say anything last night, but thank you for reconsidering and calling. Sure. No problem. I'll check it out and call you back later."

When he snapped his phone closed, Savannah could tell something was up, just from the look on his face.

"What is it?" she asked. "What did she want?"

Dirk reached over and locked the other cuff around the bedpost. Then he said to his prisoner, "Ms. Elizabeth Fortunato just told me something very interesting about you. She says I should check your pool house. Do you think I should do that, Suzette? Should I see what I can find in your pool house?"

Savannah was confused, but all ears. "What's in the pool house?"

Dirk gave her a strange look. He, too, looked confused, but excited.

"Elizabeth says that she and that kid who takes care of her office helped Suzette here move a particularly heavy box into the pool house. She says it had a weird, bad smell to it. That Suzette here told her it was books that had suffered some water damage.

But Elizabeth says she opened the trunk of her car today and it still stinks."

"Oh, really?" Savannah's own brain gears were spinning. "The smell was that bad, huh?"

"Yeah, and in light of what we told her at the bar last night, she was thinking that maybe she might get in trouble if she admitted she'd helped move such a . . . stinky, heavy box. So she slept on it and this morning, she decided she'd better tell us about it."

"Well, there's only one thing to do," Savannah said, her heart pounding in her throat. "Let's go check out that box of smelly books."

They were still at least fifty feet from the pool house when Savannah got her first whiff and nearly gagged.

"Oh, Lord," she said, "there's only one thing in the world that smells like that."

"Yeah, a DB," Dirk said, wrinkling his nose. "My favorite call."

Savannah agreed. If there was anything in the world that cops hated to hear on their car radio it was the term "DB"—dead body—or just as bad, "suspicious smell."

In all her years on the job, Savannah had seen and heard plenty of things that made her old before her time, things that scarred her soul and kept her awake at night. But there was only one thing that made her barf.

And she was smelling it now.

The stench of death.

"You go in," she said, holding her sweater over the lower half of her face. "You know I can't take it. I'll hurl. I always do, and that makes things so much worse."

"Pansy."

She raised her hands in the air. "I admit it. I have no pride in this respect. None at all. I'm a total wuss."

"Sissy girl."

"I am. That's me. Prissy Pants, that's me. You go in and I'll owe you."

He shook his head, stood at the door of the pool house, and opened it. Then he took a deep, deep breath . . . and shuddered from head to toe.

Dr. Liu had told her long ago, "Here's how you handle the smell, Savannah: just take a big deep gulp of it, fill up your head and your lungs. It's such a shock to the system, you won't smell anything else for hours."

Yeah, right, she thought. *Maybe it works for Dr. Liu and Dirk, but I'd rather bite a skunk in the ass and suffer the consequences.*

"What is it? Do you see the box?" she asked.

He was frozen in the doorway, staring, his mouth hanging open.

"Well?" she asked, inching forward, her curiosity getting the best of her. "What do you see?"

"Oh, my god," he said. "Weird. This is so creepy! Van, come here! You gotta see this."

She might be squeamish about smelling dead bodies, but Savannah's primary character attribute was nosiness. It overrode absolutely everything else in her system.

She held one hand over her mouth and with the other hand pinched her nose together. Then she ran over to the door and looked inside.

The interior was dim, lit only by one small window. But the late morning sunlight was shining in enough to illuminate the macabre scene.

A woman sat on a folding chair, pulled up to a card table. Across the tabletop was spread a game of solitaire. She held a stack of cards in her hands.

"What the hell?" Savannah said, forgetting all about the stench.

The woman was dead.

No doubt about it.

She was tied to the chair with yellow nylon rope and was sagging limply against her bindings. Her flat, milky eyeballs stared sightlessly at the opposite wall.

She was wearing a white physician's smock and her platinum blonde hair was nicely coifed on one side, and stuck to the other side of her head with a mass of black, matted gore that Savannah knew was the result of a terrible head wound.

On her smock pocket was a small, black, plastic name tag.

Savannah read it aloud. "Suzette Du Bois, M.D."

She and Dirk stared at each other for a long time. Finally, he said, "So, if this is Suzette . . . who do I have handcuffed in there?"

They ran back to the house and rushed into the master bedroom, where the maid was offering the lady on the bed a glass of water with a drinking straw. The woman pushed the water away, spilling it across the bed.

At her feet, Sammy the poodle whined and licked the water off his paw.

"Who are you?" Dirk shouted, jostling her shoulder. "Devon? Clare Du Bois?"

"No, go away," the woman mumbled with swollen, bandaged lips. "Get out!"

Savannah looked down at the woman's hands. She was clutching the bedspread, digging her nails into the fabric. Her long, bright red fingernails.

Savannah had seen those fingernails before . . . swirling a drink.

"Myrna," she said. "Myrna, it's you."

The woman on the bed began to sob; it was a horrible, high-pitched shriek, like a hurt animal caught in a trap.

The maid backed into the corner of the room, pulled her apron up over her head, and began to softly cry.

Dirk looked at Savannah in surprise. "How do you . . . ? Is it her?"

Savannah nodded. "It's Myrna," she said. "The body in the pool house is Suzette. She killed her."

"But why?" Dirk said. "For the money?"

Savannah thought back on the grisly scene that had been staged in the pool house. "I don't think so," she said. "You wanted her to be alone, too, didn't you, Myrna?"

The woman stopped shrieking and nodded her head ever so slightly.

"Suzette fixed your ex-boyfriend up really good, didn't she," Savannah said. "So good that he left you, found himself a younger woman with his new, younger-looking face that you paid for."

Again, Myrna nodded.

Savannah continued. "She's playing solitaire out there in your pool house. And you're here, in a fancy house, with all her money and Sergio's, too. And under those bandages you've got a new face, a new life . . . or so you thought."

Myrna nodded, still crying, still clutching the bedclothes.

"There's just one problem, Myrna," Savannah told her, "you can't create a nice, new life for yourself by robbing two other people of theirs."

"Yeah," Dirk said, uncuffing the bedpost and placing it on her other wrist. "Lady, you just bought yourself one shitload of really nasty karma."

Chapter

24

"I'm never going to look at that island the same way again," Savannah said as she gazed out across the water at Santa Tesla Island, where it appeared to be floating on the horizon atop a cloud of haze.

"I just wish we'd been there with you," Abby said as she bit into one of Savannah's chicken salad sandwiches and helped herself to a handful of potato chips. "I would have given anything to sleep in a hotel right under that lighthouse. To have its beam shining right inside your room! That must have been a wonderful experience."

Savannah cast a quick warning glance toward Dirk, but he pretended not to hear as he stretched out on his back on the beach towel and adjusted the bill of his baseball cap to shield his eyes from the sun.

"It was okay," she said. "Maybe we can take you over there for a day trip before you go back home to New York."

"Count me out on that one," Dirk grumbled. "I've had all of that stinking island I can stand. You couldn't pay me to go back there again."

Savannah laughed. "He's just irked because nobody over there was all that impressed with his gold shield."

"I shoulda showed 'em my big gun," he said with a smirk. "That would have put the fear of Dirk in them."

"Yeah, yeah, we all live in terror of the Almighty Dirko." Tammy picked up a slice of fresh mango and squirted him with it.

"Myrna Cooper was pretty scared of him," Savannah said. "She was a babbling idiot on the way home in that medical helicopter. Told Dirk everything he wanted to know and then some."

"Okay . . ." Tammy nudged him with her foot. "Why did she dye her hair blond and take the name Norma Jean Baker? She isn't a big Marilyn fan, is she?"

Dirk groaned and rolled over on his side to face them. He looked terribly put out to have to answer all these questions. But Savannah knew better; Dirk was never happier than when he could complain about something. He was loving every minute of it.

"No, she's not all that into Marilyn," he said. "But she figured if we were on her trail, it would be better for us to think she was Suzette. Then, she could supposedly shake us if she needed to and start up again somewhere else, and we'd never know it was her we were chasing. So she wore a blond wig her first few trips to the island. Then the day before we caught up with her, right before her surgery, she colored it permanently."

"But she's so much older than Suzette," Abigail added. "How could she hope to pass for her?"

"She did a pretty good job of it," Savannah told her. "She wore large sunglasses and scarves and depended on her big cleavage to keep the boys' eyes off her face. It worked. The guys on the catamaran thought she was a lot younger."

"How exactly and where did she kill Suzette?" Abby wanted to know.

Savannah cringed, remembering Myrna's cold-blooded description of the murder. "Suzette used to take Sammy for a walk in some woods near her house, first thing, every day when she got home from work. Myrna knew the route well, from taking him for walks herself. She hid herself and her car among the trees and waited for Suzette to come along. Then she ran up behind her, smashed her in the head with a big rock, and dragged her body into her trunk."

"Primitive," Abby said.

Savannah nodded. "Very, but effective."

"So, Myrna was the one who installed the spyware on Sergio's computer?" Tammy asked.

Savannah shook her head. "Actually, Myrna claims that Suzette put it in there to spy on Sergio's e-mails and see if he was chasing other women. But Suzette told Myrna about it, and Myrna used the software to get his bank account number and password. That's how she was able to steal the money out of his account and put it into one of hers."

"But the password *rosarita*?" Tammy asked. "Wasn't that a reference to the place where Suzette caught Sergio with Devon?"

Savannah stretched out on the towel beside Dirk and kicked off her shoes. "Myrna overheard the big fight between Devon and Suzette that day after Suzette found them at the Rosarita Hotel," Savannah said, wriggling her toes into the cool, damp sand. "Again, she made choices based on misleading us into thinking it was Suzette we were after."

"And . . ." Abigail said, ". . . Myrna was the one who put the botulism solution into Sergio's syringe. But why kill *him*?"

"Because," Savannah told her, "she was worried when she heard he had hired me, a private detective, to find his money for him. She figured he might stop at nothing to get it back. If he kept looking, he might have realized it was her that had stolen his money, not Suzette. She decided it would be safer just to have him dead, too."

"And it was all because she was mad at them for fixing her boyfriend up with a new face and him leaving her for another woman?" Abby shook her head. "If I'd been her, I would have just knocked off the ungrateful, two-timing boyfriend, not them."

"It wasn't just that," Savannah said. "She had worked for Suzette and Sergio for years and resented them the whole time. She was addicted to the surgeries and procedures and was constantly paying off one or the other with her paychecks. She was living below the poverty level because of it, with no way out."

"But that was her fault, not theirs," Abby argued.

"Like that has anything to do with whether people commit murder or not," Dirk said. "These days, people blow other folks away just because they look at them cross-eyed on the freeway."

"And it wasn't just revenge," Savannah continued. "With that kind of money, Myrna figured she'd have a whole new life, all the money she'd ever want for new procedures to keep her looking good, a great house, leisure time to lay out on the beach and attract young studs who don't mind being supported by a rich older woman. She had it all planned out."

Abigail shook her head. "She must have been a bit off her rocker, though, saving Suzette's body, setting it up like that in her pool house. That's just gross and sick."

"You think?" Tammy laughed. "You should see what Savannah's got in *her* garage."

"What? What have you got?"

"Nothing," Savannah told her. "Your cousin is pulling your leg."

"Really?"

"Probably."

"You Californians are weird," Abby said, "I'm going back to New York City where it's safe."

"Not just yet." Savannah gave her a smile and a wink. "Now that we've got this case wrapped up, it's time for you and me to go have ourselves some fun."

"Just you two?" Tammy asked, pouting just a little.

"Yeap, just us two."

"Where?" Abby wanted to know. "Where are you taking me?"

"Someplace special. You'll see."

"Does it have anything to do with murders or stinky dead bodies playing solitaire alone in pool houses."

"No," Dirk said from under his baseball cap. "Savannah only does that fun stuff with *me*!"

"Yes, because you're so-o-o special." Savannah poked him in the ribs.

He grabbed her and held her in a headlock until she nabbed a bit of his midriff and pinched it hard enough to make him howl.

"See what I put up with," Tammy told Abigail, shaking her head. "We're just a big dysfunctional family around here. And, would you believe, those two are the *parents*?"

Abby grinned. "Looks pretty good to me. I think I'll visit more often."

Chapter
25

"What is this place?" Abigail asked as Savannah ushered her into the tiny cubbyhole called "The Oasis."

"Usually, it's your ordinary, run-of-the-mill bar," Savannah told her as she guided her toward the corner of the dark little room where a slightly elevated platform was surrounded by a circle of chairs and tables. "But not on Friday night."

"What happens on Friday night?"

"You'll see."

Savannah pulled out a chair, and Abigail sat down on it, facing the platform.

"Actually, I have someplace I have to be in an hour or so," Abby said, glancing at her watch. "I already arranged for somebody to pick me up here and—"

"Sh-h-h-h . . ." Savannah said, finger to her lips. "It's going to start pretty soon. They're usually quite punctual with the show."

"What show?"

Savannah just grinned and motioned to the waitress. "Two glasses of your house white here," she told her. Then, to Abby she said, "The first time I saw this, a few months ago, I was blown away. I think you'll really like it."

"What is it?"

"Belly dancing. The real thing, not some cheap, sleazy, Hollywood imitation."

"Belly dancing?!" Abby's nostrils flared. "You brought me to a stupid strip club?"

"Not even close. Sit still and watch."

As if on cue, the room's lights dimmed, and a soft blue light flooded the platform stage in front of them.

Music began, a slow, sensual drumbeat that slowly increased in tempo. Other exotic sounding instruments joined in, and the crowd began to clap in time to the rhythm.

Abby leaned over to Savannah and said in her ear, "If you think I'm going to sit here and watch some skinny gal with boob implants shake her stuff in my face, you've got another—"

Savannah nudged her and motioned to the door. "Look."

Through the front door of the place came a dancer. Slowly, she made her way through the crowd to the platform, pausing here and there to drape a brightly colored chiffon scarf around someone's neck, to place a kiss on a forehead, to trail her fingertips along someone's shoulder or tweak somebody's hair.

Her movements were light and playful, energetic and bouncy, as she moved onto the stage and continued to sway to the lively beat.

With their seat next to the stage, Savannah and Abby had a full view of the woman. She was middle-aged and full-figured, more than a little overweight according to society's current standard. But she was exquisite.

Her costume was a cloud of swirling scarves of every color that floated around her when she moved. Tucked here, gathered there, they moved along with her, accenting her every sway and shimmy.

As she moved around the stage, smiling down at individual

members of her audience and dropping the scarves among them, she looked like a young girl at play, lighthearted, carefree.

Savannah leaned close to the transfixed Abigail and whispered in her ear, "A real belly dance is the story of a woman's life," she said. "This part represents her girlhood. She's clothed in innocence and happy-go-lucky, the way we all start out."

As the veils were dropped, more and more of the woman's body was revealed—her arms, encircled with golden bracelets that jingled when she moved, her legs that, while hardly slender, were muscular and obviously very strong as her skirt parted to reveal and then hide them, her abdomen that rolled and moved with the beat of the music that was slowly changing.

The tempo slowed, the volume increased, and the tone became less playful.

The dancer reached down to a nearby table, and someone in the crowd handed her a couple of candles.

Holding one candle in each hand she continued to dance, moving them in circles under her arms, then over her head. Their light illuminated her skin, causing it to glow like living, breathing, fluid gold.

With unbelievable grace, the woman bent backward, her long, dark hair sweeping the floor. Still holding the candles, she sank to her knees on the stage as the other instruments faded away, leaving only the drumbeat as accompaniment.

From her kneeling position, she lowered herself straight backward, until she was lying on her back . . . all the time still swaying and rolling to the beat.

"What's she doing now?" Abigail whispered.

"This part represents the travails of womanhood. The difficulties and pain we all encounter that change us from girls into women."

The dancer placed the candles on her belly and by flexing her muscles, caused them to move in time with the drum. Her arms stretched upward, she seemed to be reaching, striving, grasping for something just beyond her reach, then grabbing it and pulling it toward her.

Lifting the candles from her abdomen, she held them in her hands again and managed to roll across the stage, holding them level all the while, managing, keeping everything in balance.

Slowly she rose to her feet and handed the candles back to the crowd.

The drum beat faster and faster, and her movements matched the tempo, shaking, swaying, and shimmying, until her body glistened with the sweat of extreme exertion. Just when it seemed she surely couldn't continue, the music paused, then switched back to the original playful, happy song.

But this time, as the woman danced off the stage and through the crowd, interacting once again, there was a distinct difference in her movements. She was stronger, more confident, more decisive in her motions.

"See," Savannah said, "she's still happy, still joyful, but with all the authority of a grown woman who's been through the fire and emerged whole."

Abigail nodded as they watched the dancer bow to her audience —who responded with wild applause—then disappear out the door.

"She's beautiful!" Abby said, her eyes sparkling, her face flushed. "She's so, so, so . . ."

"I know."

Abby shook her head in disbelief. "And she's not even skinny."

"Or especially young."

"I'd say she's downright plump. But she's so graceful, and look at them . . . they love her!"

Chapter
25

"What is this place?" Abigail asked as Savannah ushered her into the tiny cubbyhole called "The Oasis."

"Usually, it's your ordinary, run-of-the-mill bar," Savannah told her as she guided her toward the corner of the dark little room where a slightly elevated platform was surrounded by a circle of chairs and tables. "But not on Friday night."

"What happens on Friday night?"

"You'll see."

Savannah pulled out a chair, and Abigail sat down on it, facing the platform.

"Actually, I have someplace I have to be in an hour or so," Abby said, glancing at her watch. "I already arranged for somebody to pick me up here and—"

"Sh-h-h-h . . ." Savannah said, finger to her lips. "It's going to start pretty soon. They're usually quite punctual with the show."

"What show?"

Savannah just grinned and motioned to the waitress. "Two glasses of your house white here," she told her. Then, to Abby she said, "The first time I saw this, a few months ago, I was blown away. I think you'll really like it."

"What is it?"

"Belly dancing. The real thing, not some cheap, sleazy, Holly-wood imitation."

"Belly dancing?!" Abby's nostrils flared. "You brought me to a stupid strip club?"

"Not even close. Sit still and watch."

As if on cue, the room's lights dimmed, and a soft blue light flooded the platform stage in front of them.

Music began, a slow, sensual drumbeat that slowly increased in tempo. Other exotic sounding instruments joined in, and the crowd began to clap in time to the rhythm.

Abby leaned over to Savannah and said in her ear, "If you think I'm going to sit here and watch some skinny gal with boob implants shake her stuff in my face, you've got another—"

Savannah nudged her and motioned to the door. "Look."

Through the front door of the place came a dancer. Slowly, she made her way through the crowd to the platform, pausing here and there to drape a brightly colored chiffon scarf around some-one's neck, to place a kiss on a forehead, to trail her fingertips along someone's shoulder or tweak somebody's hair.

Her movements were light and playful, energetic and bouncy, as she moved onto the stage and continued to sway to the lively beat.

With their seat next to the stage, Savannah and Abby had a full view of the woman. She was middle-aged and full-figured, more than a little overweight according to society's current standard. But she was exquisite.

Her costume was a cloud of swirling scarves of every color that floated around her when she moved. Tucked here, gathered there, they moved along with her, accenting her every sway and shimmy.

As she moved around the stage, smiling down at individual

"Of course they do," Savannah replied. "She's courageous enough to let her spirit shine through, to express her joy and pride in herself through movement and music right here in front of everyone. And she allows the rest of us to feel it too when we watch her. That's quite a gift."

Abigail nodded thoughtfully. "It *is*. For her *and* for us." She turned to Savannah and smiled, then gave her a hearty hug. "Thank you so much. I'll never forget her . . . or you, for bringing me here."

Savannah returned the embrace. "Miss Abigail, you're pretty darned unforgettable yourself."

"Now," Abby jumped up from her chair and glanced at her watch, "if you don't mind, I have a date. He should be arriving here any minute now." She glanced toward the door. "Hey, there he is now."

Savannah turned toward the entrance and was surprised to see a smiling Jeremy Lawrence standing there, looking as gorgeous as ever in a pale blue silk shirt and navy slacks. He was holding a red rose in one hand. He spotted them right away and headed in their direction.

"Oh . . ." Savannah gulped. "Oh, I didn't . . . I mean . . . wow! You go, girl!"

Abby laughed. "He's taking me to Santa Tesla Island to look at the lighthouse."

Savannah glanced at her own watch. "But it's almost nine o'clock. You'll barely even make it out there before you have to turn around and come back. The last ferry leaves there around eleven, you know."

"I know." Abby smiled, reached for the grinning Jeremy and gave him a lusty kiss on the lips. "And with any luck, we'll miss it . . . just like you and Dirk."

The two of them hurried away, leaving Savannah standing

there with a sappy grin on her face and a warm feeling in her heart. "Well, hopefully not *exactly* like me and Dirk," she said. "*Bon voyage.*"

The next day, Savannah and Tammy sat next to each other on Savannah's sofa, looking through the latest Victoria's Secret catalogue, which had just arrived in the morning's mail.

"I loaned Abby my cell phone," Tammy said with a slight pout. "I've called her four times. You'd think she'd at least pick up and tell me she's okay over there on that island."

Savannah smiled. "She's fine. She'll come up for air eventually."

Someone knocked on the front door and Savannah yelled, "Who is it?"

"The big bad wolf."

"Come in, Dirk," she yelled back. "Use your key."

He entered, wearing a contented, peaceful smile.

"You must have just busted somebody," Savannah said, looking up from her catalogue. "You have that all's-right-with-the-world look on your face."

"I just heard that Loco Roco's back in for at least another three years."

"I knew it was something like that."

He glanced over to see what they were looking at. "What're you two doing there?"

"Ordering new undies," Savannah said with a chuckle. "Wanna help?"

"No."

"You sure?"

He grinned. "I'll take the catalogue home with me when you're done with it though."

Tammy snatched it up and held it to her chest. "No way, you

perv. We're going to be ordering for weeks. We've got money to spend. Lots and lots of money."

"Yeah," Savannah said. "Clare Du Bois came by earlier and dropped off a really nice check for us. The money that Myrna embezzled, it goes back to Suzette's estate, and Clare's her beneficiary. She wanted to reward us. So we let her."

"Must be nice to be a civilian," he grumbled, "and be able to accept a reward." He glanced up and saw Diamante and Cleopatra sitting on top of the bookcase. "What's up with the cats?"

"Clare brought Sammy over with her. She's adopted him. The kitties are still protesting."

"How long are you going to be doing . . . that?" He pointed at the catalogue.

"All day long and into the night," Savannah replied. "Why do you ask?"

"I just heard they're releasing Jake the Snake this afternoon."

"No way! But you just locked him up last year!"

"Actually, it was three years ago. Time flies when you're having fun . . . or getting old."

"You gonna go watch him?"

Dirk smiled. "Oh yeah. I figure he'll head right back to his old lady's house and beat her up again. It's just a matter of time before the call goes out on a domestic over there and I want to be the first to respond."

"Need company?"

"No, I don't need nobody."

"Oh, right. Mr. Macho. Do you want company?"

"Well, I don't know. I guess you could come along if you really wanna. You got any more of those pecan chocolate chip cookies?"